Praise for Elizabeth Palmer's
OLD MONEY

"Palmer's literate, understated, meticulous style
makes *Old Money* a delight to read."
—*The Boston Globe*

"A triumph of understated comedy, an interesting
examination of the fall-out of incomplete
relationships, and ultimately an enjoyable vicarious
slice of the lives of the rich and famous."
—*San Antonio Express-News*

"Palmer's third novel is an acerbic tour de force."
—*Publishers Weekly*

"A finely written romp."
—*Arizona Daily Star*

"The spoof on high society, money, family,
and power remains a great deal of fun."
—*Library Journal*

ELIZABETH PALMER

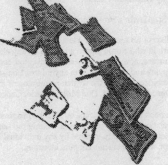

old Money

MIRA

ISBN 1-55166-547-6

OLD MONEY

Copyright © 1995 by Elizabeth Palmer.

First published by St. Martin's Press Incorporated.

Visit us at www.mirabooks.com

Printed in U.S.A.

In memory of my grandmother, Mary Jane Woodland,
born and bred in Northumberland

December/January

1

Did she fall or was she pushed? Tumbling downstairs and into oblivion, Chloe Post was never to know the answer, not in this world, at least. Off balance and top-heavy anyway because of her pregnancy, she slipped and slid and twisted, failing in her efforts to clutch the banisters as she did so, and then turned right over like a rag doll. Throughout, her main feeling was one of surprise. In slow motion a parade of photographic stills passed before her mind's eye. She and Morgan and Tom and Joanna meeting at that cocktail party. *Click.* She and Morgan in bed together. *Click.* She and Morgan in Northumberland, meeting Leonora Steer and Cassandra and Clara and Julia for the first time. *Click.* She and Morgan at their own wedding, smiling, smiling, smiling. *Click, click, click.* And, lastly, saying to Morgan, heart secretly sinking because she was afraid of having a child, afraid of the pain and indignity, 'Darling, isn't it wonderful, I'm pregnant.' *Click.* One more for the photograph album. My marriage has been fatal, went through Chloe's mind in a moment of rare perspicacity just before she hit the wide elm boards at the bottom, where, brittle in death as in life, she snapped her narrow neck. *Click.* The last still.

2

Almost a year earlier, Morgan Steer and his house guest, Tom Marchant, who had arrived late the previous night, walked down the same staircase. Crossing the hall, they turned right into the large, gloomy drawing room, where they both sat down. It was nearly lunch time.

'Drink?' enquired Morgan.

'Whisky and soda,' replied Tom, who had never been known to refuse.

Morgan poured one for his friend and made himself a gin and tonic.

'So she really has thrown you out. What are you going to do?'

Tom thought regretfully of all Primrose's money, now out of his reach, and shrugged. Lamenting the existence of the Married Woman's Property Act, he wished that they were still in the era of the Rake's Charter. 'No idea,' he said.

'Well, at least you've got a job. An awful lot of people haven't.'

Remembering that Morgan was one of those who hadn't, Tom said without enthusiasm, 'Yes, at least I've got one of those.'

'Maybe Primrose will come round.'

'I don't think so. She's already filed for divorce, and is refusing to communicate except through lawyers.'

Morgan was silent, remembering the erratic and un-scrupulous Marchant progress through school, and how later those same qualities had cost Tom both his inheritance and his lucrative job. He and Tom went back a long way, and were an old force for disorder. Previously dazzled, Primrose Marchant had plainly seen the real light at last. A dedicated trawl through the gossip columns had probably aided this illumination. Morgan wondered why she was initiating a divorce now, when he knew for a fact that the bad behaviour had been going on for almost the whole two years of their marriage, and that everybody had always assumed she knew all about it. Perhaps, after all, she had not. He was opening his mouth to ask what had finally capsized it, when Tom pre-empted him by saying, with a sheepish grin, 'She caught me *in flagrante delicto*. In her bedroom. With Tessa Lucas.'

Picturing this scene, Morgan drew in his breath. He could see that Primrose, who was unremarkably handsome and whose main attraction had been what her husband had crudely referred to as her stack of cash, must have found the sight of Tessa's naked beauty between her own sheets more than even she was prepared to stomach.

It was no laughing matter, of course, but still they both laughed, just as they had laughed their joint way through a misspent youth. All the same, the financial deprivation was going to be severe.

'I'm just going to have to marry more sterling. Or better still, dollars. You ought to do the same.'

On one level it was impossible to disagree. A similar thought had already occurred to Morgan, who was currently dependent on a frugal allowance doled out by his Edwardian grandmother, whose notion of what constituted subsistence level had hardly advanced in the course of the last fifty years. All the same, he was not comfortable with the prospect of marrying for money. Unlike Tom, Morgan was something of a romantic.

'Maybe. Of course I'm due to get most of the family cash in the end, but Grandmama is tough as old boots and quite likely to hit the hundred before she finally pops her clogs. And then there are the Aunts. And Mother. They're all in line for some too.'

Mindful of his own past disappointment, Tom observed, 'I shouldn't bank too much on getting that if I were you.'

Morgan had his lines well rehearsed.

'Well, I don't know who else she would give it to. She doesn't like animals, never goes to church, and the only charity she believes in is the Leonora Steer charity. The Aunts are all too long in the tooth, and at least one of them is dotty, plus, unlike you, I don't have an upright brother to step in.'

'No, I suppose not.'

Swallowing his whisky, Tom let his eyes rove over

the bottle-green room in which they sat. He felt as though he was sitting in a plushly overdecorated and very claustrophobic museum. It was the sort of room where it was hard to move without tripping over a footstool or being gored by the sharp, low edges of a sofa table. On the floor in front of the fire was a tiger, reputedly shot by Spencer Steer during his Indian period. Its body and paws were as flat as those of a steamrollered cartoon cat, but its massive, three-dimensional stuffed head constituted another hazard for those not looking where they were going. Knick-knacks, lamps, screens and pieces of occasional furniture were everywhere, and no concession of any sort had been made to the modern obsession with clean uncluttered lines. In one corner, there was even a large bird under a glass dome, preserved in mid-flutter amongst a dusty riot of fruit and flowers.

Outside the windows, framed by heavily fringed dark green velvet curtains, the bleakly magnificent Northumbrian landscape stretched as far as Tom's eye could see. Rugged rather than unwelcoming, it was still much less hospitable than the gentler variety surrounding his own family home. Nor was this house anything like as substantial as the Marchants', although there was rumoured to be a great deal of Steer money currently residing in the clawlike hands of the ancient, and apparently indestructible, Leonora Steer.

The door opened, and Leonora herself entered. Ramrod straight in refined tweeds, she carried her own formidable atmosphere with her, somehow managing to convey to the world the impression that she was viewing it through a pair of lorgnette.

Both men stood up. It was well known that Morgan's grandmother took no nonsense on the manners front.

'Tom,' said Leonora, acknowledging his presence and slightly inclining her head.

'Mrs Steer,' said Tom, with a half-bow.

'Morgan, I should like a gin and tonic, please. You may make it a double. The prospect of Clara's soup indicates the need for some Dutch courage.'

Watching her empty her glass and then send Morgan back for a refill, Tom thought it was no wonder she had achieved ninety if she drank gin at that rate. She must be practically pickled in the stuff. Silence fell. As with royalty, people in Leonora Steer's presence tended to wait for her to speak first. Eventually deigning to resume, she said, 'And I'm afraid Clara is also in charge of the roast. This is likely to be a gristly happening, I fear.'

'Grandmama, I don't know why you don't go back to employing a cook.' Morgan had been looking for an opportunity to advance such a suggestion for a long time, and felt he could not afford to let this opening pass.

Leonora, whose household meanness was legendary, tucked her chin into her pearls, stared at him for a full minute, and then said, 'Quite out of the question. We can't afford it. It is all in aid of preserving your inheritance, Morgan. One day you will thank me.'

Possibly, he thought, but not if he starved to death in the process. Thwarted, he decided to shut up.

Having dealt with Morgan, Leonora turned to Tom. 'I learn from Morgan that your wife has left you. May I ask why?'

Reflecting that only a patrician ninety-year-old would have the sheer rudeness to ask such a question, and tempted to answer, 'None of your business, Mrs Steer,' Tom in fact replied: 'Bad behaviour!' And then, in response to the question implicit in her raised eyebrows, 'Mine, I'm afraid, Mrs Steer.' Sizing up this woman, he was contritely flirtatious.

She loved it.

'Naughty, *naughty* boy!' Archly, she tapped his lean wrist with a stringy, ringed forefinger. 'Wine, women and song I daresay!' Leonora had always liked a stylish cad, and in her time had taken quite a few as lovers, but she had never made the cardinal error of actually marrying one. Though on the other hand, she thought, maybe that was why both marriages had been so dreadfully boring. Spencer in particular had been extraordinarily dull, and in such a worthy, boneheaded, handsome, English, upper-class sort of way, too.

Watching the strong, cunning face, whose nose and chin had, like two continents, moved almost imperceptibly closer together with the passing years, Tom said, 'Women, wine and gambling, actually, but broadly speaking that's correct.' Leonora's low, throaty laugh could have come from someone half her age, and Tom was suddenly aware of her ageless, irresponsible magnetism.

'Got any money?'

Mrs Steer appeared to spend the whole of her conversational life out of order.

'Not enough I'm afraid.'

'Oh, of course, you're the one who didn't get the Marchant riches, aren't you? Well, no one ever has enough! You'll just have to marry it. Marry money, sire a few children, and then do as you please! So will you, Morgan. Morgan! Are you listening? Of course, I shall leave you something when I die, always provided you are nice to me, but that probably won't be enough either.'

'Times have changed, Mrs Steer,' said Tom. 'You can marry money these days, but you can't get your hands on it unless your wife lets you.'

'Sounds like a good idea to me,' said his female sparring partner, who seemed to want it all ways round. She signalled to her grandson. 'Another gin and tonic, Morgan, please!'

A gong, beaten with unnecessary force in such a medium-sized house, began to boom and continued to do so for at least three minutes before finally vibrating to a stop. Leonora stood up, displaying no signs of having imbibed the equivalent of five substantial gin and tonics, and led the way to the dining room. Like an empress, she took her seat at the head of the table. Behind her was a large oil painting of the young Leonora. Feline and distinctly predatory, the earlier incarnation leant out, wearing a décolleté evening dress and a look of frank invitation. At the opposite end of the dining room hung the male counterpart in the shape of Spencer Steer, also in evening dress.

What a stuffed shirt, Tom had thought the first time he saw the picture. The fact, learnt later, that Spencer had accidentally managed to shoot himself with his own gun had done nothing to diminish his first impression of genial stupidity. Now, mindful that his late arrival the night before meant he had not yet greeted the Aunts and, in particular, Julia Farrell, Morgan's mother, Tom put his head round the door of the kitchen before taking his place at the table.

The kitchen looked as though a troop of cavalry had ridden through it. Toppling piles of dirty pans were everywhere, and in one corner the fragments of what looked like a substantial breakage had been swept into a heap. Clara Steer was standing with her back to him, stirring a very large, seething pot. At least twice the width of her mother, and box-shaped in whiskery wool she stood there, sturdy, thick-stockinged legs apart, engrossed in keeping what he supposed must be the soup on the move.

Turning her head as she heard the door, Clara was the first one to see Tom. Feminine, just, in twin set and pearls, she twittered unconfidently, thoroughly put off her stroke by his saturnine materialization in the hell-hole that was the kitchen. Kissing her papery cheek prior to passing on to Cassandra and then Julia, Tom wondered how the three ageing women stood it, stranded there waiting for Leonora Steer to die.

The food, when it finally arrived at the table, was dire. After the soup had come and gone, Morgan began to carve what he supposed, judging by its colour, must be pork, although there was no sign of any crackling. It was mainly fat, through which meandered elusive strands of meat. In the end he decided to slice the joint like bread, reasoning that if he tried a more aesthetic approach they would be there all day. After one or two false starts, the conversation was desultory and finally died away altogether as they all prospected for meat. However the pudding, when it eventually made its entrance, was a pleasant surprise, being the lightest of light lemon mousses. Perhaps, thought Tom, Julia had learnt to cook during her brief marriage to the flighty Major Fred. Famished and gratefully eating a large, unfilling plateful, he decided that in order to avoid more of the same, he would take himself and Morgan out to dinner that evening.

Later that night, lying in the guest-room bed on cold, white sheets as stiff as cardboard, Tom thought about the Steers rather than dwell on his own problems. Of course he had stayed in Northumberland before, but on the whole he and Morgan tended to conduct their friendship more at the London end, where Morgan had the run of the Steer Knightsbridge flat.

The Steer history was an eccentric one even by English upper-crust standards. Leonora had married twice, and, Tom was willing to bet, hadn't liked it much. In an odd way her hard sparkle reminded him of Camilla Vane, a woman with whom he had once been obsessed. Remembering caused a flare of the old desire (where was she now?), but resolutely putting the whole episode and the humiliation it had caused him out of his mind, he pursued his analysis of his hostess. The first husband, Maxwell, whose portrait hung in the hall, where it had probably been demoted from the dining room when she had married Spencer, looked as though he had been another amiable duffer. Perhaps, he mused, that was the way it was done in those days. You married for convenience and money and then went your own merry way, making as many discreet sexual forays as you felt like from within holy wedlock's apparently respectable confines. On the whole, Tom, whose polygamous heart had never been at one with the marital state, approved. Legend had it that Leonora had had many lovers, including, during a particularly busy summer when she was married to Maxwell, the Prince of Wales. Presumably Maxwell had done the same until he died of TB and when Spencer came along and stepped into his Lobb shoes, after a brief honeymoon the old roundelay had no doubt resumed.

Tom yawned. The air here was so different that it usually took him a day or two to acclimatise.

His thoughts wandered to the Aunts and from there to the prospect of Leonora, who had never struck him as even mildly maternal, pregnant, and not once but three times. She must have been trying for a son. I'll bet that cramped her style, thought Tom. He looked at his watch. Twelve fifteen. He put out the light.

3

Tom rose at eight the next morning. He drew back the curtains and looked out. The grey sky was low and bulbous, with a hint of yellow about it. Occasional flakes of snow drifted this way and that in the still, dense air. High winds were forecast. The possibility of being imprisoned in Armitage Lodge was a dismal one and Tom hoped fervently that any severe weather would hold off until his and Morgan's departure for London.

The room in which he slept did not possess a bathroom of its own, but had a washbasin in one corner. Tom, whose day always began with a Gauloise and then a shower, considered the prospect of the linoed and extremely Spartan nursery bathroom, which was the nearest one to him, and rejected it. It was probably freezing cold too, if past experience was anything to go by.

He turned on the basin tap and found that there was no hot water. This depressing discovery which reminded him of school, also raised the question of how to shave. Aware of the fact that shaver points did not exist in the house, he had brought with him the means for a wet shave. In the end he used the tepid contents of his hot-water bottle.

When he got down to breakfast only Morgan was in the dining room. This was a welcome deliverance.

'Where is everyone?' enquired Tom, helping himself to coffee and cold toast.

'Grandmama always has her breakfast in bed. Mother is reading in her room, and I have no idea where the Aunts are. I thought we might go for a hike this morning. Finishing up in a pub. Maybe drive to Housesteads, if no one else needs the car, and walk along the Roman Wall. We'll take Jardine. He needs a run.'

Hearing his name, Jardine, Morgan's black Labrador, stood to attention, ears pricked.

'I'm on!' The opportunity of getting out of the house appealed to Tom, as did the prospect of a square meal. 'What's the weather forecast?'

'Not too good, but if it looks like really deteriorating we'll cut and run. Cab it to the station and then get the train to Newcastle and on to London. Don't worry, I've got no intention of getting stuck here.'

That was a relief, anyway.

'Why do you feel you have to come up so often? After all, it's one hell of a trek.'

Morgan shrugged.

'To pay homage to Grandmama, and because it's where the money is. A casual attitude could be fatal. She doesn't have to leave the bulk of it to me, and she likes deference.'

Yes, I'll bet she does, the tyrannical old trout, thought Tom, then, mindful of the household arrangements, he observed, 'Well there should be plenty of it, since she doesn't ever appear to spend any.'

'That's true. Anyway, if we're going, let's get cracking.'

They both stood up and on hearing them Jardine came in carrying his master's cap. His dry pads rattled on the polished floor-boards.

'Thank you, Jardine. And now gloves, please.'

Obediently Jardine went out again, followed by Tom in search of his own walking clothes.

Visibility that day was poor. In places the bulging sky seemed almost to touch the earth and they struggled along the top of the Wall into a steely, sleeting wind. Both men had been brought up in the country and neither minded the weather. Ahead of them ran Jardine, sniffing and questing and occasionally cocking his leg. As they walked, they talked.

'So what *are* you going to do next?' Morgan wanted to know.

'No idea. Find myself somewhere to live is the first task, probably. I'm in a hotel at the moment.'

'Why don't you come and stay in the Knightsbridge flat until you do?'

'It belongs to your grandmother, doesn't it?' The thought of sharing digs with Leonora Steer did not appeal to Tom.

Following his drift, Morgan replied, 'Yes, it does,

but she only goes there twice a year. To shop in Harrods. It's the only store she's heard of.'

'What do you do when she's there?'

'I usually move out for the duration, leaving Mrs Pratt to look after her.'

It was a distinct possibility. He and Morgan had always got on well, and presumably he wouldn't have to pay anything, apart from contributing the odd case of Hardwick-Smith's claret.

'I just might take you up on that.'

By now they had reached Mile Castle and they decided to press on towards Cuddy's Crag and beyond. In places the Wall dizzily skirted the precipitous edge of the crags whose black, spiky summits appeared to touch the clouds, and where this happened Morgan called a reluctant Jardine to heel.

'How often do you see Caroline Barstow these days?'

Tom had hesitated before deciding to bring up this sensitive subject. Caroline and Morgan had been close childhood friends, and probably because he had known her so well for so long, Morgan had not noticed this old friendship slowly, almost imperceptibly, evolving into love. By the time he became aware of it, she was married to someone else and it was too late.

'From time to time.' Morgan's face darkened. 'It's not that easy. As you know, her husband's an actor and since he's always out of work, he's always around. And even if he wasn't, it probably wouldn't make much difference. Cheating isn't Caro's style.' Although she appeared unattainable, just talking about her caused his spirits to rise.

Tom shot a sidelong look at his friend. Morgan's profile carried an air of the country in which he had been born. Striding into the gusts with his dog at his heels, he looked the epitome of a well-heeled country Englishman and exuded the self-assurance endemic to the type. Morgan was attractive to women, but as Tom knew from their shared school days, whilst not stupid, he was no great brain either. Caro Barstow, on the other hand, had been something of a blue-stocking and had gone to Oxford, where there had been no question of Morgan following her. The day she had married Patrick Holland had shown Morgan with great clarity the real nature of his own feelings and Tom remembered that he and Morgan had gone out and got very drunk together.

Why Caroline Barstow?

'She's not even very pretty,' Tom had pointed out in his efforts to effect a cure for the disease of love. '*And* she's heavy going. Would rather read a book than go to a party. Moreover, she hasn't got a bean.'

Suddenly stern, Morgan had said, 'Shut up, Tom! Where Caro is concerned I don't *care* about money. I love her! And I know *you* can't see it, but *I* think she's beautiful.' After a short, brooding silence, he had pursued the point. 'It's more than that, though. It's an affinity. I can't explain it any other way. I feel as if I'm part of her and she is part of me.' And then, by now in his cups and very maudlin, 'Do you believe in reincarnation? I feel as though I've known her for centuries.'

'No, I don't, and nor do you when you aren't plastered.' Giving up on it, Tom had reflected that it was probably a good thing that the actor had happened along, thus saving Morgan from his own irrational obsession with a very ordinary girl.

They walked on for a while. The temperature had dropped again, and sharp diagonal sleet had given way to large feathery flakes of snow, as though punctured by the crags, the pillow of the sky had finally burst. Beyond Rapishaw Gap, the Wall became hazardous and finally disappeared completely. As a result they were forced to take the Roman military way instead. With the onset of the blizzard, the landscape had become a silent one, probably because all the wildlife had gone to ground and Tom and Morgan were silent, too, as they tramped. Abruptly the Whin Sill crags rose before them, wearing the weather like a garment, their austere profile bedizened by spiralling veils of snow. Below them the black waters of Crag Lough were all but obliterated.

'I think we should probably turn back,' said Morgan. 'It was in my mind to hike as far as the Twice Brewed Inn and then hitch a lift back, but this is showing no sign of letting up and I think we'd do better to pick up the car while we can. What do you think? We can do most of it along the military way.'

'I think', replied Tom, whose mind was on other

things, 'I'd like to take up your offer of a billet in the Prince's Gate flat.'

'Sure.' Morgan whistled for Jardine. 'Damn that dog. Where the hell is he?'

They arrived back at Armitage Lodge after a convivial pub lunch in the nearby market town of Hexham to find a tea party in progress. Leonora, Clara, Cassandra and Julia were all in the drawing room, entertaining Meredith Barstow and her father, Brigadier Sir Arthur Fielding, VC.

Meredith, who was the same age as Julia, whose close childhood friend she had been, had taught in one of the local schools for years. Mother of Caro and Emily, whom she saw all too rarely these days since both lived in London, and now at home all day looking after her cantankerous and mostly ungrateful parent, Meredith wondered more and more often what the point of it all was.

Or rather, Meredith thought, I can see the point of it for other people. People with fulfilling lives. But not for me any longer. And never for Julia and Cassandra and Clara, all of whom have been sucked dry by Leonora. I'm simply a victim of my own lack of adventure, with no one to blame but myself, but Leonora undereducated those girls and then, when the first signs of independence began to appear, withdrew all support, financial and otherwise. Apart from Julia, who must have learnt during her brief marriage, they can't even drive. All their lives she has dominated and bullied them, so that even when she does eventually die, it will be too late. They are all institutionalized, or, rather, Armitage Lodged. Even Julia, who nearly got away, had to stand by and watch her mother destroy her marriage. Wasted lives and empty hearts. Such a pity.

Sighing, she stirred her tea.

Morgan, too, was conscious of a sense of loss. He remembered a much younger Meredith Barstow. In those days she had been busy and efficient, a JP he seemed to recall, as well as holding down the school job, and there had been endless tennis parties. He wondered what she did with herself now, with only the Brig for company. It was a dismal thought.

As though telepathically prompted by Morgan's musings, the Brigadier suddenly uttered: 'I call it a bloody mess. Damned shame if you ask me!'

The general conversation, which was about gardening, stopped and they all looked at him. It was as though a statue had spoken.

'What is?' Clara's consternation was reflected in her wrinkled brow and open mouth. She hoped he did not have her vegetable patch in mind.

'Suez!'

Suez? Nobody had mentioned Suez.

Just as suddenly as he had spoken, the Brigadier retreated back into a dismal, preoccupied silence, as though his own interjection had not taken place. Looking at her father where he sat straight-backed on the edge of his armchair, knees apart, veiny hands on his silver-knobbed cane, his feet in their conker-coloured, highly polished shoes placed exactly together, Meredith was conscious of a sinking heart. For most of the time he was himself, that was to say he was autocratic, short-tempered and more often than not difficult. Most importantly, though, he was lucid. But lately Meredith had increasingly noticed unnerving non sequiturs, sudden small lapses of concentration. She hoped that these were not the first straws in the wind of senility.

Trying to bridge an awkward gap in the conversation, Morgan said, 'Ah yes. Suez!' and then, knowing nothing about it, stopped, uncertain how to proceed. Conversationally stranded, he smiled encouragingly at the Brigadier.

Sir Arthur drew his tufted eyebrows together, cormorant-like. 'Suez? Who said anything about Suez? I don't know what you're talking about. What's he talking about?'

'Would you like another cup of tea?' Clara hastily reached for the teapot. 'Shall I do it, Mother, or would you prefer to?'

'You do it. Try not to drop it.'

Meredith stood up. 'Thank you, no. I think we really must be going. Come along, Father.' They said their farewells. Julia and Meredith embraced. Himself again, the Brigadier kissed Leonora's hand in courtly fashion. She was a damn fine woman. Damn fine! He had always thought so.

As she was leaving, Meredith said to Morgan, 'Caroline is coming up on a visit sometime soon, with Minerva.' The moment the words were out, she was conscious of a sudden flicker of misgiving.

Carefully casual, Morgan placed a log on the fire. 'What about Patrick?'

'Probably not. It looks as though he may have a small part in a West End play.'

Cassandra saw them out. It was beginning to snow again. The parchment-coloured air would shortly be thick with it. Noticing this, Morgan said to Leonora, 'Grandmama, I think Tom and I should travel back to London tonight rather than tomorrow. In case the snow closes in.'

Leonora was easier to deal with than he had expected, her mind evidently on something else entirely. 'In my heyday we never let a covering of snow stop us doing anything. However, if it worries you that much, then of course you must leave.' She indicated that his audience was at an end, and then appeared to change her mind. 'And when may we expect the honour of another visit? When Caroline Barstow is next here, I daresay!' (Laughter) 'Bring Tom Marchant with you when you do come. I find him amusing.' She waved her hand in queenly dismissal. He had the feeling that she expected him to exit backwards bowing, like a courtier.

Once outside the door, Morgan said, 'How did she know about my feelings for Caro? I've never told her.'

'Maybe she has a crystal ball!'

'No, that's Aunt Cassandra.'

*   *   *

The next morning Leonora sat like a spider at her desk. One by one the usual affairs of state passed across it, and when she had finished these and counted out the money with which Julia and Clara would go into Hexham to do the week's shopping, she turned her mind to the intricacies of her web. Rather like Elizabeth Tudor, though without the aid of either a Walsingham or a Cecil as her eyes and ears, there was hardly anything Leonora did not know about the private lives of her immediate family, manipulation long since having replaced sex as her passion.

To Morgan she afforded more leeway than her daughters, well aware that he was securely bound to her by the gossamer but unbreakable thread of the family money. When she drew him in, he would come. The girls, Leonora despised. Despised, in fact, for what she herself had made them into. She also bore them a grudge for not being sons.

Although, God knows, she thought, most men are useless. But not as useless as Clara, for instance.

On the other hand, she had a certain amount of time for Julia, if only because she was the mother of Morgan and had very nearly achieved a successful bolt. Just the same her admiration of this had not stopped Leonora from seeing off Major Farrell.

In her mind's eye she saw him again. Getting rid of him had not been difficult. What had he been after all? Just another dashing dimwit. Handsome, though.

She had always liked handsome men. And how they used to flock round her.

Maybe that was one of the reasons she had been determined that Julia should not have him. If she, Leonora, could not, then nobody should. She remembered the look on his face when she had explained how Julia would get not one penny of her money while the marriage endured.

'What's it worth to you,' he had asked, 'if I go without a fight?' and she had named a sum. And the next day he had gone, leaving Julia behind, pregnant, although that fact had not become apparent until some time later. In the event, Leonora had rated this unlooked-for outcome very satisfactory, if not for Julia herself. After all her own tedious attempts to produce a son, her daughter had a fifty-fifty chance of bringing it off, and without the disadvantage of a husband cluttering up Armitage Lodge. A splendid state of affairs in Leonora's view.

Leaving the past, she turned back to the present. With her thin gold pen she wrote and signed a series of cheques to tradesmen, and then one by one put them in their envelopes, which she addressed and sealed. These would be given to Julia to distribute during the course of the shopping trip. Finally, all that was left in the in-basket was an unopened bank statement, which was apparently destined to remain that way, since Leonora disdainfully tucked it into a pigeonhole in her desk within which reposed more of the same.

She put the cap back on her pen, leant back in her chair, and turned her mind to disruption. Probably, she mused, the best way to achieve this would be for her to instruct Julia to take the car for its service on Thursday. Leonora was well aware that on Thursdays, Cassandra, with Julia's connivance, managed to snatch an hour or so in the company of Deirdre Ricketts, on whom she had a crush. Aided by Cassandra when she succeeded in getting away, Deirdre, who was prone to drooping cardigans, always did the church flowers on Thursdays. While this was happening, Clara, also with Julia's connivance, went to her weekly assignation with Seth Murgatroyd, a farmer who lived near St John Lee. Well aware that the absence of a car would dish both these arrangements, Leonora picked up the telephone receiver and rang the garage.

February

4

In the comfortable but shabby kitchen of their Clapham house, Patrick and Caroline Holland sat drinking tea.

'If you do get that West End part, that'll help,' said Caroline. They were discussing their financial affairs, not on a grand scale, but rather how they were going to continue to make ends meet on a day-to-day basis.

'It's an actor's play, and as such, likely to have a run of about a month, if that. What I need is a part in _The Mouse-trap_.'

'We could always sell the house. Move into something smaller.'

The Hollands had bought it years before, at the bottom of the market. Unfortunately, with the country in the stranglehold of recession, it was once again at the bottom of the market.

'No point in doing that. Sighting a house-buyer these days is like spotting a dodo.'

Pensively, Caroline stared at the scrubbed wood tabletop, mentally agreeing with him. Looking at her, Patrick was struck by her beauty, which was subtle enough to go unnoticed by the vast majority. Eyes the colour of purple pansies were currently veiled by smooth eyelids, whilst the oval of her face was emphasized by the curved, shining fall of her dark bobbed hair. It was not a modern face, but rather that of a Leonardo madonna, with all the attendant mysterious containment. Caroline did not efferversce, she contemplated, which was probably why many, among them Tom Marchant and those in a hurry, missed her point.

She stood up and went to the window. Pulling aside the lace curtain, and noticing as she did so that it needed washing, she looked out on to the February garden. The time of year was a sad one. Drifts of soggy brown leaves covered the uneven lawn, piling themselves against the collapsing fence at the end. A solitary cat, not one of theirs, was daintily digging a hole in the flowerbed that ran along one side. How do other people ever find time for gardening? wondered Caroline, thinking of the pile of marking sitting on one end of the kitchen table, flanked by a large heap of clean but unsorted laundry. There was no answer to this. Maybe other people's husbands helped more than hers did. Hers was, after all, almost permanently 'resting', and it was her private view, never openly expressed to Patrick himself, that he could have lifted a finger rather more often than he did. It simply never seemed to occur to him. But then, thought Caro, remembering his spoilt and extraordinarily silly mother, who had been an actress of the old-fashioned, refined, Rank variety, perhaps that was hardly surprising.

She decided to break the bad news sooner rather

than later, and said without looking at him, 'I've asked Emily and Jonathan to come and stay for a few days.'

Patrick jumped to his feet.

'Oh, Christ! What on earth made you do that? And by the way, don't think of consulting me before you make these generous offers, will you?'

'She burnt her kitchen down again. Until the insurance pays up and it's rebuilt, there's nowhere for them to cook. She's my sister. I really couldn't refuse.'

'What happens if she burns our kitchen down next? I suppose we all go and stay with your mother, and then hers goes up in flames and we all move on again, a sort of kitchen caravan-train growing all the time, and so on and so on. And it won't be days, either, it will be weeks.' He groaned theatrically, head in hand, and then strode over to the door, where he struck a heroic Shakespearian pose, careful to present her with his better profile.

Watching him, Caro reflected that Patrick had never used to be like this. The trouble was that when one lived with someone, change came so slowly and so subtly that it was perfectly possible to miss it until it had become profound. And by then the new persona was a *fait accompli*.

He began to pace up and down. It occurred to her that as the work had dried up, so he had become more and more stagy at home. Acted all the time, in fact.

'Look, I'm very sorry. I should have asked you.' (So why didn't I? Because I knew he'd veto it, that's why!) 'We both love Emily.'

'And hate Larch.'

No point in denying it.

'And hate Larch.'

'He's poisonous.'

'He's poisonous,' she agreed demurely. Her husband threw her a suspicious look.

'That man has raised interference to the level of an art form.'

'Well, he *is* a social worker.'

'Quite so, and we don't need a social worker, especially living in the house!'

Murmuring soothing agreement, Caro passed on the next piece of bad news. 'They're turning up at seven this evening.'

'This evening!'

'Shouting again?' Streetwise, though only thirteen, Minerva Holland entered the room. Patrick glared at his daughter and then exited majestically, slamming the door.

'"Hello, Minerva darling. Have you had a good day at school? Why don't you tell me all about it?" Yes, I've had a lovely day, thank you, Daddy dear,' said Minerva.

'Don't start, Minerva!' Suddenly feeling bleak, Caro sat down at the kitchen table.

'Why is he in such a strop, anyway?' Minerva began to unlace her Doc Martens.

'Aunt Emily and Jonathan Larch are turning up for an indefinite stay.'

This news rocked even Minerva. 'Aunt Emily's lovely.' She pulled off one boot. 'He's a twat.'

'How many times have I told you—'

'Not to use the word "twat". Sorry, I forgot. Although when you think about it, it is only a word, just like any other.'

'Got any homework?' Caro felt too dispirited to join battle on this one.

Minerva gave her mother a slippery look. 'Some. I've done most of it.'

'Well, go and do the rest. No television until you do. And take those great, clumping boots with you.'

Minerva went. Caro heard her hurl them into a corner of the hall with a loud clatter and then slowly make her way upstairs.

Consulting her watch, she saw that it was four thirty. Lackadaisically she began to sort and fold the laundry. Performing this dull task, she thought about Morgan Steer. The years had taken the edge off her schoolgirl passion for Morgan, but lately she had noticed a tendency to think of him again, mainly after she and Patrick had had a row. Caro was aware of a malaise within her marriage, almost as though with the passing of the years there had been an imperceptible emotional seepage to the point where, suddenly and surprisingly, there was almost nothing left. An empty shell.

It's funny, mused Caro, I waited and waited for Morgan to ask me to marry him. Right up to the day I married Patrick I still half expected it. And if he had, I would have thrown Patrick over.

Instead he had waited until she was safely wed to declare himself, by which time it really was too late, for by then she was pregnant.

And here she was. Part-time wife, part-time mother, part-time teacher, full-time bored, a misfired person living with a man she no longer rated, whilst Morgan himself had never married. The perversity of life never ceased to amaze her.

Heavy of heart, she stowed the basket on the side, intending to distribute the contents when she next went upstairs, and reached for a cookery book. For naturally, Jonathan Larch was a vegetarian.

Looking at him across the table that evening as they ate supper, Caro wondered afresh what her sister saw in Larch. Opinionated, and not above putting his partner down publicly when he felt like it, he was, in her opinion anyway, an unqualified pill. And Emily, attractive but vulnerable Emily, with so much to offer, deferred to him, let him get away with it. Incomprehensible! Her gaze dwelt on her sister with affection. Emily's Pre-Raphaelite auburn hair sprang back from the high Barstow forehead they had both inherited from their mother and spiralled in curls down her back. Tonight she was wearing a loose, short, ethnic dress. Really, Caro thought, we don't look very like each other at all. Funny how the same genes produce such different people.

'I blame this Government,' Larch was saying. He would, of course. There was an awful righteousness about him that could only bode ill for anyone he was employed to help.

'Sorry, what for?' asked Caro, rising above her reverie and suppressing the impulse to add 'this time'.

'For the dismal mess education is in today. This move back to examinations and streaming is entirely misguided. A return to intellectual élitism.'

What a pompous ass he is, thought Caro, before observing, 'But there are intellectual haves and have-nots. Brains are not given to everyone, after all. What is comforting, and should comfort you, Jonathan, is that intelligence is such a very democratic gift.'

'Shouldn't that make it doubly important that the state system gears itself to its own high-flyers? Goes back to levelling up rather than down?' The speaker was Emily.

'Since you yourself were privately educated, I should keep quiet on the subject of the state system,' bullied Jonathan. 'You know nothing about it.'

'I think what Emily has just said makes perfect sense,' said Patrick, defending his crestfallen sister-in-law, 'and I'm surprised that it doesn't appeal to a radical like you.' He was very tempted to use the word 'Trot', but in the interests of avoiding a fight on the first night decided not to. Although it was entirely possible that Larch would not have objected to this sobriquet. 'After all, if we don't teach the hoi polloi to read and write, the best jobs are going to continue going to the upper-middle-class products of the private

system who do know how to, and that won't advance
your cause much.'

'I probably know more than all of you, since I'm in
it,' announced Minerva witheringly, herself a pupil at
the local comprehensive and the victim of mixed-
ability teaching, 'and where I am they're so busy
teaching the thickos that the rest of us get forgotten
about. It's a relief, actually,' she added, one eye on
her mother. 'I hate school.'

Caro decided not to rise to it and began to clear
away the plates. Emily helped her. Neither the men
nor Minerva did anything.

'Come on, Minerva, you can help.'

'I've got homework to finish.' Impossible to argue
with this excuse, which was advanced every time her
daughter was asked to do something domestic.

'Well, if that's the case, go away and do it. Right
now.'

Caro was crisp. Preparing to scrub the pans that their
antediluvian dishwasher had long since ceased to cope
with adequately, she ran hot water into the sink amid
a froth of washing-up liquid. Watching her, Jonathan
said, 'You are going to rinse those properly afterwards,
aren't you?'

Caro counted to ten.

'No, you are. In this house the cook doesn't wash
up.'

'What, even when he's been treading the boards all
day, you make poor old Patrick wash up?'

This speech even succeeded in offending the person

it was ostensibly defending, for Patrick did not like
'poor', and relished 'old' even less. Both together
made him feel like an elderly sheepdog about to be
put down.

Thinking 'patronizing prig', and further reflecting
that the only boards her husband trod these days were
the ones on which they were all currently standing, she
said, 'Yes, that's right. In this house we all work, you
know.' She would have liked to pull his ridiculous
ponytail until his eyes watered. 'And talking of work,
I have a stack of marking to do, so if you'll excuse
me…' Aware of sounding curt, she went, leaving them
to it.

The next morning dawned dove-grey and surprisingly mild. There was no sign of either Emily or Jonathan. On weekday mornings when she drove Minerva
to school, Caro usually rose at seven thirty. Most of
the next thirty minutes until they left were spent trying
to instil a sense of urgency vis-à-vis the passing time
into her ungrateful child.

Minerva had got into the habit of making her day's
début at eight exactly, by which time, she had worked
out, it was too late for Caro to send her back to begin
again. Though officially the school uniform, the
clothes she wore had been anarchically assembled. The
regulation knee-length skirt was turned over at the
waist three or four times, so that it barely covered her
navy-blue knickers. On top she wore a t-shirt whose
black, two-inch-high legend, LOVE SUCKS, was

stretched over her small breasts, and was clearly visible through the regulation (though untucked) white school blouse she had put on over it. Feeling exasperated, as she did every morning and as she was no doubt meant to, Caro asked, 'Where's your sweater?'

Minerva shrugged. 'No idea.'

'We aren't going anywhere until you find it and put it on.' She was aware that swimming, which Minerva liked, was the first double period. Sulking, her daughter slowly complied. At long last in the car, Caro let out the clutch and switched on the news.

'Why can't we have Capital Radio? All the other mothers listen to Capital Radio.'

'*Do* shut up, Minerva. Do you realize that ever since you got up this morning you've done nothing but complain?'

There was a brief respite, which proved to be a regrouping exercise and was followed by, 'I *hate* the name Minerva. *Hate* it.' This was a familiar litany. 'It wouldn't have mattered if you'd sent me to St Paul's or somewhere where they've all got posh names, but the other girls at the comp really give me grief.'

'Well, when you're old enough and can afford to pay for it, you can change your name by deed poll to Sharon.'

'Oh, ha ha, Mother!' Minerva lapsed into sullen silence, aware as she did so that she was behaving badly and at a loss as to how to stop it.

She must have the curse, thought Caro, who by now felt as though she had been up all night. She drew up outside the school. Thirteen really was a ghastly age, and no doubt fourteen would be worse. And yet there were still days when consensus reigned, and her daughter was not only positive but positively helpful. Perhaps the name Minerva had been a mistake. Caro had wanted it because it reminded her of the Wall and summer walks with Morgan years before. She remembered that in one of the museums (Chester's?) there had been an altar dedicated with the inscription, *To Minerva, Quintus, architect, pays a vow.* Standing looking at it, Caro had wished that Morgan would pay such a vow to her. Without knowing any of this, Patrick had also liked the name, deeming it distinguished and picturing his daughter in the years to come on the stage, a classical actress.

They both got out of the car and Caro opened the boot. Minerva took out her school bags, hesitated for a moment and then abruptly said, 'Sorry!' Although sincerely meant, this expression of contrition still sounded ungracious, even defiant. Minerva knew that she loved and depended on Caro, but at the same time was confused by her own feelings of aggression towards her mother, whom she blamed, without exactly knowing why, for the precarious equilibrium of her parents' marriage. Dad was difficult, but Mum shouldn't let it get to her, was Minerva's opinion.

Conscious of the tumult within her daughter and equally unsure how to deal with it, Caro took Minerva in her arms. 'Don't worry about it, darling! Don't even *think* about it again.'

They hugged one another.

'Off you go. Have a lovely day.'

'Yes…'

Unseen by Caro, a tear fell.

With a combination of dejection and bravado, Minerva brushed it away and set off towards the school gates. Watching her go, Caro noticed a large ladder creeping up the right leg of her navy-blue tights. She reversed the car into somebody's drive and then set off in the direction from which she had come.

Letting herself into the house twenty minutes later, she was conscious of the fact that she resented her own generous offer to have Larch and Emily to stay. No, not Emily. Only Larch. Dear God, I hope she has the sense not to marry him, thought Caro in heartfelt prayer. This was reinforced by his unwelcome presence in the kitchen, where she found him inspecting the back of a packet of stock cubes.

'Hydrogenated vegetable oil, sodium glutamate, curcumin, capsanthin,' he incomprehensibly read aloud to himself, clicking with disapproval as he did so. Noticing Caro's entrance, and without even saying good morning, he observed, 'A great deal of the food in your cupboards appears to have passed its sell-by date.'

Aware that she was by no means Housewife of the Year, Caro was profoundly irritated by the idea that he had trawled through her food stores. Ignoring his last remark, she said, 'Aren't you going to work today?'

'I am.' He replaced the stock cubes on the shelf. 'I

have to give evidence in the juvenile court. Are you quite sure you don't want me to throw—'

'Quite sure,' said Caro, who had not in fact used that particular brand for years and would have thrown them away herself if she had found them first. He must have located them right at the back.

Indicating a row of tins, he said, 'I lined these up for your inspection. They are all very ancient. You might like to consider them. Oh, and while I'm on the subject, the fresh orange juice in the fridge is one day over.'

Once again treating his last utterance as if it had not taken place, Caro said, 'Has Patrick put in an appearance yet?'

'No, he hasn't.' Seeing his lover lifting her coat off the bentwood stand in the hall prior to entering the kitchen, Jonathan was momentarily distracted from his food purge by the need to criticize her appearance.

'You look like a rather dull secretary in that suit, Emily.'

With a certain edge that was new to Caro's ear, and a bright spot of colour on each cheek, Emily said, 'Well, I am a secretary, though not a *particularly* dull one, I hope. And after today's interview I may not be one at all. I may, if all goes well, be a dull receptionist instead!'

She turned on her heel and walked out. Following her, quite unabashed, Larch said in a jocular tone to Caro, 'Emily's sense of humour seems to have deserted her this morning.'

Hearing the door slam behind them both, it was with a feeling of relief that Caro went in search of Patrick.

She found him lying naked on their unmade bed with his hands behind his head, whistling to himself.

'You sound very cheerful!'

'I know. I've just had Smollet on the phone.' Smollet was his agent. 'I've got a part! But it's better than that. They've given me something much more substantial than the one I actually auditioned for. It could be my big chance.'

'Darling, that's wonderful.'

Caro experienced a spontaneous rush of pleasure on her husband's behalf, and with it came a resurgence of something that had been conspicuously lacking lately, namely the desire to celebrate such good news in bed. Sitting down beside him, she kissed him.

'Congratulations.'

'Why don't you take off your clothes and put on some scent?'

Without saying a word, she slowly, which made her actions all the more interesting, complied. Though not exactly thin, his wife was slim enough for the eye to notice line before flesh. Linear and honey-coloured, thought Patrick, with a body whose beauty, like that of her face, lay in its understatement. Modigliani should have been Caro's painter. Watching her with desire, Patrick was conscious that he had not been easy to live with recently, and the thought of it made him suddenly afraid, for what if she should ever leave him? Putting both his hands around her long neck, he drew her down towards him, kissing her breasts as he did so, and as the dark bell of her hair fell forward, he buried his face in it, obscurely convinced that by doing so, like a small child he could blot out all his fears and insecurities and disappointments.

Lying in his arms afterwards, Caro decided that her marriage was probably what she wanted. If Patrick could only lift himself out of the slough of despondency into which months of unemployment had cast him, then perhaps it would be possible for them to make up the marital ground that had been lost.

Almost as though he divined her thought, Patrick said, 'I'm sorry. I'm afraid I've been an awful bastard lately.'

There was a short pause while she weighed up whether to let him off, as was her natural generous inclination. On balance it seemed better to get it out in the open. Anxious to avoid spoiling the moment, Caro chose her words with care.

'It's true to say you haven't been very easy.'

'Why didn't you ever say so?'

'Because, as you well know, it isn't my way. I don't like confrontation if I can avoid it. I just kept hoping that you yourself would notice what was happening and stop it.'

'Stop what exactly?'

Caro took a breath. Nothing for it now but to tell him.

'Oh, the artificiality. The self-absorption. The petulance.' Like many people who normally do not complain, she was aware of having said far too much.

'Oh, I see.' Frowning, he fell silent.

'I'm sorry. But you did ask me!'

'No, *I'm* sorry it has all been such an uphill struggle for you. Perhaps you ought to be married to a bank clerk!'

'Patrick, that's unfair. You yourself just admitted you've been very difficult.' As she said the words, she recognized that there was a world of difference between her uttering them and Patrick uttering them himself. 'Oh, come on, don't spoil it all. Please, darling!'

A door banged downstairs.

'Anyone in?' It was Jonathan Larch, who must have forgotten something.

Christ! thought Caro. Now the opportunity to sort out that particular marital blip had gone, and Patrick would be sulking in his tent for the next five days.

Aloud, she called back, 'Patrick and I are having a private talk.'

'Oh really?' The innuendo was unmistakable and extremely irritating. 'Well, don't let me stop you!'

'Nothing to stop.' By now in his underpants, Patrick began to pull on a pair of cords. 'We've finished. My wife has just dotted the last i and crossed the last t.' He shot her a furious look.

Caro gave up on it. She pulled the sheet over herself and closed her eyes, registering another promising moment of closeness that had suddenly and surprisingly metamorphosed into an unpleasant row. Sometimes I 'wonder what I'm doing here, thought Caro. No, not sometimes, almost all the time lately.

Another door slammed, this time the one belonging to their bedroom, as her husband exited. She listened to his retreating footsteps descending the stairs. At the foot of them she heard him have a perfectly ordinary and apparently good-humoured exchange with Larch about the weather, as though their quarrel had never taken place, before he left the house, banging the front door with unnecessary force. That evening, Caro knew, there would be more of the same. He would be perfectly normal with the others and only address her when he absolutely had to, at which point he would be glacial and brief. He was quite capable of keeping this up for a week.

Escaping from the unpalatable present, Caro remembered the episode in Northumberland during which Morgan had told her that he loved her, and she had told him that she was pregnant.

'Why on earth didn't you say all this before,' she had wept, 'it would have saved us all so much trouble. Now I'm married and having Patrick's child and I *can't* leave.' Patrick had been spear-carrying in a London production of *Coriolanus* at the time. Standing on the Roman Wall with the wind whipping around them, Morgan had kissed her again and again. Perhaps he had needed her absolute unavailability to put him in touch with himself. It had been the beginning of a very cold October and there were few tourists about. To those who were there, she and Morgan must have appeared to be just another pair of lovers.

'Let me make love to you,' Morgan had said urgently. 'If we do, I know you'll never go back.' He would never know how close she had come to doing it. And he was quite right. Had she done so, going back to Patrick after such a betrayal would have been inconceivable. As it was, Meredith's strict upbringing had asserted itself and she had told him no, and had regretted this on and off ever since.

It's amazing that it all took place fourteen years ago, reflected Caro. And, after all, my marriage hasn't been so bad. There have been long periods when I've hardly thought about Morgan. She had always been conscious of his presence, however, and conscious, too, though they met infrequently these days, of his enduring obsession with her.

Downstairs she heard the unmistakable sound of someone's key in the lock. With a lift of the heart she hoped it might be Patrick returning to apologize. Getting out of bed, she wound the sheet togalike around her naked body, and walked out onto the landing. A quiet closing of the door rather than a masculine slam indicated that the entrant was probably Emily back from her job interview. Caro sank on to the top stair, drew her knees up to her chest and wrapped her arms around them. She was suddenly reminded of the Priest's Seat, a beauty spot on the brow of a hill near Hexham, and of all the times she had sat there as a girl. She waited patiently for her sister to come up.

Emily did not come. Caro heard her fill up the kettle. This normally untraumatic act was followed by the sound of loud sobs. The grade of sob one only allowed oneself when certain there was no one else around to hear it. Stormy crying was followed by furious railing, by more heartbroken keening, and by much agitated rattling of crockery. In spite of her distress, Emily must have decided to press on with the idea of a cup of tea.

Quietly, Caro stood up and softly, like a cat, made her way down and materialized in the kitchen.

'Em?' said Caro. 'Em! What's the matter?'

Confronted by the unexpected apparition of her sister, Emily was so het up that she barely broke her emotional stride.

'The matter is', shouted Emily, knocking over her cup of tea without noticing she had done so, 'that I'm living with a complete bastard.'

Temporarily forgetting her own problems, Caro took her sister in her arms and for a few minutes they wept together. Making an effort to compose herself, Emily suddenly became aware that she did not have a monopoly on distress. She drew back.

'Caro, what's the matter with *you?*' Then, noticing her sister's attire, 'And why are you wearing a sheet?'

'The matter is,' said Caro, through her own tears, 'that I am living with a complete bastard, too, but I'm married to mine.'

That evening's meal was a classic of its kind. Patrick did not speak to Caro, and Emily did not speak to Jonathan. Jonathan apparently did not notice this and did speak to Emily, who did not reply. They all spoke to Minerva, who did not particularly want to talk to any of them and was disconcerted to find herself a conversational catalyst. Finally, Minerva, who had just begun to keep a diary to whose pages she confided her inmost thoughts and who couldn't wait to get back to it, stood up, announcing loftily though untruthfully, 'I have to go. I have homework to do.'

In the wake of her departure, they all washed up in silence.

March

5

Morgan met Chloe Post at a party given by Tom Marchant's business partner, Michael Hardwick-Smith. It was at his flat in Chelsea and appeared to be composed almost entirely of bankers and their wives.

'I think we might give up on this, don't you?' said Tom as the two of them lounged in one corner of the room surveying the pinstriped horde. 'It must have taken a really dedicated trawl through his old address books for Michael to have come up with quite such a relentlessly dull gathering.' He ate a canapé. 'Perhaps he left the guest list to his secretary. What do you want to do? Shall we go to the cinema, or shall we take ourselves out to dinner?'

Without female company, each was privately of the opinion that this was a dismal prospect.

Morgan was just about to answer when, suddenly on the alert, he said instead, 'Who's that? Over there.'

Tom looked. Two women stood by the door evidently having just arrived. One was tall and blonde and probably, he estimated, around thirty. The other was petite with a razor-sharp short bob, and, as Tom put it to himself, reeked of chic. Both, his expert eye noted, were expensively dressed, and both had the indefinable aura of women currently without men in tow. Perhaps, like Morgan and himself, they were hunting as a pair.

'Yes?'

'Yes.'

Without exchanging another word, both men languidly moved across the room homing in for the social kill.

Later, over dinner, Joanna and Tom and Morgan and Chloe appraised one another.

How attractive Tom Marchant is, thought Joanna, and extraordinarily pleased with himself. Dangerous. I could fall for him. I wonder if he's married?

Tom considered Joanna Blackstock. Not exactly a beauty, he concluded, but she does have a certain sparkle. And good legs. I'll have a small bet with myself that if I play my cards right, I can get her into bed tonight. I wonder if she has any money?

Observing Morgan over the top of her menu, Chloe thought how handsome he was and how much his unusual name suited him. But he's bound to try to get me into bed tonight. They always do. I do wish I liked it better and that sex wasn't quite such a chore. All the same, I'm tired of trawling London on my own and a regular escort would be useful. I wonder if he's married?

And Morgan had decided there was a look of Caro about Chloe Post: something to do with that dark, sleek head.

Because conversation was of the stilted, exploratory sort, born out of the fact that they did not know each other, no light was shed on the questions raised in their hidden agendas. Like Morgan and Tom, Joanna and Chloe had been at school together. Of the two women, Tom preferred Joanna, though he was not bowled over by her. There was a curious lack of substance about Chloe, as though she was hardly there at all. Maybe this was why it was so easy for Morgan to project the image of Caroline Barstow onto Chloe. There was simply nothing to stop it.

Standing on the pavement afterwards, they discovered that between them they had two cars, Tom and Morgan having turned up in one and Joanna and Chloe in the other. It was therefore decided that Tom would drop Joanna off before proceeding to the hotel to which he had been exiled by his estranged wife, and Chloe would drop Morgan off at the Steer flat in Prince's Gate on her way to W8. In the event, this only half happened. As they turned into the service road in front of Prince's Gate, Morgan said to Chloe, 'Can I tempt you in for a last drink? Cup of coffee, even?'

'Why not?' Chloe had decided to get the whole thing over with. Sex may not be my bag, she thought, but these days nothing much seems to happen without it.

Beyond the front door was a black-and-white tiled floor and a rather grand wrought-iron staircase. Chloe was struck by the familiar stuffy smell that the cream entrance halls of all blocks of flats, Victorian or otherwise, seemed to acquire. The large, artful flower display, *de rigueur* in a place such as this, looked artificial, though in fact (she tested one bloom between finger and thumb) it was not.

Letting them both in at the top of the second flight, Morgan switched on the lights. It was like entering a time warp. Crimson was the predominant colour of the walls, on which were hung a series of ponderous portraits, all male, presumably ancestral Steers. The drawing room was more of the same, but dominated by a fine full-length painting (a Sargent?) of a woman wearing cream satin and pearls. Titian hair was piled above an unlined brow from beneath which almond-shaped, tobacco-coloured eyes imperiously challenged the onlooker. It radiated will and hauteur. Not a shrinking violet, thought Chloe.

'Grandmama,' said Morgan briefly, seeing her look. 'What can I get you to drink? Whisky? Gin? Brandy?'

'Brandy, please.' Walking across to the windows with their undrawn velvet curtains, Chloe looked out. The flat was at the end of the terrace, so that Exhibition Road ran along one side, and in front was Kensington Gore, along which coursed the lights of the Knightsbridge traffic, whose faint hum could be heard. Beyond that lay the park. Turning back into the room, she found Morgan at her elbow with her drink.

'Thank you, Morgan,' she said, taking it. It was the first time she had used his name. Eyeing her, he was struck afresh by her elusive resemblance to Caro, which was not so much a physical thing as something to do with the air of repose she carried with her.

'You remind me of someone I used to know.' He could have said, 'Someone I still know and am in love with,' but did not.

'Do I?' Chloe could not claim to be very interested in this statement, but was adept enough at conversational nuances to divine that he was referring to unrequited love. 'I really think I prefer not to be compared with past mistresses. Are you married by the way?'

'Would it matter if I was?'

'No, not really. It's just tidier if you aren't.'

'Do you have affairs with married men?' asked Morgan.

'Not if I can help it.' Chloe was deliberately vague. 'Although in America married couples get bored with one another so quickly that it's hard not to.'

She looked at Morgan, who had loosened his tie and removed his jacket and was leaning, pink-shirted, against the mantelpiece. He bore a strong facial resemblance to his handsome grandmother, and his careless elegance put Chloe, devotee of the novels of Georgette Heyer, in mind of the Regency period. She wondered how Joanna was making out with Tom Marchant. Tomorrow they would compare notes.

'Did you spend all your childhood in the States?' Morgan was asking. 'I only ask because you don't have an American accent.'

'No, that's because my mother is English, and I

went to school here. She's now based in Boston. Some years after their marriage broke up, she went to live in New York and took me with her. But that wasn't until I was fifteen.'

Chloe was silent, thinking of her shallow, neurotic parent, whose main preoccupation had been deciding what to wear the next day. On her passport, under the heading 'Occupation', Chloe's mother had entered the word 'Socialite'. Her father had married his latest mistress after her mother left, the upshot being that Chloe had a stepmother who was younger than she was. It had long been Chloe's view that her frigidity derived from the fact that her birth into a wealthy and privileged family had brought her a substantial trust fund but no love or affection of any kind.

'Why don't I get you another brandy?'

Morgan held out his hand for her empty glass.

When he returned, he handed it back to her and then sat beside her on the sofa. Putting down his own drink, he slid an arm around Chloe's shoulders and kissed her. His aftershave smelled of musk. Chloe was conscious of the usual trepidation stirring within her, plus something else. Could it be desire?

Morgan put one hand on Chloe's narrow, silken knee, which was as smooth as a stone, and then slid it up to the top of her thigh. Heart fluttering, Chloe did not stop him. Like a small child, she closed her eyes and he kissed her again. Stopping for a moment and looking at her heart-shaped, painted face, Morgan said, 'You're very beautiful, Chloe Post.'

'Am I?'

'Yes.'

'Oh!'

Morgan leant sideways, moving away from her as he did so, and having located his glass of wine, drank it at a swallow.

'Why don't I show you the rest of the flat?'

Reflecting that the art of seduction really wasn't very various, and well aware that by the rest of the flat he meant the bedroom, Chloe said, 'Why not?'

She rose and followed him. His grandmother's bedroom, which was where they ended up, had the largest bed Chloe had ever seen. It was a stylish room rather than an intimate one, with fine mahogany furniture and mirrored wardrobe doors. On one of the chests of drawers stood a collection of silver-framed sepia photographs. Interested, Chloe picked one up. It depicted Leonora Steer riding side-saddle, and Chloe saw at once that here was none of her own mother's vapidity. Cutting a dash at a canter, Leonora had the air of a female brigand rather than of a gently reared daughter of the upper classes.

'That's Grandmama again.' Morgan took the photograph from Chloe and replaced it on the chest. Turning her around, he began to unbutton the jacket of her Armani suit.

'Let's go to bed!'

'Yes, all right.'

Yes, all right?

She did not sound very passionate, or even interested. Morgan, engaged in achieving a smooth seduction, registered this rather disappointing passivity but decided to disregard it. He slipped off the jacket, revealing her small, pointed breasts, which he kissed before slipping off everything else.

Later on, but not much later on, feet in the air as Morgan drove into her, and watching her lacquered toenails as he did so, Chloe was ambushed by her first and, as it was to turn out, last orgasm.

Joanna Blackstock's house was in SW7, in a pretty cobbled mews with window boxes. Drawing up outside it, Tom put the car into neutral and then drew his companion towards him and kissed her. His advance was reciprocated with enthusiasm, and in the light of this, what happened next was surprising.

Tom got out of the MG and went round to open Joanna's door for her.

'Thank you,' said Joanna.

On the doorstep, fishing around in her bag for her key, she said, 'And thank you very much for dinner. I really enjoyed this evening.'

The words had a valedictory ring. Suddenly aware that he was in danger of losing the bet he had made with himself earlier, Tom urged coaxingly, 'So why don't we prolong it? Surely you aren't going to send me off into the night without even a cup of coffee?' He saw his bleak hotel bedroom in his mind's eye.

By now she was inside and he was still on the step.

'Yes, I'm afraid I am.'

Joanna was very conscious that allowing herself to be seduced by a man like Tom Marchant on the night they first met would be a road to nowhere, much as she would probably enjoy it. If she wanted to see him again, she would have to play a longer game than that.

Having allowed himself to regard spending the night with her as a certainty, Tom was inordinately disappointed. Resisting an overwhelming impulse to put his foot in the door, since if he did and she made a fuss, in a tiny mews like this they would no doubt be instantly surrounded by upper-crust vigilantes toting unreliable shotguns, Tom said, 'If you're sure.'

'I'm quite sure. But there's no reason why we shouldn't meet again.'

Huh! thought Tom. Aloud, he coolly replied, 'No, none whatever. Well...goodnight!'

His small, unsatisfactory revenge would be to go without even bothering to take her telephone number.

'Goodnight, Tom.' And then, 'You can kiss me again if you like.'

Here was hope. He should have known she would change her mind. He took her in his arms, and she kissed him back with abandon. There was no doubt that Joanna Blackstock was hot stuff, Tom thought, enjoying himself and anticipating the treats to come. Then to his astonishment, she slipped out of his embrace, stepping smartly backwards over her threshold as she did so.

What the hell was happening now?

'Where are you going?'

'To bed. Where do you think?'

Of course! He was an idiot. Stepping forward to follow her in, he heard her say as she firmly shut the door in his face, '*Au revoir*, Tom.'

Tom and Morgan met for lunch the next day.

Tom decided against revealing just how far he had not got the night before. Morgan had no such inhibitions. Morgan and Chloe, it transpired, had enjoyed a very sexy time together. Tom was just rationalizing that it was too bad, that you won some and you lost some, and that Joanna Blackstock wasn't exactly God's gift to men anyway, when Morgan said, 'You really fell on your feet!'

'Did I?'

'Yes. Do you mean to say she didn't tell you? She's Harry Blackstock's only daughter. The millionaire property developer.'

'The *what*?' Remembering that he hadn't even asked her for her telephone number, Tom was aghast.

'I get the impression that you really screwed up there,' observed Morgan, watching his expression. 'That's not like you.'

They were silent for a few minutes whilst they ate their first course, then Morgan said, 'Tell me, does Chloe Post remind you of Caroline?'

'Not particularly,' answered Tom, who couldn't really be bothered to address the question, preoccupied as he was with the property heiress. All of a sudden, Joanna seemed much more desirable.

'Chloe's one of the American newspaper-chain Posts,' added Morgan, 'so she isn't short of a bob or three either.'

'If she reminds you of your lost love and she's wealthy, it sounds to me as though you may have fallen on your feet too.'

'Maybe,' said Morgan absently, remembering Chloe's slender nakedness with a flicker of desire. 'Maybe.'

Joanna and Chloe also had lunch together. Joanna noticed that Chloe had an oddly replete look. In the way that women often do not talk intimately about these things, as opposed to men, who often do, Joanna did not remark upon this fact, but drew her own conclusions.

'Do you intend to see him again?' she asked Chloe.

'Yes. What about you?'

'Certainly. I intend to marry Tom Marchant!'

6

Chloe never had another orgasm. Once or twice she thought Morgan might be going to bring it off again, but he never quite did, or rather they never did. In the event, Chloe went back to simulation, and let her mind wander afresh through the pages of the latest *Vogue* while Morgan laboured. Sometimes she remembered the day she had lost her virginity, or, to be more accurate, had given it away, and how she had lain there afterwards thinking that it had all been so undignified, verging on the ridiculous, and so, well, *un-chic*. At the age of seventeen and following the social trail blazed by her grasping and shallow mother, Chloe had decided that sex was more a means to an end than for delectation. She did not, of course, tell any of this to Morgan, and in spite of the unsatisfactory nights, which she had in any case already grown accustomed to with previous partners, she enjoyed his company and liked being squired by him at the parties they attended almost every evening.

Watching her one morning as she sat naked and cross-legged on Leonora's bed, inscrutable as an Egyptian figurine and drinking a cup of black coffee he had made her, Morgan wondered if he was in love. But then there was Caro, tantalizing, unobtainable Caro, whose elusive beauty still haunted him. If only we had actually fucked one another that day on the Wall, I wouldn't be suffering like this, thought Morgan, for either we would still be together or we would not. Either way, things would have been brought to some sort of conclusion. Perhaps he should go and see Caro, make a last appeal, then if she remained obdurate, concentrate on Chloe.

Chloe replaced her empty cup in its saucer and said, apropos of nothing in particular, 'I think we should go to Ireland for a weekend.'

Struck by this novel proposition, and mindful of his own Irish ancestry, through the parentage of the dubious Major Farrell, Morgan said, 'I don't believe I know anybody who lives in Ireland.'

'Oh, but I do. A Brazilian tin magnate! He's a billionaire.'

Naturally! thought Morgan, at the same time finding the idea of a Brazilian in Ireland inherently unlikely. To Chloe he said, 'Really? That sounds promising. Whereabouts? But why would your friend the billionaire want to have us to stay?'

'Dublin, and he's already invited me, and I'm perfectly prepared to wangle an invitation for you if you'd like to come. The occasion is a horse show. Roberto owns a stud.' Chloe yawned at the prospect.

Curiouser and curiouser!

'I didn't know you—'

'Liked horses,' she finished for him. 'I don't particularly. But this is different. It will be a huge house party and an ongoing beano.'

'And how do you—'

'Come to know the magnate? My mother used to be his mistress.' The way she delivered this, she might just as well have said, 'My mother used to be his bridge partner,' noted Morgan, struck afresh by his lover's detached attitude to sex and unaware that this extended to himself. 'But that all ended when he married for the fourth time,' continued Chloe.

'So he didn't want to marry your mother,' stated Morgan. 'Why not, if they were having an affair at the time?'

'No, he didn't, and if you met my mother, you'd know that that was the right thing to do, or rather, the right thing not to do. Mummy is not cut out for domesticity, even domesticity as well heeled as that. And certainly not in Ireland. Although he does have houses elsewhere, of course.'

Of course.

Chloe sighed briefly, thinking that if she had had one of those warm, comfortable mothers instead of a social termagant, perhaps things would have gone differently for her. She stood up and, lithe as a cat, drew on first a pair of knickers and then a pair of black leggings. Her hair fell forward, its sharp, dark shape as glossy as a blackbird's wing. Morgan eyed her with interest mixed with desire. He put a hand on her thigh. Momentarily stopping what she was doing, Chloe gave it back to him.

'Sorry, darling, but I'm afraid I have to be some-where at ten.'

'Where do you have to be?' Morgan was conscious of a twinge of jealousy.

'I have a dress fitting.' By now she was in the act of slipping over her head a loose, silky, oatmeal-coloured sweater that covered up her small, firm breasts as it fell.

'Why don't you ring them and tell them you'll be late. Better still, cancel it!'

He clearly did not understand the importance of clothes at all.

'I couldn't possibly do that. Once you upset a dress-maker, nothing fits properly for months.' She started to apply her make-up.

'Well, what about lunch? We could have it here. I'll get a takeaway.'

'No, I'm afraid I can't do that either. I'm having lunch with Joanna today.'

In spite of himself, Morgan was interested.

'Did Tom ever contact her again?'

'No, she contacted him. Joanna's very liberated.'

Reflecting that on the whole Tom Marchant and lib-erated women did not go together, Morgan was further taken aback when, spraying herself with scent, Chloe observed, 'I think she intends to marry him.'

It didn't sound as though Tom was going to have much say in the matter. Bearing his friend's heartless romantic career in mind, Morgan said doubtfully, 'I really don't think that's very advisable. Tom doesn't have much staying power where monogamy is concerned.'

'No, but I'll bet he has plenty of staying power where money is concerned, and Joanna's loaded. *Au revoir.*'

Blowing him a kiss, she went.

Marriage.

Inconclusively wandering about the flat in the wake of her departure, Morgan thought about it. He was now in his thirties, so if he was going to take the marital plunge it should probably be sooner rather than later. And the thought of escaping his grandmother's tyrannical rule via the delectable Chloe and her money was definitely appealing. The brake on proceedings was his (probably) futile obsession with Caroline Barstow. On impulse, he picked up the telephone receiver and dialled her number.

Over lunch, Chloe said to Joanna, 'How did you make out with Tom Marchant?'

'I haven't as yet. We set a date for dinner, but unfortunately I had to cancel. He wasn't very pleased. I get the impression that that sort of thing doesn't happen to him too often.'

'So when *are* you getting together?'

'Tonight. But dinner is all that's on the agenda. He won't like that either.'

'No, he won't.' Chloe stared at her strong-minded friend. 'Sounds as though you're going to keep him on a very short rein.'

'A *very* short rein.'

Joanna drank some of her wine.

'What about Morgan? He seems like rather good news to me.'

Chloe gave her a bright, blank look.

'Yes, in so far as any of them are, he is. But it's still no good in bed. For me, I mean. It's fine for him.'

Joanna, who had divined a long time ago that her friend's gift for acquaintance was unable to extend itself as far as physical love, had often wondered how Chloe, who had no job, passed her time. She glides along on the surface of everything, apparently unaware of any depth whatsoever, thought Joanna. She's like an icon: very decorative, but two-dimensional.

Their friendship went back a long way. Back to that old-fashioned, largely brainless institution the finishing school, where Chloe had been sent as a matter of course, because that was what happened to all the Post girls. Joanna, the first generation of her family to experience such a thing, had been dispatched there by her father, an intelligent rough diamond who was ambitious for his only child to acquire the sort of polish he himself had never had. Joanna had been drawn to Chloe by her soignée elegance, and in those days had been oblivious to her oddly bloodless personality. Perhaps her own spontaneity and dash had obscured this fact. Later, when other friends had drifted off into predictable marriages, Chloe and Joanna had continued to knock about London together.

'So what are you going to *do* with Morgan?'

Chloe was silent for a moment before she answered, 'Not sure.' And then, 'What do you think I should do with him?'

Joanna looked at her, at the same time experiencing a sudden, inexplicable anxiety. 'Well, for heaven's sake don't marry him unless your heart's in it.'

'Do you honestly think I would?' parried Chloe, searching her shoulder bag for her chequebook, her face veiled by the triangular fall of her hair. Sensitive to her evasion, Joanna was to wonder in years to come whether she herself hadn't put the idea in Chloe's head, thereby sowing the seeds for what was to come.

Morgan rang Caroline three times before he finally got hold of her. She sounded harassed.

'I wondered if I could come round to see you. Today if possible.'

'I really do have an awful lot to do…' Her voice faded and she was aware of a treacherous lightening of her heart at the sound of his voice.

'It's important. Very important.'

Holding the receiver, Caro stared at a plastic army of carrier bags standing in rows on the floor, waiting to have their contents decanted into food cupboards and fridge. Struggling around the local supermarket with a recalcitrant trolley that had run sideways, crablike, she had brooded on her marriage, which also seemed to be moving sideways. And now here was Morgan wanting, if past form was anything to go by, to review this very situation. Well, one never knew. He just might have something new to contribute.

'Caro? Caro? Are you still there?'

'Oh, sorry! Yes, I am. Look, why don't you come over now?'

It was, she thought, the best time, or more to the point, probably the only time. Getting the house to herself these days was becoming increasingly difficult, what with Larch's odd hours and Patrick's unpredictable rehearsal schedule. Although it had to be said that since he had begun to work again, the two of them were getting on better. Though maybe rubbing along was the way to describe it. Caro wished she did not feel quite so joyless.

'I'll be with you in half an hour!'

At least he sounded elated.

Caro began to disperse her shopping. How, she wondered, does one know when a marriage is past redemption? After all, advance nuptial publicity in the form of 'for better for worse, for richer for poorer,' and so on, clearly signalled that a bed of roses was not necessarily on offer. And given that there were bound to be ups and downs, at what point did the whole thing become untenable? The trouble was that she had no idea how much she should realistically expect. All the same, to feel as flat as this couldn't be right.

Stowing some tins in one of the cupboards, she came across an ancient bottle of tomato ketchup bearing the suggestion 'Best before July 1985' which

Larch must have missed, and replaced it right at the front.

Morgan drew up outside the Holland house and parked the car. A bottle of milk was still on the step, and he picked it up before ringing the doorbell. There was a long pause, and he was just going to ring again when the door opened and Caro stood before him.

Christ, she looks tired, he thought. Absolutely exhausted, in fact. He followed her into the kitchen.

'I brought you this.' He gave her the milk. 'And this.' It was a bottle of champagne, glassy green and very cold. 'I think we should crack it now, don't you?'

'Morgan, it's only eleven o'clock!'

'So what?'

Caro's smile transformed her, taking him back to their childhood in Northumberland, and more particularly to the day on Hadrian's Wall when he had failed to persuade her to elope with him. Looking at her with love and concern whilst he eased the cork, he decided to resist the temptation to take her in his arms.

Better not to rush things.

Instead, he poured her a glass of champagne. As he did so a brief and decorative vision of a naked Chloe Post sitting on his bed the previous night after they had made love passed before his mind's eye.

But I was desolate and sick of an old passion,
When I awoke and found the dawn was gray:
I have been faithful to thee, Cynara! in my fashion.

'Shall we adjourn?'

Caro's voice brought Morgan to himself.

He followed her, curious to see her sitting room. It was comfortable but shabby. More like a study, in fact, with books everywhere, so that Morgan had to move a pile of them in order to sit down. One wall was covered with photographs, mainly of Patrick. There was Patrick improbably dressed as a robin in what looked like his nursery-school play, Patrick at Oxford, Patrick at RADA, Patrick spear-carrying, quite a few of Patrick spear-carrying, in fact, in various productions, and Patrick and Caro on the day they married. Morgan averted his eyes from this one, which still evoked painful memories, not the least of which was his epic hangover. Its presence also reminded him of the purpose of his visit.

'I've come to ask you for the last time,' said Morgan, deciding to go for broke and taking a deep swig of champagne, 'if you will marry me. Because I've met somebody else.'

'Why are you asking me if you've met somebody else?' Caro was mystified as well as upset.

'Because I'd rather be married to you. I've been in love with you for years. You *know* that.'

'But Morgan, if you're in love with me, *if* you are, you shouldn't be thinking about getting married to anyone else. It isn't fair. To them I mean.'

'Well what am I to do? If you won't leave Patrick,

I can't be expected to live like a Trappist monk for the rest of my life.'

He stood up and Caro watched him walk restlessly up and down the room. Although youthful grace had long since matured into lean manhood, there was a lingering boyishness that was very appealing to women. The looks which had caused Morgan such problems as a small boy at Eton had changed surprisingly little over the years. Thick, coppery hair fell forward over finely drawn dark eyebrows and was constantly tossed back. With his straight nose and strong chin, both inherited from his grandmother, and his striking eyes, which were of an intense Celtic blue, courtesy of Major Fred, Morgan was very handsome.

Caro longed for him to take her in his arms and, at the same time, feared it.

'Nobody's asking you to live like any sort of monk!' She felt perilously close to tears. 'But there's no need to mess up somebody else's life for the duration as well.'

'WILL YOU MARRY ME?'

It was a cry of desperation.

Wanting to shout back, 'YES I WILL!' she looked at the school photograph of Minerva standing on the mantelpiece, still in its original cardboard frame. Out of it her clever, vulnerable, uncompromising child stared at the camera with hostility as if defying it to take a flattering likeness.

'No, I won't,' said Caro. 'I can't!'

Following her forlorn gaze, Morgan also eyed Minerva's picture, deciding as he did so that the words 'baleful brat' summed up this example of the photographer's art.

'Yes, you can! We'll take your daughter with us.'

Pulling her towards him, Morgan began to kiss Caroline, and as he slid one hand inside her shirt and over her breast, she felt his signet ring cold against her flesh.

I'm tired of fighting this, thought Caro, and kissed him back. Oblivious to everything except one another, neither heard the door open.

'Well, well!' said Jonathan Larch.

Later that night he said casually to Emily, who was sitting in front of the dressing-table mirror wearing a pin-tucked white cotton nightdress and removing her make-up, 'Were you aware that your sister is two-timing her husband?'

Startled, Emily stared at him through the medium of the mirror.

'I don't know what you're talking about,' she said adding, 'And I don't think you do either.'

'I caught them at it!' Jonathan was smug.

'Who? And at what?'

'Some fellow I've never seen before. Tall, thin, with an awfully, awfully upper accent.' He imitated it. 'I think she called him Morgan.'

Morgan!

Emily put down the hairbrush she had just picked up. Of course she knew—the whole family knew—that

Morgan had carried a torch for Caro, but Emily had assumed that the apparent success of her sister's marriage had effectively extinguished this.

'You must mean Morgan Steer. I think you've misunderstood the situation. They're childhood friends.'

Attempting to dismiss the subject, she seized the brush again, but Jonathan was not about to let the topic drop.

'Oh really, and do childhood friends usually kiss each other passionately and tear each other's clothes off?'

There was no answer to this. What on earth had Caro thought she was doing? Emily began to brush her hair with sweeping, agitated strokes until, charged with electricity, it sprang back from her face, forming itself into a shining, curling auburn halo.

'The question is,' Jonathan resumed, 'what do we do about Patrick?'

'What do you mean, what do we do about Patrick?'

'Well, don't you think I have a duty to tell him?'

Livid, Emily slammed down the brush, stood up and turned around to face her lover.

'If you say one word of what you've just told me to Patrick, I'll never speak to you again! Do you hear me? Never! And that's not all I won't do!'

There was no mistaking that she meant what she said.

'Just joking,' said Larch, surprised by her vehemence and backing down. 'Where are you going?'

'Out of here!'

He heard her go into the bathroom and then the faint click as she turned the key in the lock. Reflecting that Emily really was getting out of control these days and that he would have to have a talk with her about it tomorrow, Larch went to bed alone.

Some time later, Emily noiselessly let herself out of the bathroom. There was no longer a pencil of light beneath the door of the spare bedroom, which meant that Jonathan must be asleep. Long hair streaming and white nightdress billowing, she ran silently past and then down the stairs towards the kitchen, where someone appeared to have left the lights on.

Caro was sitting at the scrubbed pine table staring into space and so engrossed in her own thoughts that she did not hear Emily enter.

'Caro?'

'Em! You made me jump! What are you doing up at this time of night? Where's Jonathan?'

'Asleep. Where's Patrick?'

'Also asleep. Electrifying aren't they?'

'I *want* Jonathan to be asleep.' Emily spoke with feeling.

'I expect he told you what happened.'

'Some of it. I wasn't aware that you and Morgan…'

'We aren't. But I can quite see that there was room for misunderstanding.' Caro sounded dry.

'So what was going on?'

'Morgan wants to marry me, and if it wasn't for Minerva, I'd probably do it.'

'What about Patrick?' Emily had always had a tenderness for her brother-in-law.

'Patrick and I ran out of steam a long time ago.'

Emily was silent for a moment, and then said, 'Do you mean to tell me that Morgan has been palely loitering all these years?'

'I do. What about a stiff gin? I feel I need one.'

'Sounds to me as though he needs one. Still, it's *so* romantic,' was Emily's irresponsible reaction. 'But you're not going to run off with him?' What a pity! she thought privately. If someone asked me to run off with him, I'd go like a shot! 'So what *are* you going to do?'

'Strikes me that if Jonathan tells Patrick what he saw, the decision may well be taken from me. Ice?'

'I've told him not to, on pain of excommunication on every front. But maybe it would be better if he did. You really don't seem very happy to me, Caro.'

'I'm not.' It was a relief to say it. 'But in my saner moments I can't believe that uprooting Minerva and running off with Morgan, who hasn't even got a job, is the answer.'

'Patrick hasn't got a job either most of the time.'

'No, he hasn't, but you know what I mean.'

'Yes.'

Caro drank half her gin at a swallow. It was the last of the duty-free, and at one o'clock in the morning tasted like nectar.

'So what actually did happen, and where's Morgan now?'

'What happened was that Morgan turned up here with a bottle of champagne, raving that he loved me, he had always loved me and that he wanted to marry me, but if he couldn't do that he was going to marry someone else instead.'

'Wow!' exclaimed Emily, breathless with delight and hanging on to every word. 'And?'

'And then, gentle reader, he took me in his arms and kissed me!'

'It is *just* like a Victorian novel.'

'Well here the similarity stops, because then he began to undress me, and I was just doing the same thing to him when Jonathan arrived. You should have seen his face! Let's have another gin.'

'Yes, please! Who's he going to marry, by the way, if he doesn't marry you?'

'No idea.'

'I was going to say, if you don't want him, I'll have him.'

'I don't know if I want him or not. But it's probably too late anyway, since I've sent him away now.' Caro was conscious of a poignant feeling of regret and an unnerving sensation of opportunities missed, of life slipping past and nothing to show for it. 'I told him to go and he went.'

'What about Jonathan? What did he do?'

'Morgan told him to fuck off, and he did!'

Emily hugged herself with glee.

'Why would you want him anyway, when you've

got…' Here Caro did not speak the name but pointed to the ceiling.

'I think in a funny way I've outgrown Jonathan, actually,' said Emily. 'But with a shared mortgage and a fire-ravaged kitchen, plus an outstanding insurance claim, separating is going to have its complications.'

'He can go back to the conflagration and you can stay here. What do you think attracted you to him in the first place?' Caro had often wondered.

'I think it was partly the fact that he's ten years older than me. When I met him I needed someone to look after me.'

'And you don't now.'

'No, not anything like as much. I mean that *was* five years ago. It's trying when you can't do the smallest thing without reams of advice being offered.'

Reams of instruction, more like, thought Caro, listening to this.

'Of course he's very intellectual,' continued Emily, 'and I so much admire the selfless way he chose to do social work because he feels he wants to put something into the community, when with his brains he could easily have gone into some much more lucrative profession.'

Watching her sister persuading herself back into Larch's bed, Caro decided to say nothing. Her own opinion of Larch's intelligence and potential was nothing like as exalted as Emily's. In Caro's view he was probably functioning in precisely the right job for him, although it was highly likely that some of the over-organized families in his care might have disputed this. But then her dearly loved sister was not very clever either, and probably would not have presented a great brainwashing problem for her lover.

Emily held up the gin bottle.

'There's hardly any left. Shall we finish it?'

'Might as well.'

Caro looked at her watch. Heavens above, it was two o'clock. Dropping in some ice, Emily handed her a drink and for the next five minutes they sat and serenely tippled in sisterly silence.

Feeling more than a little tipsy, Emily had just opened her mouth to say, 'Peaceful, isn't it?' when she suddenly saw the handle of the kitchen door slowly begin to turn and in an anxious whisper said instead, 'Caro, you did lock the house up, didn't you?'

Caro followed the direction of her mesmerized gaze, and the two of them stared as the door soundlessly opened.

To their combined relief, through it arrived not the burglar but Larch, wearing only his underpants. His hair, which was long and wispy, floated free of its usual rubber band and his appearance reminded Caro of nothing so much as a particularly humourless Old Testament prophet.

The sight of this bizarre apparition was too much for Emily, who pointed at it wordlessly, at the same time dissolving into gales of giggles.

Her lover was not amused. His pale eyes rested briefly on the empty gin bottle.

'What's going on here?'

'Nothing illegal,' said Caro, who did not like his tone. 'No need to summon the vigilantes.'

Deciding to treat these remarks with contempt, Larch said sternly, 'Emily, you are drunk!'

Through tears of merriment, Emily gasped, 'No I'm not, I'm *very* drunk.' Then trying, and failing, to get a grip, she added, 'Sorry, darling!' More infectious shrieks of mirth. Caro smiled, despite her desire not to upset him more than was strictly necessary, for then her sister would surely suffer.

'*And* you are hysterical!'

Observing his censorious mien, Caro decided that it was very like having John Knox living in the house. Although John Knox would probably have been more fun.

Aloud she said, 'Emily, I think it probably is time for bed.'

Larch ignored this helpful contribution.

'Follow me, Emily! I shall talk to you about this in the morning,' and turning on his heel, he left.

Sobered, but only slightly by his displeasure, Emily put out her tongue at his retreating back, and then complied. Caro could still hear her laughing to herself as she mounted the stairs in his wake.

Wearily she rinsed the glasses, dried them and put them away before following her sister upstairs.

April

7

Morgan went to Ireland with Chloe. Sitting beside her on the plane, while she leafed through the pages of the latest *Tatler*, he reflected on his last, disastrous meeting with Caro. Once again matters had not been resolved and Morgan was now beginning to perceive that they probably never would be.

Because of his vacillation, they had taken the decision to go at the last minute. As a result, they had been unable to get seats on a plane to Dublin and had been forced to go via Cork. Now, sitting in a hired oar scrutinizing the map and taking on board the fact that the drive was going to take them at least three hours, Morgan said, 'Surely it would have made more sense for us to fly to Belfast?'

"Really? I'm afraid I've never been very geographical,' was Chloe's uninterested response. 'Would you like me to read aloud your stars for you?'

He declined.

Driving along the roads of Ireland, where he had never been before, Morgan, son of an Irish father, experienced an unexpected affinity for this green country. Roots, perhaps, he thought. All the same, it surprised him.

A fine grey drizzle hung in the air like gauze, and this, coupled with the fading light, made the drive a slower one than it might otherwise have been. Chloe proved to be a less than adequate map-reader, and Morgan got the impression that she expected him to drive and navigate at the same time. After copious breaks to check their route, they eventually stopped at a bar, of which there were a very great many, and rang ahead to say that they would be late.

During the days that followed Morgan's visit, Caro avoided Larch as much as she could, and mealtimes tended to be even more stilted than usual. Patrick, who was clearly enjoying his work and was therefore much easier to live with, appeared not to notice the tensions and regaled them all with theatrical anecdotes. These were received by Minerva in particular in glum silence.

Finally she spoke: 'Dad, I've been press-ganged into being in the school play because you're an actor, and right now it's all I get when I'm at home as well. Can't we talk about something else for a change?'

Patrick was interested. 'Which play are you doing?'

'*A Midsummer Night's dream.*'

'Oh, marvellous! And what part have you got?'

'Fairy Mustardseed.' Minerva was dour.

Larch guffawed. 'Aren't you rather large for a fairy?'

Listening to this, Caro thought that it would serve him right if Minerva punched him.

'When's your kitchen going to be ready? Soon I hope.'

It was an unsubtle blend of rudeness and enquiry, but Caro, who normally stamped on that sort of insolence, decided to let it go. He had, after all, asked for it.

With that increasingly familiar bright spot of colour on each cheek, Emily intervened. 'By the end of the month it should be more or less usable. I expect you'll be glad to be shot of us.'

'No, no!' chorused the Hollands insincerely, separately savouring the prospect of the Larch departure.

'Oh, yes, yes!' Larch, his eyes on Caro. 'I'm sure our presence must have put a brake on some of your more exciting extracurricular activities.'

'What extracurricular activities?' Patrick was startled. 'You haven't told me about these, Caro. Is this something else the school has asked you to take on?'

'No,' said his wife through gritted teeth, 'it's just Jonathan's little joke.'

'Oh really?' said Patrick, losing interest. 'I have to admit I don't get it.'

'That's because it really isn't very funny.' Emily stared furiously at Jonathan.

Not understanding any of it, and bored by all of them, Minerva stood up. 'Since it's not my turn to help wash up,' she said, 'I'm going off to do my prep,' spoiling the laudable intent by adding the words, 'in front of the television.'

This little conversational hand grenade had the desired effect, for as she left the room, she heard Larch saying disapprovingly to her mother, 'Surely you don't allow that, do you?'

The tin magnate lived in a mansion. Unlike many similar English mansions, where central heating did exist but was never turned on unless the temperature fell below zero, this one was both extremely warm and very comfortable, having been extensively, but unjarringly, modernized throughout. Their bedroom was, quite simply, vast, with windows that looked out across gardens and beyond them to fields where comatose cattle stood knee-deep in lush grass and wild flowers.

Morgan took in the peaceful scene with appreciation, reflecting as he did so that this was how he should like to live.

It was the morning after their arrival. Dinner the night before had been a buffet affair for forty, the other guests being an eclectic mixture from the worlds of show business, horse racing, the gossip columns and, presumably, tin, plus a scattering of other Brazilians. Meeting a film star, Morgan wondered why it was that a person who looked so impressive on screen, in the flesh always turned out to be half his own height and not as good-looking. Perhaps he, Morgan, should become a film star. As for Roberto Vargas, their host, he was short and fat and wore a double-breasted suit of absurd cut that made him look as broad as he was long. His hair was very black and very shiny, and to Mor-

gan's disapproving English eye looked as though it
might be dyed. He was plainly very taken by Chloe.

'And how's your lovely mother these days?' Morgan heard him asking her. The buffet was over, and
Vargas and Chloe were sitting side by side on one of
the large white sofas.

'Just as lovely, but no easier,' had been Chloe's reply, accompanied by something of a sigh. 'I don't see
very much of her since she moved to Boston.'

Roberto, it transpired, probably saw more of Veronica Post than her own daughter did, and sizing up his
man, Morgan would not have been surprised to learn
that he and Chloe's sociable parent were still con-
ducting an affair, regardless of his recent marriage. In
the meantime, however, neither relationship seemed to
hinder his current intentions, and Morgan, who was
struggling on with a lack-lustre conversation divided
between himself, the film star and a man who trained
racehorses for a sheik, could only watch as one of
Roberto's hands placed itself on Chloe's silken knee.
His cufflinks, which appeared to be of solid gold, were
the size of pullets' eggs. Chloe did nothing, but simply
went on talking as though the knee was nothing to do
with her, and the hand even less. Morgan noticed the
fourth wife, a statuesque blonde, also hawkishly
watching this little scenario over the shoulder of the
film producer she was talking to. Catching his wife's
basilisk eye, Vargas reluctantly removed his hand, allowing himself a furtive squeeze as he did so.

Standing up, Chloe prepared to retreat. With one eye

on the rustling advance of his spouse, Morgan heard her companion say, 'You must let me take you out to dinner the next time I'm in London. What about the Gavroche?' And was disconcerted to hear his lover treacherously reply, 'Thank you, Roberto, that would be very nice.'

Morgan, who knew all about jealousy having suffered from it throughout the years of Caro's marriage to Patrick Holland, now discovered that on top of his inconvenient obsession with her, he also profoundly disliked the idea of anybody but himself taking out Chloe.

Mildly hung over, therefore, the following morning, Morgan, staring out at the garden, whose soft, sad, watercolour green veiled by a fine, silvery rain looked as though it ran into the cloudy wash of the sky, took the decision to put aside his unrequited passion for Caroline Barstow and concentrate instead on Chloe Post.

He turned towards her. Chloe was sitting up in bed, supported by a heap of pillows. Mermaid-like, her naked body rose out of the sheath of the sheet. Without her make-up there was a frailty about her that touched Morgan's heart. He crossed the room, taking off his dressing gown, and got into bed beside her. Slipping one hand between her thighs, he kissed each rosy nipple and then her pale, unpainted mouth.

'Chloe, darling, will you marry me?' he said.

A poignant and unnerving memory of kissing Caro

the last time he had seen her rose before his inner eye,
stayed for a second, and then was gone.

'Will you?'

'Yes, I will,' said Chloe.

'Oh, darling! Let's make love. To celebrate!'

Closing her eyes, and wishing they could celebrate
in some other way, Chloe said, 'Yes, all right.'

On the endless drive back to Cork the day after the
horse show, Morgan wondered whether he had done
the right thing. Would he have proposed to Chloe if
she had not been rich? he asked himself. The perfectly
honest answer to this was that he probably would not
have, for although he found Chloe very attractive and
on that level desired and even loved her, he was not
in love with her. And if Caroline Barstow had been
prepared to leave her husband for him, he certainly
would not have.

But maybe, thought Morgan, pursuing a familiar ar-
gument for the nth time, once we are married I will
fall in love with her. After all, people do. Nevertheless,
it did not alter the fact that her wealth had tipped the
balance and that, at this stage anyway, this was primarily marriage for money, not marriage for passion.
Acknowledging this fact, Morgan, who was basically
an honourable man and lacked the total amorality of
Tom Marchant, for instance, felt ashamed. Nothing
had been announced, and it was still not too late to
pull out, though if he did so he would lose Chloe altogether, for there could be no question of things re-

verting to the way they had been before. The whole thing was a fuck-up. Giving the cameo of her profile an oblique glance, Morgan decided that he did not want to forfeit Chloe, for if he did there would be nothing left.

At this point in his internal debate Morgan took the decision to cut short the agony, and said to Chloe: 'Presumably you'll want to inform your family before we put a notice in *The Times*? And I'll have to inform Grandmama immediately. Anything less would be regarded as lese-majesty. After that, we'll have to go to Northumberland to meet her and the Aunts.'

Morgan quelled another *frisson* of anxiety. London life was one thing, but the Northern set-up was quite another. He could not imagine a hothouse plant like Chloe thriving amid the rigours of Armitage Lodge. On the other hand, aside from the regular northbound treks to butter up his grandmother, they would live mainly in London. It would probably be all right, he decided.

That night, he wrote to Leonora.

The morning his letter arrived, Leonora, who had a dental appointment, had got up for breakfast rather than be ministered to in bed by Clara as usual. Watching her slit open the envelope with the butter knife, the sisters, all of whom recognized the handwriting, wondered what on earth Morgan, not renowned as a correspondent, could be writing about at such length.

Leonora did not immediately enlighten them.

'Interesting!' she said, scrutinizing it through pince-nez. 'How very interesting!'

'What is, Mother?' Cassandra was all agog.

'What's in this letter.' Being tantalizing had become a way of life for Leonora, who had once reserved this skill for the many men in her orbit and now used it to baffle her immediate family instead.

After reading it again, during the course of which activity they all sat watching her, she said to Julia, 'Your son writes to inform me, and therefore you, that he is getting married.'

Julia looked at her mother and was conscious of a feeling of resentment. He writes to her and he doesn't write to me, she thought. He's my son and he doesn't write to me. I'm disenfranchised in this house.

Clara stared open-mouthed at Leonora. Cassandra studied the tea leaves in the bottom of her cup. The same thought occurred to them all simultaneously: How will this affect the will?

'He tells me that his bride-to-be is a newspaper heiress,' stated Leonora. This, she reflected, was good, except that being well off through the medium of his marriage might make Morgan insubordinate. 'Her name is Chloe Post.'

'I've heard of the Posts,' said Julia.

'Really!' pronounced Leonora dismissively, who never had but was not prepared to allow Julia centre stage in order to be enlightened. 'He is going to bring her up here quite soon to meet us all. We shall have to push the boat out.'

Since Leonora's idea of pushing the culinary boat out was to serve ham instead of cucumber sandwiches for tea, no one was too excited by this prospect.

'How old is she?' Clara wanted to know. 'How did they meet?'

'He does not say.' Leonora folded the letter, which was a long one and clearly imparted more than she was prepared to tell them, and put it away in her handbag. 'No doubt we shall learn more during the course of their visit. Now, who is going to drive me to the dentist?'

'As I'm the only one who knows how to, I expect I am.' Julia was tart. Once they were in the car, which was an ancient Ford, she felt furious and let out the clutch so suddenly that it bucked in a scatter of gravel like a fractious horse before setting off in its usual sedate mode down the drive.

Joanna prevailed upon Tom Marchant to take her to the opera. They sat through hours of *Xerxes*, which Joanna, who liked the music of that period, enjoyed, and Tom, who did not, privately thought was an awful lot of Handel or a lot of awful Handel, depending on how you looked at it.

Sitting in the Café Pelican in St Martin's Lane afterwards, he decided that the better he got to know Joanna Blackstock the more he liked her. Joanna had the gift of charm. What she was like in bed remained a mystery, however, since the three evenings they had so far spent together had been entertaining but otherwise disappointingly decorous. After his bruising experience with Camilla Vane, Tom knew better these days than to rush his fences, and was therefore forced to await the signal that a pounce would be appreciated. So far there had been no hint of such a thing.

After Morgan's revelation about the Blackstock cash, Tom had been careful not to bring up the subject of money, though several times during the evening he had asked himself if he would have been prepared to sit through interminable Handel if he had not known her to be rich. It was a tribute to her growing attraction for him that he found himself unable to come up with the answer.

Joanna put down her knife and fork. 'Have you seen Morgan lately?'

'I saw him a week ago. He and Chloe were about to go to Ireland. To a horse show.'

'Really? I wasn't aware that horses were one of Chloe's passions.'

'They aren't, but apparently sybaritic house parties such as those thrown by Roberto Vargas are.'

Tom was aware of feeling mildly envious. Not of Morgan's relationship with Chloe, whom Tom considered decorative but vapid, but of the hectic social roundelay that his friend was currently enjoying. 'Before he met her, Morgan asked me if I would like to move into the Prince's Gate flat. Presumably he hasn't raised the subject again because it would now cramp his style.'

'Can't see why,' said Joanna succinctly. 'Chloe has

a very large flat of her own. Whatever his reason, it can't be lack of space.'

'It's probably that he likes to keep his options open.'

'And what about you? Do you like to keep your options open?'

Tom was stumped by this. It was not the sort of question women usually asked him, probably because they did not want to hear the answer. Lamely he sidestepped it. 'Living in a hotel means I don't have any options.'

Joanna said, 'If you like, you can move in with me. Into my spare room, I mean. If we don't get on, you'll just have to move out again. We could give it a month's trial. Shall we order some coffee?'

Her unexpectedness quite took his breath away.

'Are you serious?'

'Perfectly serious.'

'Just supposing the answer's yes, when would you want this arrangement to commence?'

'Well, not straight away. Let's soldier through another month of getting to know one another, and then review the situation. Or, rather, you review it. I think we'd get on very well, provided certain ground rules were observed.'

Tom had never encountered anyone so practical. She must have French ancestry. It occurred to him to wonder what rules she had in mind. It also occurred to him that it had not been made clear whether a romantic cohabitation was the order of the day, or simply a platonic cohabitation. On the other hand, what did it matter if it extracted him from his present prison?

She gave him a sudden brilliant smile, the candour of which could not be doubted. 'Think about it! Shall we go?'

Driving back to her flat, Joanna asked, 'What's your opinion of Morgan and Chloe as a couple? Would you say they were compatible?'

'Possibly, except for the fact that Morgan has been besotted by someone called Caroline Barstow for years.'

'Really?' Joanna was alerted. 'And is he still?'

'He certainly was up until the last time I saw him.'

'Why on earth didn't he marry her if it was such a grand passion?'

'Search me. In the end she married someone else, an actor called Patrick Holland.'

'I see.'

Joanna was silent.

'Sometime, if you could bear to tell me, that is, I should like to hear all about *your* marriage.'

Tom was surprised to hear himself saying, 'It was a complete disaster. I married Primrose for all the wrong reasons.' It struck him that for the first time in his life he was suddenly dimly aware of what the right reasons might be.

'Which were?'

'I prefer not to answer on the grounds that I might incriminate myself.' He turned the car into the mews and drew up outside her house. 'Or, rather, on the grounds that I *would* incriminate myself.'

'The important thing is to marry for inclination, not for money. Although money is a very useful addition.'

Unwilling to get further into this discussion since it was altogether too near the bone, Tom said, 'What about dinner tomorrow night, and I'll tell you all about it then?'

He wouldn't, of course. That is, he would tell her some of it, but not all. Joanna made a resolution to get Chloe to pump Morgan about it.

Anxious to regain some of the initiative, Tom escorted Joanna to her front door, but tonight did not kiss her.

'Shall we say eight o'clock? I'll pick you up here.' He went.

Once inside, the first thing Joanna did was to take off her shoes, and the second, out of habit, was to check her phone. There were several messages, the first of which was from her father.

'Hello, Joanna love,' said Harry Blackstock's Yorkshire accent. 'It's your dad speaking. Just ringing to find out how my little girl is, and to say stay away from Tom Marchant. I'm in the City on Thursday, so let's have lunch. Give me a ring at the office.'

How on earth had he found out about Tom? Whatever it was that he had found out, he plainly didn't like it. She passed on to the next and the next. The last one was from Chloe. True to type, Chloe had seen nothing strange in purveying the news of her engagement through the unemotional medium of an answering machine.

'Morgan has asked me to marry him.' There followed a substantial pause. 'In Ireland,' she added inconsequentially. 'And I've said yes.' Another pause. 'I'm very happy.'

Actually, thought Joanna, she sounded very flat, but maybe that was because she was giving the happy news to someone who was not actually there to receive it in person. She replayed the message and this time the impression of blandness was, if anything, even stronger. Listening to it and remembering Tom's words vis-à-vis Morgan Steer's infatuation (what was the name again? Caroline? Yes, that's right, Caroline Barstow), Joanna experienced a feeling of disquiet.

8

A week after the arrival of Morgan's letter, Julia, Cassandra and Clara sat in the kitchen drinking their morning tea. Leonora was still in bed, presumably eating the breakfast Clara had prepared for her.

Into the silence, Cassandra said, 'How do you think Morgan's marriage will affect Mother's will?'

'There's no need for it to affect the will at all. The Post family are extremely rich, so Morgan should be able to get by very comfortably with his allotted tranche without needing any more. No, as usual what will affect it will be Mother's attitude to all of us the day she dies. And as we know, she is capable of anything. Woe betide anyone who offends Mother.'

The speaker was Julia, whose private thoughts were even more vehement. I loathe being shackled to Mother and this house. Loathe it! I've never forgiven her for refusing to send me to university, and probably never will. Meredith went and I was left behind, and I've been left behind ever since. She remembered eating her heart out over Meredith's letters, avidly reading them, living her life vicariously as she did so.

'Girls do not need degrees,' Leonora had scornfully proclaimed. 'In my day dancing and a little French sufficed. Oh, and playing the piano rather badly, of course. Most important!'

It was pointless explaining to her impervious parent that times had changed.

'But I should like to get a job,' persisted Julia.

'A job? I can assure you, Julia, there is plenty to do here!'

Leonora had proved impossible to move. And so, poorly educated and untrained for anything, except possibly, for working in a shop, which did not appeal either, Julia had stayed where she was and the country days had succeeded one another, one more or less the same as the last, until the monotony of her existence had threatened to drive Julia mad. The high points had been the holidays, when Meredith had come home with various young men in tow, Rollos and Bunnys and Ralphs and there were tennis parties and picnics. When they had eventually gone back, she had sunk once more into lethargy and depression.

'If you must mope, Julia, please mope somewhere else.' Leonora had no sympathy for the tragedy queen in her drawing room.

It had been after just such a holiday that Julia had met Major Farrell. At a dance. She was aware even then that all was not quite right about Major Farrell. That his eyes were perhaps a little too close together, and his voice a little too loud. But beggars couldn't be choosers, and she was desperate for some fun in those days. Still wouldn't say no to it even now. And he had been a good horseman and an amusing raconteur, in a very Irish sort of way. He had made her laugh.

For the first month or so of their acquaintance, although Cassandra, who had wallflowered at the same dance, and Clara, who had not, both knew about Frederick, Julia instinctively kept the existence of her first beau a secret from her mother, unaware that Leonora knew anyway, gossip being what it was in a town like Hexham.

Eventually, having first made discreet inquiries about the Steer money and having ascertained that Julia stood to inherit a substantial amount, Major Fred had proposed, at which point it had become necessary to expose him to Leonora. Julia still remembered the occasion with a shudder. Over the cucumber sandwiches, and in front of Julia herself, her mother had blatantly flirted with her prospective son-in-law. *And he had reciprocated in kind.* I should have known then what a shit he was, thought Julia, but I was so unworldly in those days. And so desperate to get away.

When he had finally, gallantly, taken his leave, Leonora, wintry in white and very treacherous, had said, 'I'm afraid he really won't do at all, Julia. Rather a vulgar man. You must, or I must, tell him that an engagement is *quite* out of the question.'

'No!'

'No?'

'No! I won't do it, Mother!'

'Then I shall have to do it for you.'

'You will do no such thing!'

'If you insist on this ill-advised liaison, you will not receive one penny from me. Do I make myself clear?' And when Farrell receives that piece of information, she thought to herself, he will show us a clean pair of heels, thereby saving me the trouble of seeing him off personally.

In fact, Julia had not passed this threat on to Farrell, maybe because in her heart of hearts she had no confidence in his reaction to it. The upshot was that a week later she had run away with the Major, reserving the news of her disinheritance until some months after they were married.

Marriage was not the unalloyed pleasure she had expected, and sex, which Julia had been given no information about whatsoever, struck her as bizarre. She could not imagine Leonora ever indulging in such a thing, though clearly she must have. Most unnerving of all was that Frederick suddenly seemed to be very short of money, and on top of this appeared to have nowhere to live. As a result, after a week's honeymoon in a seedy hotel, they moved in with his sister Lettice and her husband. Lettice was sympathetic to her new sister-in-law and taught Julia how to cook, as well as suggesting that she should learn to drive.

By now it was becoming apparent to Julia that she had married a man she knew nothing about.

One evening, she voiced her concern to Lettice.

'When is Frederick planning to return to his regiment?'

'Return to his regiment?' Lettice was dismayed. 'But my dear, has he not told you?'

'Told me what? I try to talk to him, but he flies into rages and won't answer me.'

What an innocent abroad, reflected Lettice, finding herself in the disagreeable position of having to say, 'Frederick is no longer in the army. He was cashiered, I'm afraid.'

Since her husband had given Julia to understand that he was simply on leave, the shock was immense.

'So he has no income?'

'Not until he gets a job.'

There had been no sign of Frederick even looking for a job.

Dreading the answer, Julia asked, 'What was he cashiered for?'

'For not honouring his debts.' Lettice fervently wished that the conversation was at an end. 'Cards mainly, but horses too.'

And that, thought Julia, was how I learned I was married to a compulsive gambler.

Later that night, when her husband returned home from heaven knew where, Julia said, 'I know all about it. The army, I mean. Lettice told me. Why, Frederick, didn't you tell me yourself? And what are we going to do?'

Frederick replied curtly, 'I wish Lettice would mind her own business!' and then, seeing Julia's stricken look, became reassuring 'Don't worry about it, old girl.

We'll ask your mama for an advance on your inheritance. You're her daughter. She'll cough up.'

Reflecting that if that was what he thought, he really hadn't read Leonora at all, Julia said, 'She has disinherited me. I shall never get any money out of my mother.'

The look on her husband's face as she spoke told Julia everything. He had always thought Leonora would come round. In short, he had married her for her money, and now there was not going to be any.

Abruptly, he stood up and left the room, and the next day he went to visit Leonora. What transpired during this interview, Julia was never to know, but after it she did not see him again. He simply decamped, telling no one, not even Lettice, where he was going.

Sitting thinking about it all these years later, still married to him, though in name only, Julia wondered at her own naivety. The sad recognition that this was a house of wasted lives and empty hearts refused to be denied. All the same, thought Julia, although it's late, it's not too late. When Mother dies, I'll travel, see the world, make up for lost time. Maybe I'll take Meredith with me. Although Meredith was saddled with her own difficult parent.

The bell for Leonora's room began to jangle, then stopped, and then jangled again. In so far as a bell could, it sounded bad-tempered.

Nobody moved. 'Your turn!' they all said as one.

'Oh, go on Clara,' said Cassandra, pouring herself

another cup of tea, 'you've probably forgotten the salt.'

The habit of obedience was well ingrained. Clara heaved herself to her feet and prepared to set off. There followed further knocking from above.

'Better hurry. She's hammering her stick on the floor now.'

'I wonder if it is the salt!' Clara was flustered.

'Why don't you take it with you, just in case?'

'Oh, good idea!'

She went.

'The older Mother gets, the more impossible she is.' Julia put on the kettle.

'I'm afraid Mother is a monster.' Cassandra put three sugars into her cup.

'Yes. A direct descendant of Messalina quite likely,' agreed Julia. 'What are you going to do when she dies?' They had this conversation every so often, usually when Leonora was at her most overbearing.

'I'll probably buy a small cottage, maybe share it with someone.' Cassandra was vague.

With Deirdre Ricketts at a guess. The two of them had always been very close.

'Have you ever thought of doing that sooner rather than later?'

'Not really. I couldn't afford it for one thing. Obviously, like you, I would prefer to get out of this house, but unlike you, I do enjoy village life. Everything I want is here, apart from financial independence, and my inheritance will eventually provide that.'

A waiting game.

'Do you think there'll be enough for that?'

'No idea. Mother's so secretive. She's like a squirrel with a nut where that will is concerned. I hope so!'

'I can't see why she won't give it to us now, or some of it anyway.'

'Fat chance.' Cassandra was dismissive. 'Mother's heavily into blackmail. A one-woman Mafia. If we had the cash, she would no longer have any hold over us. As it is, we're all stuck with her.'

The tyranny of money.

Clara returned carrying the breakfast tray. 'It was the butter. No butter. She's in an awful bate. It's all cold. I have to start again.'

For the hundredth time, Julia said, 'Clara, why don't you make a list? A breakfast list? And check it before you take the tray up.'

'Yes, I should.' Clara was contrite. Filling a saucepan with water in order to boil another egg, she said, 'You're not going into Hexham today, are you?'

'Yes I am, but not until this afternoon. Why, do you want a lift?'

Clara blushed. 'I just wondered if you could possibly drop me off at the Murgatroyd farm, that's all.'

Once again, in this house of the hidden agenda, Clara's affair with Seth was never even acknowledged, much less openly talked about. And just as well, thought Julia, certain that Leonora would have had a particularly scathing field day at Clara's expense, since Seth, unlike the gentlemen farmers they used to encounter at dances in the old days, was one of the hands-on variety. A real farmer, in other words, who did a great deal of it himself, with only the aid of a man and a boy. Furthermore, Seth was uninterested in his surroundings and, probably because he was a bachelor and had no one to look after him, resided in a house that was barely as clean as his own mucky farmyard, though lately, rumour had it, he had employed a girl from one of the villages as some sort of domestic.

'No problem,' said Julia, 'but how will you get back?'

Clara had no desire for her sister to see the interior of the Murgatroyd farmhouse. 'Would you be able to pick me up on your way home? From the end of the lane?'

'Yes, if you think that will give you enough time to do what you want.' On the whole, Julia thought, it would. It was unlikely that Seth was an imaginative lover, which would mean that the whole thing would probably be over in minutes rather than hours.

By this time Clara had finished reassembling Leonora's breakfast.

The bedroom bell jangled into life again.

Watching her sister's retreating back, Julia said, 'Let's hope Clara's remembered everything. Mother is perfectly capable of sending her down to begin again. Again.'

'Don't I know,' said Cassandra.

'What about you? This afternoon, I mean.' Julia was used to being the family chauffeuse.

Cassandra pondered this question, picturing Miss Ricketts, the object of her desire, arranging flowers with long, thin, Virginia Woolf fingers, using vases that she, Cassandra, had lovingly filled with water.

'Well, we were going to do the church tomorrow, but since you're going past it today, maybe that would be better. Yes, on the whole, that's a good idea. I'll give Deirdre a ring.'

In London, Morgan decided to burn his boats and telephone Caroline with the news of his decision to marry Chloe. The first time he telephoned he got Patrick, or maybe Larch. He hung up. A day later he tried again, and this time got Caro.

'I've decided to get married,' announced Morgan, starkly.

Caroline was surprised by how bereft she felt. It put her in touch with the degree to which the reliable presence of Morgan had allowed her to hedge her bets where her marriage was concerned. As the years had passed, it had become inconceivable to her that he would not always be there, and the idea of a romantic elopement that one day would enable her to leave behind the dross of her marriage, was a silly but nevertheless sustaining one. Suddenly Caro felt herself without a prop of any kind.

Pulling herself together, she said, 'Congratulations,' recognizing as she did so that it was just possible that if he were to ask her once more to run away with him, she might actually do it.

He did not.

'Who is she?'

'Her name is Chloe Post. Her family owns an American newspaper chain.'

Well, that sounded useful, anyway. Morgan could do with some money. But then who couldn't?

'Have you told your grandmother yet?' It never occurred to Caro to ask whether he had told his mother yet. Indubitably the one who mattered at Armitage Lodge was Leonora Steer.

'I've written. Shortly I'm going to take Chloe to Northumberland to meet them all.'

A silence unnerving in its completeness slid between them like a cold blade. It fell to Morgan to break it.

'Well, that's it, really. I wanted you to be one of the first to know. I hope you and Patrick will come to the wedding.'

'Of course we will.' Caro felt as though she might be about to faint. 'Is it going to be in London or Northumberland?' She sat down.

'London. Look, I must go. No doubt we'll be in touch before then.'

She did doubt it.

'Yes, I'm sure we will… Goodbye, Morgan.'

'Goodbye, Caroline.'

No longer Caro, but Caroline. A new, formal dimension to their friendship. Caro buried her face in a cushion and wept.

* * *

Chloe rang first her mother and then her father.

As usual, Veronica Post was in a hurry, although not having any occupation of any sort except the gratification of her own desires, it was hard to know what she was always hurrying for. On receiving the news of her daughter's engagement, her first reaction was, 'Really! What are you going to wear?'

Reflecting that anybody else would have asked, 'Who to?' Chloe said, 'Don't you want to know who to?'

'Will I be any the wiser if you tell me?'

'No, you probably won't,' Chloe conceded.

'Then there's no point.'

Veronica was nothing if not incisive, her cut-glass tones traversing the Atlantic Ocean to such good effect that she could have been in Chloe's sitting room instead of thousands of miles away.

Thank heaven she isn't, thought Chloe.

Reviewing the possibilities, Veronica was asking, 'And *where* are you getting married?'

She seemed to want to know everything about everything, except about Morgan himself, but then her mother always had seen men as a means to an end, rather than as an end in themselves.

Choosing to disregard the last question, Chloe was determined that her husband-to-be should not be disenfranchised. 'Have you got a pen, Mother? His name is Morgan Steer.' She spelt it out.

Her maddening parent let her do it and then said, 'No, I haven't got a pen.'

Giving up on it, Chloe said, 'His family home is in Northumberland.'

'You can't possibly have your wedding in Northumberland.' Veronica was definite. 'Nobody would come. Unless they have the misfortune to live there already, of course.'

'They also have a Knightsbridge flat.'

'It is very important that we get the guest list right.'

This was a dialogue of the deaf. Noticing the threatening use of the word *we*, Chloe said, 'Please don't worry about that, Mother, I'm perfectly capable of drawing it up myself.'

'Very well, but under no circumstances send out the invitations until I have seen them. As the mother of the bride, whom you ask will reflect on me. Have we set a date yet?'

Chloe felt very much as though it was turning into her mother's wedding rather than her own. She said, 'Probably June.'

'June is perfect for weddings. My own took place in June.' Mindful of the short-lived disaster that had been her parents' marriage, Chloe felt that this did not augur well for June.

'Or maybe July.'

'August would be better. Have you told your father yet? He will need time to come to terms with the amount this is all going to cost him.' Veronica uttered these words with some satisfaction.

'No, I haven't. It's my intention to ring him when I've finished talking to you.'

Noticing her watch, Veronica said, 'Good Lord, look at the time. I must go. I have a hair appointment. What did you say his name was again?'

'Whose?' Chloe felt suddenly mulish.

'Your fiancé's, of course!'

With a sigh. 'Oh, him! Have you got a pen, Mother?'

'Yes, I have.'

She had probably had a pen all along.

'It's Morgan Steer.' Once again she spelt it out. 'M-O-R-G-A-N S-T-E-E-R.'

'Got it,' said Veronica, deciding as she wrote to do some research into the Steer pedigree. 'I'm thrilled for you, darling. So very thrilled. Must dash now. Goodbye!'

'Goodbye, Mother.'

A click. She had gone.

After this exacting exchange, Chloe decided to reward herself with a drink before starting afresh with her father. It was ironic, thought Chloe, that her very English mother lived in America, whilst her very American father lived in England. What on earth had made them marry when the only way they could achieve mutual tranquillity was by having an ocean between them? Chloe could not begin to guess.

She dialled the number. To her relief it was her father who answered and not the Child Bride.

'Hello, Daddy.'

'Chloe, honey! How's things?'

In the background she could hear what sounded like a television. She waited for him to turn it off, and finally concluded that he had no intention of doing so. Resuming, she pictured him one-quarter listening to her and three-quarters watching whatever it was. Reflecting that no amount of money could compensate for being almost permanently ignored, Chloe said, 'I'm getting married!'

There was a sharp click and the drone of the television stopped abruptly. There was no doubt that she had his full attention now.

'Does your mother know about this?'

'Yes, she does. I've just rung her.'

'We'll have to make sure that you are properly protected financially. You're a very rich woman, Chloe.'

Properly protected financially? From the person she was planning to spend the rest of her life with?

'Daddy, you don't even know who he is!'

It was beginning to frustrate Chloe that whilst neither of her parents appeared to want to know who it was she was marrying, or, indeed, anything about him, both in their different ways were limbering up to interfere in peripheral arrangements that Chloe felt perfectly capable of sorting out for herself.

'No more I do. Who is he?'

'His name is Morgan Steer. I thought you might like to meet him.'

Another click. The hum of the television started up again in the background.

'Well now, you tell Morgan that I *would* like to meet him. Why don't you ring my secretary in the morning, Chloe, and book an appointment for lunch.'

Chloe said she would, reflecting as she did so that she was the only person she knew who had to make an arrangement through a secretary in order to see her father.

In Northumberland, in the privacy of her bedroom, Leonora reread Morgan's letter. The prospect of a wedding and with it the possibility, later on, of grandchildren, gave her more strings to her bow and demanded some public tinkering with her will. She would not, of course, allow any of her daughters to know what these alterations were, but the simple fact that she was making certain adjustments would put the cat among the pigeons, she herself being the cat.

Accordingly, she went to her desk, which she kept locked, and from the top drawer extracted a fat bundle bound in dark green ribbon. She undid this and then spread out in a fan shape eight Last Will and Testaments. There was one where she had disinherited the lot of them, one where she had disinherited Julia only (that was when the disruptive and oily, though ultimately useful, Major Fred had been on the scene), and two where she had rejigged the dispersal of her jewellery (one had been made the day Clara had dropped the gin bottle, the other after an acrimonious exchange with Cassandra). The remaining four had been occasioned by boredom or inclement weather, when she had inserted small, spiteful deprivations mainly to pass the time. Now she would indulge herself in one more manipulative will. Meanwhile, what to do with the redundant eight?

She decided to burn them. Standing them up in the grate so that they formed a tepee, she struck a match. Tentatively, the pale yellow flame curled and licked along the borders of the thick white papers, turning them brown. Then, as if gaining confidence, it deepened in colour and began to envelop the tepee, which crackled most satisfyingly. As Leonora leant like a priestess over her small, sulphurous fire, the light it shed threw her narrow, imperious face into dramatic relief, emphasizing its deeply etched lines, and with them her great age.

The success of her auto-da-fé gave Leonora an idea. Standing up, she went back to the desk and from the envelope slots at the top removed some fifty or so unopened bank statements. These she added to her bonfire, where the flames shot through them, showing none of the circumspection they had accorded the wills, and reducing them in seconds to a heap of ash.

'Cheap and nasty,' murmured Leonora with distaste, picking up a poker and stirring the ashes, fragments of which flew up and floated, still flaming, before slowly descending again.

There was one will left in the desk, the ninth and most recent, which she would destroy as soon as the next had been drawn up and witnessed.

Leonora peered at her watch. It was almost time for

dinner, and certainly time to bully her daughters over a stiff gin and tonic. She found all three of them in the drawing room.

'A gin and tonic, Clara,' commanded Leonora. 'And I should like lemon but no ice. Ice dilutes the gin! Now, who would like to know what I have been doing?'

'You've been burning your old wills.' The speaker was Cassandra.

Leonora was mightily offended to be so completely upstaged and made a silent resolution to take her pearls away from Cassandra and give them to Julia instead.

'How *did* you know that?' Clara's mouth was open in amazement.

'Quite simple. I went to Mother's room to alert her to the fact that it was time for dinner, but she wasn't there and I couldn't help noticing the matches and the green ribbon on the floor by the fireplace, as well as the ashes in the grate.'

'I should prefer it if none of you entered my room when I am not present.' Leonora was glacial.

'So when am I supposed to clean it and make the bed for you?'

Annoyed by Julia's tart delivery, Leonora moved the pearls on again, this time to Clara, around whose fat neck they would be wasted, of course.

'You know perfectly well what I mean, Julia, so please do not take that tone with me. And tomorrow I shall require you to drive me to Hexham, to the solicitors, where, in the light of what Morgan has told me in his letter, I intend to revise my latest will.'

Silence fell as all three dependants stared at their mother, waiting for elucidation. None, it seemed, was forthcoming, for having made this intimidating statement, Leonora simply said as she prepared to lead the way, 'Shall we go in to dinner?'

9

_____

Sometime after this unsettling conversation, Clara sat in the kitchen of the Murgatroyd farmhouse. Opposite her, wearing the sort of shirt onto which a collar should have been buttoned, a waistcoat and trousers held up with braces that had belonged to his father, sat Seth. Five years younger than Clara and used to hard physical work, Seth was of medium height and muscular. His light, foxy eyes and mop of curling hair, together with his ruddy complexion and paisley neckerchief, gave him a gypsyish look that was not unattractive.

Today, the kitchen itself was cleaner than usual, though not all that much. The milk pan, for instance, which Seth never washed but went on using night after night for his cocoa, was upside down, apparently draining, and the stone-flagged floor looked as though it might have been swept. Through the curtainless window a yellow duster that had been washed and hung out to dry was visible. Although she disliked housework and got more than enough of it at Armitage Lodge, Clara experienced a stab of jealousy.

'Has somebody been helping you out in the house?' she enquired, carefully neutral.

'Yes,' said Seth, a man of few words, as he proceeded to fill his pipe.

'Oh. Who?'

'Martha.'

'Oh.' There was a dying fall in her inflexion. No need to ask who Martha was. Martha, in Clara's view, was a slatternly girl, and Clara did not like the idea of her queening it in the Murgatroyd farmhouse. Let her wash her dusters out somewhere else, she thought.

Aloud, she said, 'Why didn't you ask me to do a bit around the house for you? I wouldn't have minded.'

'No need. She's doing it now,' was his unsatisfactory rejoinder. 'She comes in Tuesdays and Thursdays.'

Really? *Two* days a week!

Mindful of the fact that he hadn't bothered about cleaning anything for years, this radical change in Seth's affairs indicated to Clara that there was more here than met the eye.

'I should have thought one day would have been quite sufficient.' Nervously she began to stir her tea.

'That's for me to decide,' stated Seth.

Temporarily silenced by this, Clara took a small revenge by imagining Martha at the sink tackling a huge pile of washing-up consisting mainly of Seth's morning-porridge saucepans, none of which he bothered to soak. She saw the head of dark-rooted, dyed blonde hair bent over the stone sink, the thin, unstockinged legs with their down-at-heel shoes, and much scrubbing going on. But that, Clara knew, was not all of it.

Martha was twenty-six, and had the firm, slim body that went with her age. There was no getting away from this uncomfortable fact, and Clara wondered whether the situation might not arise where she would have to fight for her man.

The trouble is, thought Clara, watching her lover as he sat stolidly puffing, apparently oblivious to the fact that they had not yet made love, which was what she, Clara, was principally there for, and that Julia would shortly be arriving to collect her from the end of the lane, the trouble is, Seth is my only hope of some sort of normal life when Mother dies.

In a desperate attempt to focus his attention, she stood up.

'I really must be going. Julia will be arriving soon to pick me up.'

Seth took his father's silver fob watch out of his waistcoat pocket, looked at it, and then knocked out his pipe.

'She won't be here yet awhile, hinny. You come with me.'

The bedroom was low-ceilinged, with a huge and gloomy old mahogany press all along one wall. The wallpaper, patterned with pink roses, dated from the days of Seth's mother. But at least this room had electric light. On the floor above, the spare room did not, and when Seth had guests, which was practically never, they were required to retire by candle-light. His bed, a brass one, was neither a double nor a single but something in between. With alarm, Clara noticed that someone had washed the sheets. No time to speculate on that now, though. In workaday fashion, Seth removed his clothes, dropping them onto the floor. He had a very large erection, which, like his own bull, he appeared to be able to achieve at will.

Clara, whose old-fashioned underwear was more like upholstery, began to remove her own clothes. It took her a lot longer than it had taken Seth, especially when it came to her girdle, which needed a coating of talcum powder before she was able to wriggle into it in the first place. Finally naked, she walked over to the bed where he lay. The only time she had been surprised by Seth had been the first time they had made love. Since then there had been no deviation from the original ritual.

Clara lay down beside him. Seth kissed her and then, with no further finesse of any kind, rolled over onto her and pushed himself hard inside her. The thrusting rhythm of his movement excited and disappointed her at the same time. When he had finished, he simply rolled off her and appeared to go to sleep. As usual, staring at the ceiling afterwards, Clara was uncertain whether or not she had enjoyed herself.

Eventually she rose and, carrying her clothes, crept along a draughty passage to the bathroom. Here, as was her habit, mainly because she did not want Seth to see her forcing herself into the girdle, she got dressed. Then she plodded off down the lane to where Julia sat patiently reading a novel in the old Ford.

* * *

Seth waited until he heard the door slam behind Clara and then opened his eyes. Fancying a drink, he got off the bed, fetched himself a Newcastle Brown Ale from the kitchen, and then returned and lay down again. Supine and sipping, he thought not about Clara, but about Martha. Maybe because she was new, Seth lusted after Martha in a way he did not lust after Clara. Clara, on the other hand, had great expectations, which Martha did not, and Seth had ambitions to expand his farming activities. Cannily, he had taken a decision not to propose to Clara until she actually had her hands on the money. Which surely couldn't be long, since Mrs Steer was very ancient indeed.

Still, there was a slant-eyed air of temptation about Martha that caused Seth to stop and think. Watching her as she moved silently about his house, smoking a cigarette and making very small inroads into the grime, he found himself wondering more and more what it would be like to have sex with such a creature. Martha wore short skirts and blouses that had one button too many undone. Surprisingly for one who was so slender, her breasts were full and contained only with difficulty by the tops she wore. He had not yet dared lay a finger on her. The quality of her dour, self-sufficient country silence, so very like his own, caused her in an odd way to be unapproachable, unlike Clara, whose volubility and desire to please had made her a relatively easy seduction.

Tomorrow was Tuesday, one of Martha's days. Seth, who always paid her in cash, went and checked

that he had enough in the tea caddy in which he hid
his money. Perhaps tomorrow he would touch her for
the first time.

Julia drove back to Armitage Lodge with Clara, and
then, as had been previously arranged, set off to visit
Meredith Barstow. Even though this meant driving
back to Hexham, Julia did not mind. More and more
these days, she felt suffocated in her own home.

Meredith resided with her father in a pleasant cottage near Tyne Green, the large house with a tennis
court in which she had lived while her husband was
still alive having long since been sold. Too big, said
Meredith, who in actual fact could not afford it any
more.

The April countryside was greening and turning its
milder face up to the sun, away from the snowy rigours
of the Northumbrian winter. Julia could remember one
arctic December when Leonora's stone hot-water bottle had burst, so intense had been the cold. Entering
the town, she drove down Battle Hill, and then turned
left, finally emerging into the market square, with the
Moot Hall on her right. As she passed by the abbey,
its clock was striking five. On impulse, Julia stopped
the car opposite the gates to the bowling green and
wound down the window. The day was a still one, and
she breathed in the evocative scent of moss and old
stone that she had never encountered anywhere else. I
want to get away from here, thought Julia. I *must* get

away from here, before my life is over and there is nothing to show for it.

She restarted the car, allowing it to roll gently down the steep bank before the street levelled out at the burn that flowed beside the road leading to Tyne Green.

When Julia arrived, Meredith was in her sitting room. There was no sign of the Brigadier.

'Father's having a nap,' said Meredith, 'and between you and me, it's a relief. He really is very difficult these days. Embarks on things, then forgets what it's all about and when reminded gets cantankerous and says it's all my imagination.'

'Leonora never forgets anything,' said Julia. 'I rather wish she would. She has a memory like an elephant, especially for slights.'

'Never mind.' Meredith felt rather hard-hearted as she spoke the words. 'Can't be long now.'

'Sometimes I think she might see me out.'

'Father's always had a very soft spot for your mama.'

'Mother wouldn't know what to do with anything soft. It simply isn't part of her vocabulary. Anyway, for heaven's sake, let's not talk about *her*. I've come to tell you that Morgan is getting married.'

'I know,' replied Meredith, 'Caro wrote and told me.'

'That being the case, you probably know more than I do. As usual, Mother played her cards close to her chest and simply relayed the bald fact. And now we are talking about her *again*.' Sometimes Julia felt as though her powerful parent infiltrated every single part of her life, and that nowhere was this helpful. 'What does Caro think about it?'

'She didn't really say.' Meredith was cautious. In fact, Caroline had seemed depressed, almost weepy. Meredith, who for her own reasons wanted Morgan out of her daughter's orbit, did not wish to pass on anything that might upset the applecart of his forthcoming marriage. 'Though she did say that the bride-to-be is a newspaper heiress.'

'Yes, that's the only nugget of information Mother was prepared to pass on. She's a member of the Post family, apparently.'

'When are they coming to Northumberland?'

'Not sure of the exact date, but quite soon I believe. It will mean Gentleman's Relish for tea instead of Shippam's meat paste.'

Ah, this was unfortunate, for it looked like coinciding with Caro and Minerva's visit to Tyne Green. Meredith made a mental note to try and put them off until the following week. On the other hand, that might not be possible because of the school holidays. Damn! Meredith was very aware of the strong pull Caro exercised where Morgan Steer was concerned, and very conscious too that even with the new fiancée in the offing, a Northumbrian meeting at this sensitive juncture, might cause a change of heart.

The Brigadier appeared.

'Julia! What a surprise. Meredith didn't tell me she was expecting you.'

'Yes I did, Father. It was the last thing I said to you before you went upstairs for your rest.' Meredith sounded uncharacteristically tetchy. Julia gave her a keen look. He really must be getting on her nerves.

'No you didn't, Meredith! I would have remembered. I think your memory must be going. It's probably your age. Perhaps you should see a doctor. Anyway, never mind about that.'

Dismissing it, he turned to Julia.

'How's your mother these days? She's a fine woman, I've always said so. A fine woman!'

Julia, feeling herself in imminent danger of a stream of reminiscence, stood up and prepared to take her leave.

'Oh, full of fight, you know Mother.' Uttering these words, it occurred to her that full of spite might have been a better way of putting it. 'I'm afraid I must go. I have to pick Cassandra up from the village church.'

On the way there, having said her farewells, Julia thought how ironic it was that in spite of the fact that Meredith had gone to university and then held down a succession of demanding jobs, the two friends had ended up in the same place, namely at the beck and call of a very demanding parent. Although it had to be said that Meredith had had more fun along the way. Much more fun. When she cared to think about it, Julia was forced to face the fact that her life had been something of a wasteland.

The lights were on in the little church when Julia finally arrived. Cassandra and Deirdre Ricketts were standing together admiring their flower arrangements. Was it a trick of the eye, or did they move swiftly apart as she entered? Julia had never been able to make up her mind what, if anything, was going on there. Perhaps Deirdre Ricketts's slightly smeared lipstick was a pointer. Well, whatever it was, good luck to them, thought Julia. She hoped that Leonora never found out.

But Leonora had of course found out about Cassandra's attachment to Miss Ricketts, though only the fact, not the detail. She also knew about Clara and Seth. It seemed to Leonora that there was no point in broadcasting her knowledge and that she had a potentially powerful weapon at her disposal should she ever need it.

Time was when Leonora would have been much more instantly destructive with such information. Nowadays, however, she could see the past with more clarity than the present. She found herself remembering old vendettas rather than new ones, and could recall balls she had attended, dresses she had worn and lovers she had had as if they were yesterday.

These days I'm bored, thought Leonora. Bored, bored, bored. I have an agile brain within the body of an old woman. In my mind I feel as though I am still twenty-five, not ninety, no, eighty-five. She corrected herself out of habit. The highlight of her life had been 1930. In 1930 she had been thirty-two. That had been the summer of the Prince of Wales and the naughtiest house parties. The social cachet of being, albeit briefly, a royal mistress had been heady, and Maxwell had been quite content to lurk in the background until it was over. The royal person himself had been less than a pure delight, being a petulent, tricky individual with an overinflated idea of his own cleverness. Still, it was the position that mattered, not the person, Leonora recognized, making the most of it. And then Wallis Simpson had come along, also with a complacent husband in tow, and had proved more than a match for them all, Leonora herself included. Still put out even after all these years, she sniffed at the memory of it. American parvenue! Although parvenue or not, she had still been the victor, if you could call it a victory. There had been no throne at the end of the day, just him, reflected Leonora with some satisfaction.

She stood up and walked over to the window. Sometimes she felt that her life had gone on a little too long. Leonora was susceptible to the seasons, and responded to them in kind. So the spring made her flirtatiously destructive, the summer langorously manipulative, the autumn energetically combative, and the claustrophic, harsh Northumbrian winter, socially murderous. Maybe the forthcoming visit of Miss Chloe Post would provide the required diversion. A new element was what was needed, to ginger things up. Hopefully the fiancée would be one of those modern, dangerous girls. That would cause a flutter in the dovecotes, and not before time.

* * *

Clara moped. That is to say, she performed all the usual duties but in a conspicuously lacklustre way that Julia and Cassandra tactfully kept quite about, and which Leonora did not fail to remark upon.

'You are behaving like somebody who has been crossed in love,' said Leonora cruelly.

The truth of the matter was that Clara did not know if she had been crossed in love or not and suspicion was proving very difficult to live with. Seth had cancelled their Thursday tryst, with only the most monosyllabic of explanations, asking her to come on Friday instead. Tempted to call anyway, Clara had resisted, but could not escape the feeling that something was going on.

She arrived on Friday as requested. On the surface things were the same as usual, except that the kitchen was unswept, and no washing-up of any sort appeared to have taken place.

'Did Martha come yesterday?' enquired Clara, very casually.

'Yes, she did.'

'I only ask because she doesn't appear to have done much.'

'Oh, she did plenty,' said Seth without amplification.

Plenty of what, though?

When they finally got as far as the bedroom, two things alerted Clara, one being the lingering smell of cheap scent, which Clara finally identified as lily of the valley, and the other being Seth's behaviour, for

Seth had abandoned his usual robust approach for something altogether more subtle. Benefiting from this interesting change, and moaning with unfeigned pleasure as she did so, Clara was nevertheless aware that this sudden, atypical surge of imagination could only be explained by her lover having had a tutorial elsewhere.

'Do you want to talk about it, Clara?'

Leonora and Cassandra had both left the room.

Not trusting herself to speak, Clara nodded.

Sensitive to her sister's distress but mindful that in the normal course of events Clara never discussed her lover, Julia hesitated before venturing, 'Is it Seth?' As the eldest of the three, she had always been the one in whom they had confided their troubles as girls.

Clara's lip trembled and her eyes filled with tears.

'Yes, it is. Well, it's Seth and Martha, really.' She fished in her cardigan pocket for a handkerchief.

Clara is another of Mother's casualties, thought Julia, looking at her sister with sympathy. She used to be such a pretty girl, and should never have been reduced to Seth. Now it looks as though even he is going to let her down.

'I'm sorry, Julia, I'm making an awful fool of myself.' Clara blew her nose. 'It's just that when Mother dies, I want a life of my own, and a home of my own, with a man in it to look after. I don't want to be alone.'

More tears.

Reflecting that she herself *did* want to be alone, and that she had had enough of the company of women, and men for that matter, to last her a lifetime, Julia asked, 'Are you sure he's bedding Martha?' She rejected the words 'having an affair' as too sophisticated with regard to Seth.

'Pretty well. And I don't know what to do about it.'

'If you're right, there's nothing to do. Just go on being there, and hope he gets tired of her. And don't make scenes.'

Julia had learnt this invaluable lesson when married to the unreliable Major Fred, who had a fine ability for provoking rows and then going absent without leave when, all too predictably, they occurred.

'I expect he'll get over it.' She was aware of making Martha sound like an attack of chickenpox. Sounding more optimistic than she felt, she continued, 'After all, you and Seth, well, you've been together a long time.'

With sad perspicacity, Clara said, 'Do you know, if I came into my money I think he'd ask me to marry him.'

And carry on fucking Martha, no doubt, Julia thought to herself. What a depressing scenario.

At that moment Cassandra entered.

'Oh, I'm sorry, am I interrupting something?'

She prepared to withdraw.

'No, no, don't go. I've said all I have to say to Julia. What time is it? Half-past six. Time for Mother's blood transfusion.' This was Steer speak for Leonora's gin and tonic. Clara went to the drinks cabinet and poured a stiff one with shaking hands, nearly managing to lose the bottle in the process.

Eyeing her, Cassandra observed, 'For God's sake don't drop that. She'll disinherit you!'

When Clara had gone, she turned to Julia.

'Trouble with Seth?'

'Worse. Trouble with Seth and Martha.'

Cassandra was silent for a minute or two before saying, 'Mother has a lot to answer for.'

'She does, doesn't she,' said Julia.

May

10

Both Chloe and Morgan had doubts about the wisdom of their forthcoming marriage, Chloe because of her frigidity, and Morgan because, try as he would, he could not rid himself of his enduring obsession with Caro. He dreamt about her, and she was still in his mind when he awoke. She even haunted him when he made love to Chloe, and sometimes during the day when he felt unaccountably depressed, he concluded that she must be thinking about him. Nevertheless, he knew that he had to get over this. Caro could not, no, *would not*, marry him, and somehow he had to break free of her. He was also aware that in order to avoid looking like a drone to Chloe's well-heeled family, he ought to step up his desultory attempts to find a job. On the other hand, this raised the question of how much Chloe herself would like living with someone whose availability was circumscribed by a nine-to-five office day. On the whole, Morgan thought she would enjoy it just about as much as he would. Chloe needed a lot of attention.

It underlined the lack of communication between them that for her part, Chloe herself felt as though for once in her life she was getting almost too much attention, in the physical sense anyway. It was almost as though, she thought, unaware of how near the bone she was, Morgan was trying to exorcize something.

Staring at the sapphire he had given her, a symbol of their commitment to one another, she thought about the aspect of marriage that frightened her the most, which was childbirth. Morgan wanted children. Chloe knew this because he had talked about it. Theirs being a comparatively late marriage, it meant children sooner, not later. She could see the logic of this, but not the desirability. Chloe remembered all too clearly the horror story of her own birth, as related by her mother with great relish and in gruesome detail. 'It was agony, absolute agony! I've never known such pain, and it just went on and on! Nobody can expect me to suffer like that again,' Veronica Post had proclaimed closing the matter, and with it her bedroom door. Listening to all this the young Chloe had been afraid, and because neither of her selfish parents took much notice of her, being too busy pursuing their own, and most of the time, separate pleasures, she had had an unhealthy amount of time on her hands to dwell on her mother's experience. And now the very thing she feared most was very probably going to happen to her.

Neither Chloe nor Morgan spoke of their reservations to one another. Perhaps if they had the marriage would never have taken place. As it was, careless of their silence on such pivotal subjects, the arrangements for what would be a very social wedding gathered im-

petus until, quite independently, they both came to the
conclusion that to pull out now would be unthinkable.

Veronica Post arrived from Boston, thin as a pin,
and prepared to be disappointed. Meeting her over a
cup of Lapsang Suchong, Morgan was struck by her
brittleness. There was nothing motherly about her, and
on the whole he doubted there ever had been. Her
thick, waving hair was shoulder-length and artfully
streaked, probably to conceal the fact that she was going grey. The face it framed was in good shape for its
age, though the tilted point of the nose indicated sur-
gery, and a slight tightness of the skin a skilful face-
lift. She wore a sharp little suit and a tan so uniform
in colour that it was like a body stocking. In common
with a lot of people who spend a great deal of their
time in the sun, she would have to beware of the leath-
ery look, he decided.

But it was her hands that fascinated him. They were
small and bony, with the long, lacquered unchipped
nails of one seldom forced into the indignity of manual
work, and they were never still. Veronica lightly
drummed her fingers on the side of her teacup, plucked
at her necklace, fiddled with her hair, and when she
was not doing any of that, twisted what he supposed
must be a large Post diamond round and round her
wedding finger. In short, she was nervy. He also noticed that Chloe and her mother had a curious way of
talking to one another, as if they were strangers who
just happened to be sharing the same railway carriage.

Ceasing her drumming for a moment, Veronica addressed Morgan.

'I gather your family lives in Northumberland. Such a lovely county. Where exactly are you?'

This was delivered rather in the way a royal might ask a question of a factory worker during an official tour of some plant or other, the point being that she had deigned to ask the question, not that she attended to the answer. After all, reflected Chloe, whatever he says won't mean a thing to Mother, who has never been north of Mayfair as far as I'm aware.

Not listening to his reply, Veronica sized up Morgan Steer and was more impressed than she would have expected. Morgan, who was wearing a suit in her honour, had what she called a certain air about him. And expensive shoes. Veronica always noticed people's shoes. She pictured him in morning dress at the wedding, enjoying in advance the way in which her friends would compliment her on having acquired such a handsome son-in-law. Enviable accessory would be his role in relation to her. Chloe had done much better than she would ever have expected.

A pause brought her to herself. Morgan had finished his answer. Luckily his last few words had contained no upward inflexion, so he couldn't have been asking her a question.

'How fascinating,' said Veronica. 'I absolutely adore the country.'

'Then you'll be delighted to hear that we have decided to be married in Hexham.' They hadn't, of course, but the temptation to flush out her insincere parent was more than Chloe could resist.

'Have we?' Morgan was startled.

'I don't think that's advisable,' said Veronica, and then, rapidly improvising. 'Your father wouldn't like it. He's bound to want you to invite some of his business friends and they wouldn't want to go all that way.'

'Mummy, this is my wedding we're talking about, not a business conference for Daddy!'

'Yes, darling, but you know what your father's like.' Turning to Morgan, Veronica explained: 'When we were married, I hardly ever saw John. He was always too tired to go out in the evenings. For the last year, I lived like a hermit!'

The idea of Veronica Post living like a hermit was risible. Morgan avoided catching Chloe's eye.

'Do you have a job, Morgan? And if so, what is it?'

Here it was. The question he had hoped to avoid, for the time being anyway.

'I'm afraid I'm unemployed at the moment, Mrs Post, but I am about to—'.

With a wave, she cut off his good intent.

'Please call me Veronica. You are about to become my son-in-law, Morgan. So you haven't got one. Splendid!' came the surprising response. 'If you had one, when would you and Chloe see each other? I quite decided during the course of my life with John that there is nothing more destructive to a marriage than the Office. And anyway, courtesy of her father's family money, Chloe is very rich, so you don't need a job! You can concentrate on your wife instead.'

Dazzled by the purity of her selfishness, Morgan could think of nothing to say. Veronica began to twist the Post diamond round her finger and they all sat in silence for a moment or two, mesmerized by the sheer size of it and its hard sparkle. Beside it, Chloe's more modest sapphire looked like a poor relation.

'The guest list is the most pressing item,' resumed Veronica, letting go of the diamond and beginning to tell her pearls as though they were some sort of costume rosary. Watching her silver-tipped fingers darting nervily in and out of the strands like lizards' tongues, Morgan wondered how Chloe had survived her unquiet parent as well as she apparently had. 'It is most important to get that right, and quickly,' she continued, 'otherwise nobody will be able to come and your wedding will be a dull disaster!'

Chloe was adamant. 'Mummy, Morgan and I are perfectly capable of drawing up our own guest list!'

As though this last statement had not been uttered, her mother began to reel off a list of names, most of which Morgan recognized from Euro high-society gossip columns, *Hello!* especially, finishing with the decree, 'And of course we must invite the Ponsonby-Smiths. Not to do so would be social death! Perhaps,' she mused, 'I should make discreet enquiries as to what their immediate plans are so that we may schedule ourselves around them.'

Morgan could hardly believe his ears.

Looking suddenly like a mutinous five-year-old with fists clenched, Chloe, her voice rising, said, 'Mother, I am not going to organize my wedding day around the Ponsonby-Smiths. I don't even *like* the Ponsonby-Smiths!'

The authoritative and frankly ageing use of the word *Mother* seemed to call Veronica briefly to herself. Deigning for once to notice somebody else's point of view, and looking at her daughter as if she was mad, she pronounced, 'Don't be silly, Chloe, neither do I! Nobody does. They are a poisonous couple. But I should not have to tell my own daughter that that is not the point. The point is, they are social...' She looked into the middle distance for a moment or two, searching for the *mot juste*, finally coming up with, '...trophies!'

Morgan, who vaguely knew them too, pictured two stuffed Ponsonby-Smith heads.

Her voice by now very high-pitched, Chloe reiterated, 'I absolutely *refuse* to—'

'And the church is a matter of prime importance as well. I shall have to discover which is the chicest these days. No doubt churches go in and out of fashion like everything else.'

The interruption was both impervious and expert, leaving Chloe and her protest high and dry. Watching and listening to the pair of them, Morgan began to wonder if he was really there at all. Did they always squabble like this? He appeared to be utterly redundant. Perhaps all that would be required of him would be to turn up on time on whatever day Veronica Post decided upon.

Chloe's face was set and white. She sat up very straight, her furious silence apparently by-passing her social parent.

Lighting a cigarette and inhaling, Veronica, too, fell silent. Deciding to step in helpfully, Morgan said, 'We ought to convene a meeting of the two families before the wedding.'

Momentarily distracted as he had intended her to be, Veronica said, 'Oh, would your family be prepared to leave Northumberland to travel down here?'

She made them sound like troglodytes. Reflecting that when they finally did encounter one another his grandmother would make short work of Veronica Post, and that he hoped to be there to see it, Morgan said, 'Grandmama makes two trips a year to London in order to shop, one of which is usually just before Christmas. No doubt this time she will alter her arrangements around the wedding, but if you would prefer to meet her before then, Mrs Post, perhaps you would like to travel to Hexham with us. Since you are so fond of Northumberland, that might be a better idea.' It was a calculated gamble. He held his breath, recognizing that her acceptance of his proposal would be catastrophic.

'Veronica. Please call me Veronica,' said Veronica automatically, thinking fast as she did so. Finally she said, tapping her foot, 'On balance I think that with so much to do, I would be better employed here. Such a shame, but there it is. Perhaps', she deigned graciously, 'there will be time for travelling when the wedding is behind us.' The regal tone of her voice elevated a simple train journey to the status of a royal progress.

'By then you will all have met at the wedding and there won't be any need for such an uncongenial trek!' Chloe felt she had had enough of her mother's social dishonesty.

Veronica Post stood up.

Sensing that hostilities were about to break out all over again, Morgan said hastily, 'That's all right, we'll arrange some soiree or other. Leave it to me. I'll organize it.'

'Oh, will you, Morgan? Will you really?' Veronica gave him a constricted smile, anything wider perhaps being a little hampered by the strictures of the last face-lift. 'Chloe, my bag, please!'

Handing it to her, as her daughter did not move, Morgan thanked Christ she lived in Boston.

When she had finally gone, he said to Chloe, who looked drained, 'What's your father like?'

'The same but different,' she responded. 'Do you think I could possibly have a stiff drink?'

Meeting Chloe's father for the first time, Morgan saw what she meant. John Post was tall, expensively suited and his immaculately coiffured hair had gone a distinguished grey in all the desirable areas. His tan, topped up by a recent holiday in Bermuda, was as deep and as smooth as Veronica's. It was the subtly different tan of the very rich. In tow was the Child Bride.

'Daddy, this is Morgan Steer.'

Chloe blushed, letting the glossy wing of her hair cover her face in an attempt to conceal it.

'How do you do, sir,' said Morgan, receiving in return a handshake whose dry firmness was calculated to impart a sense of integrity.

'Hello, Morgan. My wife, Annabel.' He propelled her forward by the elbow.

'How do you do.'

Annabel's hand was soft and boneless and her handshake correspondingly limp.

Dark and fair, Chloe and Annabel kissed without warmth.

Morgan could hardly take his eyes off Annabel. Annabel was a Veronica clone. She looked exactly like her predecessor except that she was half her age. Even the clothes were similar, and there was another large Post diamond on the third finger of her left hand. Maybe John Post had a safe full of them. There was, however, one significant difference between the Post wives, apart from Anno Domini, as Morgan was to learn, and that was that while one never stopped talking unless lighting one of her hundreds of cigarettes, the other never spoke at all unless forced into it.

A waiter materialized and hovered. They all sat down. John Post proceeded to order himself a complicated cocktail. The accompanying instructions on how to prepare it were so extensive that Morgan decided it would have been quicker if Post had gone behind the bar and made it himself. Without consulting her, he then ordered a different and equally difficult drink for his wife.

'Madam?' queried the waiter, finally getting to Chloe.

'A gin and tonic, ice and lemon, please,' she said, very rapidly.

'Sir?'

'The same.' Morgan was even terser.

The relief of the waiter was palpable.

'This bar is famous for its cocktails, you know,' said Post, reprovingly putting his oar in.

Undermining the legitimate preferences of others appeared to be a family pastime, thought Morgan. He tried to imagine John coexisting with Veronica and failed. Presumably they had both talked at once and nobody had listened to anybody. He wondered how on earth they had arrived at a joint decision to divorce, or even to marry one another in the first place, come to that.

'I don't *want* a cocktail, Daddy, I *want* a gin and tonic.'

Chloe sounded firm and at the same time arch. There was a little-girl quality to her voice that reminded Morgan of the way she had responded to her mother. Then she shot her father a coquettish look. The response was immediate. He was clearly tickled pink.

Watching his fiancée flirt with her father, Morgan found the whole Post-family set-up curiouser and curiouser. He looked across at Annabel, who was staring at her diamond with a sad absorption, her cocktail untouched. She looked as though she felt *de trop*. Just as I probably do, thought Morgan. Leaning towards her and taking a crisp from the bowl the waiter had thoughtfully left for them, he said, 'Do you spend much time in the States?'

'No.'

He waited for her to elaborate, and when she showed no sign of doing so, followed it up with, 'But surely all the Post newspapers are in America?'

'Yes, they are.'

This was an uphill struggle.

'Well, in that case…?'

Annabel, finding herself forced to string more than three words together, exuded dejection.

'John's money comes from the newspaper chain, but he doesn't actually work in the family business.'

She closed her mouth again. The expression getting blood out of a stone could have been coined for Annabel.

Coming to his aid, Chloe interrupted whatever it was she was talking about with her father.

'Daddy's a banker,' explained Chloe. 'And an Anglophile. He finds the States too hectic.'

Leaning back in his chair, Post drank half his cocktail at a swallow. Turning to Morgan, he said, 'And what about you, Morgan? What is your profession?'

Here it was again, the dreaded question. Too much to hope for the same favourable response.

'Well, actually, I—'

'Morgan is on the short list for a most wonderful job!' Chloe stepped in mendaciously. 'So wonderful that he isn't allowed to talk about it yet!'

'Oh really!'

Post drank the other half of his cocktail. Morgan, still reeling from what Chloe had just said and wondering how he was going to explain it later, was nevertheless aware of a sour intonation in the American's words. It was at this point that he realized that as far as Chloe's affections were concerned, he was in hot competition with her father.

John Post shot a discontented look at his wife.

'Say that's great news! Isn't it, honey?'

Glumly she assented.

'All the same, Morgan, I think it advisable that we have a man-to-man talk about money. Without the ladies present. However, before we go into the restaurant, just tell me what you were doing before you—'

'Now, Daddy!' Touching his wrist with one sapphired finger, Chloe was fetchingly firm. 'No more business talk over lunch!'

Spurred on by both his opinion that women were brainless, a view reinforced by his first marriage, and his desire to flush out his daughter's suitor as a fortune-hunter, Post found it hard to subside.

'If you say so, sweetheart! Make an appointment with my secretary for dinner one day next week, would you, Morgan?'

It sounded more like a threat than an invitation. They went into lunch.

Later, driving back to the Prince's Gate flat, Morgan said to Chloe, 'What on earth did you do that for? We both know there's no such job, and no prospect of one. And shortly your father will know that too.'

Unruffled she replied, 'Yes, but by the time Daddy finds that out we'll be married, and there won't be much he can do about it.'

Morgan, who was fundamentally honest, did not like this.

'You see,' continued Chloe, 'Daddy's very protective of the family money.'

Morgan thought it was more than that but did not say so. The unhealthy fact, made so disconcertingly apparent over lunch, that John Post was also very possessive of his own daughter, appeared to have passed Chloe by.

'So he's met your parents, but you haven't yet met his.' The speaker was Joanna Blackstock as they sat one evening in her flat. "How did it go?"

Since Chloe had no particular point of reference where this sort of exercise was concerned, her reply was uncertain.

'All right, I think. Mummy and Daddy are about to lock horns on the subject of the wedding, which will keep them both occupied. Nobody seems very interested in my views on the subject, so I thought I'd leave them to it.

Reflecting afresh on her friend's curious passivity, Joanna was suddenly assailed by a vague but nonetheless unnerving intimation of impending catastrophe. Abruptly she said, 'According to Tom, Morgan has been obsessed with someone called Caroline Barstow for years. And probably still is.'

Chloe remembered the conversation she and Morgan had had in the Steer flat the night they had met. That must be the woman he was referring to, she thought.

Aloud, she said, 'Well why didn't he ever marry her?'

'She's married to somebody else. An actor called Patrick Holland.'

'Never heard of him,' said Chloe, reflecting at the same time that being married had never inhibited anyone she knew from pursuing their sexual pleasures. 'And after all, at our age you don't expect virginity.'

'No, of course you don't, but this is rather more dangerous than that. If I understand it right, they never actually did have an affair, so, if you like, it's unfinished business.'

'I want to be married, but I can take or leave the sexual side of it. As far as I'm concerned if Morgan wants to play away, as long as he does it discreetly, of course, I'm not about to make a fuss.' Chloe was quite definite.

This practical and jarring little speech encapsulated the difference between the two women and repelled

Joanna, who had a much more Roman approach to such matters. When I'm married to Tom Marchant, she thought, if I ever find he's been cheating on me, I'll kill him. No, I won't. I'll torture him first, and then I'll kill him.

Deciding to get away from the unsatisfactory subject of her friend's forthcoming wedding, Joanna said, 'By the way, I've asked Tom to move in with me.'

'Oh really!' This caught Chloe's interest. 'So you've...?'

'No, we haven't. It's the spare room, and if we don't get on he moves out again.'

'But you're not expecting that.'

'No, I'm not.'

Chloe had her own nugget of information to disclose.

'Morgan says that a few years ago Tom was fired from his job. Insider dealing. It was quite a scandal in the City, and one of the reasons why his family disinherited him.'

'Ah!' said Joanna. 'That must have been what Daddy meant. He left a message on my answering machine indicating his disapproval of this particular friendship. I'm having dinner with him sometime in the near future to reassure him.'

'Is Tom divorced yet?'

'Nearly.'

'Morgan doesn't think he's the stuff of which faithful husbands are made,' proffered Chloe.

'No, he isn't, but by the time I've finished with him

he will be. Where are you going to be married, by the way?'

Chloe shrugged.

'Don't ask me! Ask Mummy.'

Dinner with Veronica was an event that John Post anticipated and dreaded. And a dinner where they were to attempt to discuss their daughter's forthcoming nuptials, which he was in any case very ambivalent about, promised to be even more of a trial than usual.

She arrived twenty minutes late, by which time he had almost finished his second cocktail and was exasperated before they had even exchanged pleasantries. Veronica had always been unpunctual. Post decided to rise above yet another of those acrimonious scenes that had characterized their brief marriage, many of which had centred on this irritating habit.

They kissed. Even now he still found her attractive. And she still used the same scent she had when they had been married. Nina Ricci, he remembered. There was an unfairly evocative quality about scent. It took him nostalgically back over the years, and he was conscious of his annoyance subsiding.

'John!'

'Veronica!'

Sitting down, the second thing she did was light a cigarette.

Infuriation set in all over again.

'God damn it, Veronica! Can't you exist for thirty seconds without one of those things?'

She inhaled deeply.

'No, I can't, John. Doing without the weed makes me fretful. And please don't start telling me what to do. We are no longer married and I don't have to listen.'

She had him there.

She signalled to the waiter, another maddening habit. Why couldn't she just let him organize it for her? She had never been able to wait five minutes for anything. All the same, she did look glossy. And there was a vibrance about her that the second Mrs Post did not possess. Leaning forward and preparing to be urbane, and therefore seductive, Post took the hand that was not holding a cigarette and said, "Veronica, you're still very beautiful. You haven't changed at all.'

Pointless flirtation was apparently still his forte.

'So everyone tells me.'

His vanity disappointed by the signal absence of the words 'Nor have you, John,' he dropped her hand and seized the menu instead.

'This is one of the best restaurants in town.' He handed it to her.

'Fillet steak, rare, green salad and mineral water,' dictated Veronica to the waiter, without even looking at it.

'Oh, come now…'

'Pour être belle, il faut souffrir.'

Unexpectedly she sent him a look of invitation, though not so inviting that all the fine lines around her eyes were accentuated. Remembering with distaste the depressed slope of Annabel's shoulders when he had told her that her presence at this particular soiree was not called for, and failing to recall exactly how infelicitous his first marriage had actually been, he was conscious of a resurgence of interest in his first wife. However, preparing to follow up his advantage, he was stopped in his conversational tracks by her next remark.

'I shall, of course, require a new outfit for Chloe's wedding,' said Veronica. 'I thought that perhaps you might like to choose it with me.'

And pay for it while you're there, perhaps?

The words were unspoken, but might as well have been said. He had forgotten quite how grasping she was. All thoughts of rekindling an old passion were dissipated as he remembered the size of her dress bills.

'I think I'd rather it was a surprise. I'm sure that whatever you buy will be very elegant!'

And very expensive.

Veronica shelved the subject, deciding to return to the attack later. John always had been difficult about money. Not stingy, but careful. It had been one of his less endearing traits.

'Perhaps we should talk about Chloe. It is, after all, her wedding.' This was delivered with an element of reproof, as though he had been the one putting his own sartorial concerns first. 'Chloe's dress *must* come from Paris.'

Post felt an attack of severe financial anxiety coming on.

'Can't we leave that to Chloe?'

Disregarding this remark entirely, she said, 'And then there is the reception. I have drawn up my own guest list, and no doubt Morgan will want to ask one or two people.'

'I should like access to the guest list too,' said Post. 'I have quite a few business colleagues it would be polite to invite.'

'Well, not too many, John! This is, when all is said and done, Chloe's wedding, not one of your business conferences.'

Post thought this was rich, considering that he was obviously expected to pay for the whole extravaganza.

She finished her steak, and without asking him if he minded, lit a cigarette, which she drew upon deeply before exhaling two Mucha-like plumes through elegantly flared nostrils all over his *canard à deux services*.

'Veronica—'

His intended reprimand never got any further.

'I thought Claridges for the reception. The honeymoon presumably we can leave in Morgan's hands.'

The honeymoon. Wreathed in smoke, Post's face fell. Of course he knew that his daughter had had affairs, but the idea of her being permanently locked away from him in the arms of Morgan Steer, who would no doubt prove very proprietorial, was an alarming one.

There was a brief silence, then he said, 'Are we quite sure that we approve of Morgan?'

Surprised, she stared at him. 'What can there be to disapprove of? He's about to become a perfectly presentable husband, which is all that is necessary.'

She stubbed out her cigarette and prepared to light another.

Finding himself without any sort of support, Post said tetchily, 'Can't you survive for at least five minutes without one of those? It's a disgusting and dangerous habit!'

Here Veronica actually stooped to answer this last remark, saying complacently, 'I'm probably one of the very few who still indulge in it. The statistics are quite horrendous.'

She signalled for the waiter again.

Deploring her initiative, and sighing with exasperation, he decided to press on. The sad passivity of the second Mrs Post suddenly seemed much more desirable than it had earlier that evening.

'What I mean is that apparently Steer hasn't even got a job.'

'A small black coffee, please,' she said to the waiter, who had just presented himself. Taking a lipstick out of her hand-bag together with a mirror, she proceeded to outline the shape of her mouth and then block it in, another habit he couldn't abide at the table, as she well knew. He wondered if she was deliberately trying to offend him.

'So what!' said Veronica, finally putting away her make-up. 'He doesn't need a job. Chloe has plenty of money. Chloe needs an escort for parties, not a corporate wage slave!'

By now there could be no mistake.

Very huffed, this time he signalled for the waiter.

Veronica retook the advantage.

'I think I would like a pudding after all.'

'You've just ordered coffee.'

'Nevertheless!'

Putting aside his earlier intention, which had been to ask for the bill, he requested the menu again.

It arrived.

Veronica looked provocatively over the top of it, as though it was a fan and she a nineteenth-century courtesan, and said, 'You know, John, you haven't changed a bit since the day we married!'

Post, his self-esteem badly in need of a recharge, decided to take this ambiguous statement as a compliment and not ask her what she meant exactly. He preened. Having got the meeting back on course, Veronica said, 'I think I won't have a sweet after all, but what about a brandy for you, darling?'

Darling?

Mollified, but without losing sight of the financial aspect of all this, he asked, 'Who's going to work out a budget for all these plans?'

A budget?

'I will, of course,' responded Veronica, for whom this was a foreign concept. 'But just to get the show on the road, perhaps an advance would be a good thing. Unless, of course, you want to organize the whole event yourself.'

Of course he did not.

'How much do you want?'

She named a sum. A huge sum.

And this is only Chloe's first wedding, thought Post, an American to his fingertips, as he wrote the cheque. Too many more like this and I'll be bankrupt.

Putting the cheque in her bag, Veronica said graciously, 'Thank you, John, that should do to sort out the preliminaries!'

The preliminaries!

'I think it would make sense for you to open a special wedding account. Makes things easier all around. Tidier, you know.' Even as he spoke, he knew it was too late, that he should have opened it in their joint names first and not simply handed her the cheque.

'*Such* a good idea, darling, you always did have a very acute financial brain.' She did not, he noticed, say she would do it.

Veronica looked at her watch, a small platinum affair that he had given her after one of their more spectacular rows, and announced, 'Good heavens! Is that the time! I must fly! Can I leave you to take care of the bill, darling?'

Post watched her go amid a flurry of bowing waiters, his cheque tucked in her Gucci wallet. Not sure whether *darling* was a promotion or whether that was what she called everyone these days, he decided to have another brandy.

As he drank it, he came to the conclusion that the only way to solve his problems, financial and otherwise, was to try and ensure that the marriage never took place.

11

For all sorts of reasons, it had proved impossible for Meredith to reschedule Caro and Minerva for the week after Chloe and Morgan's visit. Instead, they came earlier, which meant that Minerva had to miss some school, although because she was at the age when if Caro said black she said white, Minerva was unable to decide whether to exult or complain. However, even the new arrangement only underlined the fact that the best-laid plans can go awry. Travelling in opposite directions, Morgan and Chloe and Caro and Minerva met by accident in Newcastle Station. Morgan's heart missed a beat when he saw them, and he was about to steer Chloe away from them when Caro looked up from the copy of the *Spectator* she was about to buy for reading on the train, and saw him.

She was wrapped in a long purple cloak the colour of which echoed her eyes, and wore ankle-length buttoned Victorian boots. The effect was both bohemian and arresting, although her height alone distinguished Caro from the common herd. In turmoil, Morgan stood stock-still, and she did the same.

Following the direction of Morgan's gaze, Chloe saw her too, and with a psychic click divined exactly who she was. Chloe was impressed. Not by the clothes, which she could see were inexpensive, but by the sheer presence of the wearer. A follower of fashion, Chloe knew that certain people can make anything look good and that one such person stood before her. Morgan's rapt look left her in no doubt that, whether he knew it or not, he was still in love with Caroline Barstow.

Oblivious to the small drama going on around her, Minerva, who was wearing a partly shredded sweater, slashed jeans and the inevitable Doc Martens, the toes of which she had spray-painted with broad silver stripes, said, 'Can I have some money to buy *Just Seventeen*?'

'Please!' said Caro automatically, giving it to her. Minerva went.

Nevertheless the spell was broken.

'Aren't you going to introduce me?' asked Chloe.

It was the last thing he wanted to do, although obviously they were going to have to meet at some point.

'This is Caroline Barstow, a Northumbrian neighbour of ours. Caroline, this is my fiancée, Chloe Post.'

Chloe, who knew more than he realized, was less interested in what Morgan said than in what he did not say.

The two women appraised each other.

There was only one word for her rival, decided Caro enviously as they shook hands, and that was soignée. Amid the grime and soot of Newcastle Railway Station, Chloe looked as though she had stepped out of a bandbox.

Minerva reappeared with the magazine.

'I'm afraid we have to go. The King's Cross train goes in fifteen minutes. Have you got everything, Minerva?'

'No idea,' was her daughter's uninterested response.

'Well, could you check?' Caroline sounded exasperated.

She turned to Chloe. 'Goodbye!'

'Goodbye!'

'Goodbye, Morgan.'

Morgan felt incapable of speech. Pain predominated. He stared at her with sorrow and desire, remembering how close he had come to making love to her that day in her own house, until her ludicrous lodger, or whatever he was, had interrupted them.

She turned and went.

Wishing that he could relieve his feelings by groaning aloud, Morgan watched her walk proudly away from him, straight as an arrow, like a queen of the Iceni, purple cloak streaming, Minerva dragging her feet in her mother's dramatic wake. He saw them hesitate for a moment, apparently listening to a scrambled announcement over the tannoy, before they moved off again, and were finally lost to sight.

As they sat in the train to Hexham, Morgan and Chloe were silent. Chloe stared out at the countryside, which grew wilder the further north they travelled. They rattled through small stations with patriotic red, white and blue flowerbeds and names like Blaydon,

Prudhoe, Riding Mill and Corbridge. Unkeen on the
country, the wildness of Northumberland made Chloe
feel as though she was in a foreign land. And she now
saw what Joanna had meant about Caroline Barstow.
Her initial idea of graciously turning a blind eye to a
dalliance with a mousy little mistress, thereby dividing
the sexual chores, was quite inappropriate in the light
of the person she had just met. The day Morgan went
to bed with Caroline Barstow would be the day he left
her, Chloe.

For his part, Morgan felt like weeping. The course
his life was taking, which had appeared to have a certain inevitability about it, suddenly seemed open to
question again. Suddenly he could no longer persuade
himself that the course his life was taking was the right
one. Caro isn't on offer, thought Morgan, and so I'm
marrying Chloe. It can't be right. But what else am I
supposed to do? I can't go on pining for someone who
doesn't want me. And Chloe, as well as being very
attractive, is very…Morgan veered away from the
word rich…*suitable*. But was that enough? Probably
not. Once again he wondered if it was too late to pull
out of the marriage. Probably it was. And short of kid-
napping her, there was no way that he could see of
marrying Caro instead.

Morgan opened up the day's *Times* and pretended
to read. Chloe was not deceived. She saw that if she
wanted her lover, she was going to have to fight for
him, but combating something as intangible as unrequited love was not going to be easy, and she would

probably only succeed if Morgan himself made a conscious decision to look away from his obsession.

Wisely, Chloe decided not to raise the subject of Caroline again, even though it was on both their minds. Instead she said, 'Are we taking a cab from the station?'

Pulling himself together, Morgan replied, 'No. My mother has been instructed to meet us in the car. She's the only one of them who can drive.'

Chloe had never heard of anyone over the age of seventeen who could not drive.

'So she is, therefore, the family chauffeuse. What a cross!'

'I think she quite enjoys it. It gets her out of the house as well as out from underneath Grandma's thumb for brief periods.'

'You make it sound as if your grandmother rules the house with a rod of iron!'

'She does.'

The prospect of a few days in Armitage Lodge trying to keep his grandmother sweet momentarily took Morgan's mind off his other troubles. He wondered how she and Chloe would get on. Well, no doubt, since money and good looks, in that order, were very important to Leonora.

The train drew into the station. Unloading their cases, Morgan saw his mother standing further down the platform and waved to her. As she approached them he was suddenly struck by how much she had aged, but then perhaps it was simply the contrast with

Chloe, and the absence of the Aunts and Leonora, beside whom everyone looked young, that made him
think this.

Sitting beside Julia as they bumped along the dry-
stone-walled lanes, Chloe was interested to note that
the Ford's indicators were little orange arms that shot
out on request, and that the seats, although covered
with leather, were bald and shiny. It's a veritable an-
tique and exhausting with it, thought Chloe, who had
never driven anything that was not an automatic. She
watched Julia throwing it into first, then second, then
third and back down again, stamping endlessly on the
clutch as she did so.

Armitage Lodge, with its peeling grandeur, was
more of the same. In so far as they could, the flowers
of early summer softened its craggy face, but in the
way of a very crusty person wearing a frivolous hat.
Trees were few in number, and those there were tilted
in the same direction, indicating that the prevailing
wind came straight off the fells. The Lodge was starkly
open to the weather, and probably, thought Chloe, very
cold, especially in winter. She breathed deeply, inhaling a smell of old grey stone, moss and earth that
would be one of her abiding memories of her first encounter with Morgan's childhood home.

Julia opened the door and let them in. Inside, despite
the fact that it was the end of May, the temperature
was cold. Standing in the hall at the foot of a large
and imposing staircase, Chloe shivered.

* * *

'Mother, who is currently having her afternoon nap, has decreed that we all change for dinner. Meredith and the Brig are both invited.' The speaker was Clara, nervously excited at the prospect of a dinner party, a rare occurrence these days.

'Who's cooking?' Morgan sent up a prayer.

It was not answered.

'I am,' said Clara, 'and your mother is making the pudding.'

Morgan made a mental note to warn Chloe, although she ate like a bird anyway and perhaps wouldn't feel as hungry as the rest of them by the end of the meal.

'How clever of you! I don't know how to cook,' observed Chloe.

Neither does Clara, thought Morgan, nevertheless alerted by this statement. He cast his mind back over their relationship and realized that, apart from the occasional breakfast, she had never prepared a meal for him.

'Where's Cassandra?' enquired Morgan.

'Walking Jardine.'

'Who's Jardine?' Chloe was finding it difficult to keep up with all the members of the family.

As she spoke they heard the front door open, and close.

'Ah, here they are,' said Julia.

There was the dry rustle of a mac being hung up in the hall, and then Cassandra, Jardine at her heels, walked into the drawing room. Or, rather, it might be more accurate to say that she walked into the drawing room, saw Chloe Post and immediately sensed that life would never be the same again.

Jardine, who was well trained, waited for the signal before bounding forward to greet his master. Watching them together, it was obvious to Chloe how much Morgan loved his dog, and she was conscious that here, in the country, she was about to see a completely different side to her lover. Perhaps it was the result of all their hidden reservations about their relationship, but she was also aware Morgan had never shown her the uncomplicated tenderness he was now displaying towards his dog. Ecstatic, Jardine put both black front paws on Morgan's chest and barked.

'Oh!' Clara sucked in her breath. 'Don't do that. If Mother hears him, it'll be the outhouse for a week.'

'Sit!' commanded Morgan. Jardine sat. Loyalty personified, his eyes never left his master, and his tail rhythmically beat the floor.

'He looks wonderful!' Morgan complimented Cassandra. 'Just right, plenty of muscle and not too much fat.'

'You might need to take him in hand a bit,' said Cassandra, ogling Chloe as she spoke. 'He's getting quite disobedient when off the leash. Won't come back when called, that sort of thing.'

'I'll sort him out. Don't worry about it! Which room has Grandmama put us in?'

'Not room, rooms.' The speaker was Julia. 'You know what Mother's like, a child of the Edwardian era with all the inconvenience and hypocrisy that that implies. If you and Chloe want to commune you'll have to corridor-creep at dead of night. Right past her door. She's put you at opposite ends of the house.'

'But we're engaged!' said Morgan, hardly able to believe it.

'Try telling her that!'

Later on, dressing for dinner, Chloe took in her new surroundings. A particular culture shock had been her bedroom, which was gloomy and chilly though the bed itself (she tried it) was comfortable. Leading off her bedroom was a bathroom that was positively Spartan and had lino on the floor. The soap, Chloe noticed, was the end of two cakes that someone had economically pressed together so that an unlovely black line had formed where they joined. This was parsimony of a practically royal order. There was no hot water.

How long were they staying? Was it four days or five? Disconsolately Chloe exhumed her little black dress from the depths of her large suitcase, and then, in the interests of cheering herself up, changed her mind and decided to wear red instead.

In the bedroom next door, Clara was saying to Cassandra, 'Should it be the salmon pink or the turquoise?'

Cassandra winced. 'I should say neither, Clara. Look, what about this?' She extracted a dark green silk from Clara's gaudy wardrobe. Heaven knew how it had got there in the first place.

Reluctantly putting down the pink, Clara said, 'Oh, are you sure?'

'Absolutely!'

Cassandra, elegantly angular in maroon velvet, turned to go.

'Don't forget the food. What is it, anyway?'

'Rabbit. There's a lot of them about. I made it in advance. It's in the oven.'

'Oh, good,' said Cassandra vaguely. And then. 'Do you know, I have an odd feeling about Chloe Post, and it's bothering me. I sense something gathering around her. Something…' She hesitated, before unnervingly concluding, 'dark.'

Clara looked up, momentarily distracted from searching her jewel case for the string of coral she had been given for her twenty-first. Cassandra's premonitions struck without warning and were famously accurate.

'What do you mean, dark?' she asked, brow clouded.

'Not sure, but it's not good. Let's not talk about it. Do you want to wake Mother up or shall I?'

Leonora wore white for dinner. It was an odd choice for a ninety-year-old, thought Chloe, but in a strange sort of way it suited her. High-necked and with leg-of-mutton sleeves, the dress harked back to Leonora's youth at the same time as it drew attention to her hair.

'Miss Post!' said Leonora, meeting her grandson's fiancée for the first time.

'Oh, Chloe, please!'

'Chloe!'

Leonora looked Chloe up and down for a full minute without speaking, and then, as though the object of her interest was not there at all, observed to her grandson. 'You've done well for yourself there, Morgan.'

Her rudeness was in a league of its own. Any minute now she'll open my mouth and look at my teeth to check how old I am, thought Chloe, nettled.

She did not, in fact, do this, but simply said, 'How old are you, Chloe?'

Smarting, Chloe told her.

'Better get on with it then. Children, or, rather, a male child, must be your priority.'

With relief, Chloe heard the front doorbell jangle.

'Ah,' said Leonora, 'that will be Meredith and the Brigadier. Clara! Door!'

'Yes, Mother,' Clara scurried.

'*Courage*, darling,' murmured Morgan under his breath, noting Chloe's discomfort. 'It's just her manner. She doesn't know how she sounds.'

On the contrary, thought Chloe, she knows perfectly well how she sounds.

Clara prepared to offer the guests drinks.

'Now, what can I—'

Secure with her own very large gin and tonic, Leonora interrupted. 'No time for that now. We have to go in to dinner. What held you up, Meredith?'

'Nothing that I'm aware of,' replied Meredith, who was used to Leonora's tactics and her determination to keep the gin bottle solely for her own consumption. 'We were invited for eight o'clock and arrived here at ten minutes past, as perfect manners demand.'

'A small misunderstanding. I quite definitely said seven thirty for eight. Well, no matter. Follow me!'

Stately in her white dress, Leonora took her seat at the head of the table.

'Clara, there is no *placement*! Where is the *placement*?'

Chloe watched Clara go scarlet and then begin to panic before Morgan stepped in and verbally did it for her.

'No, no, that won't do!' Determined to corner the men, Leonora imperiously overrode him. 'Brigadier, you will sit on my right, Morgan, you on my left. Chloe, on the Brigadier's right. The rest of you may sit where you like.'

She's power-mad, thought Chloe, watching all this dictatorial behaviour. Or maybe just mad.

They all sat down. Cassandra slipped into the chair next to Chloe's. Both she and the Brigadier gave the beautiful newcomer a sidelong glance. Nothing quite so exotic had crossed the horizon for a very long time.

The conversation was less than sparkling. Picking her way through some of the most appalling food she had ever been forced to endure, Chloe felt as though dinner would never end. Desperately, she looked across the table towards Morgan, who smiled supportively back. At last the cheese arrived and Leonora authorized the opening of another bottle of wine to go with it. Bulgarian, the Brigadier noticed with disappointment, before wrapping his hand around his tiny glass and drinking the contents in one go.

Later that night, much later, stepping as light as a cat along the corridor towards Chloe's room, Morgan was dismayed to find his grandmother's bedroom door open and the light on. Hanging around in the shadows, he was debating whether to make a dash for it when she said, 'Please come in, Morgan. Don't hover around in the passage like that, it gets on my nerves.'

How had she known he was there?

Giving up all hope of bedding Chloe that night, he went in.

'I was just coming to say goodnight, Grandmama,' he lied. 'I hope I didn't disturb you.'

'Not at all.' Smiling, she radiated mischief. 'I shall be up for quite a while yet. You young people have no stamina.'

Her sudden roguishness took him back to his boyhood, when Grandmama had enjoyed repartee and had been open to discussion, though even in those days, only up to a point. And while she had never been particularly affectionate, she had been fun, with a quick brain and a quick tongue to go with it. It was easy to see why men had found her so attractive. Looking back, he decided that the sarcasm and aggression had increased in direct proportion to the gradual erosion of her beauty, which while she still had it she had no doubt taken for granted.

Deciding to respond in kind, Morgan said, 'I have plenty of stamina when I'm allowed to use it.'

Amused, Leonora understood him perfectly.

'Yes, I dare say you do!' And then, in a burst of totally unexpected benevolence, 'Well, well, run along then! Go and see your Chloe, if that's what you want, but first give your grandmother a kiss.'

She lifted up her withered cheek.

'Goodnight, Morgan.'

'Goodnight, Grandmama.'

He closed the door and set off along the corridor again, wondering as he did so why she couldn't always be so reasonable.

In their respective rooms Clara and Cassandra also considered Chloe. Clara was frankly envious, for it seemed to her that Chloe had it all. By all, she meant money, looks and a man. She herself on the other hand, because of the capriciousness of her mother, might never lay her hands on the money she felt was rightfully hers, had lost her looks, and, unless she was much mistaken, might be in the process of losing her man as well.

'It's not fair,' announced Clara aloud, beginning to tear at her fingernails with her teeth, an old childhood habit she had never grown out of.

She picked up a silver-framed photograph of herself as a young girl. She had never been very clever, but she had been bright-eyed and vivacious, with a small waist, a spring in her step and a good seat on a horse.

And her long, thick, auburn hair had been famous throughout the county. When had it all began to go wrong?

She went over to the mirror and looked at herself by the light of the sixty-watt bulb Leonora considered sufficient for what was in fact quite a large room. Disappointment and a general lack of stimulation had caused her face to slip and had encouraged jowls. Although, thought Clara, defending herself, the overhead light did not help. Puffy and pale, her image peered back at her, although her thinning hair still retained something of its earlier ruddy burnish, thanks to the semipermanent rinses she secretly bought herself from the chemist.

It had all begun to go wrong, she thought, when Leonora had decided to see off her numerous suitors. On encountering the critical stare of the terrifying Mrs Steer, they had decided they could do without it and had gone away and married other people. So that one day Clara had woken up to the fact that she was twenty-eight and on her own. Vague, panicky thoughts of escape before it was finally, absolutely too late had been dashed by the sight of Mother's rage on learning of Julia's bolt with Major Fred. Reading the note she had found propped up against the teapot, Leonora had looked to Clara to be on the verge of a seizure. Mother in a vitriolic temper was not a pretty sight.

'Serves her right,' Cassandra had pronounced irreverently when they were finally out of earshot. 'Bossy old bat. You watch. She'll go off and rewrite her will now. Good luck to them, I say.'

In the room next door to Clara, and lying on her bed rather than in it, Cassandra too pondered the arrival of Chloe Post. Never remotely interested in men and until now content with her comfortable, unscintillating relationship with Deirdre Ricketts, with whom she had thought herself in love, Cassandra thought that Chloe Post was something else again. She was... Cassandra searched for the *mot juste*, and came up with *exquisite*. Simply exquisite. But curiously detached, and from Morgan too. Once again Cassandra experienced the feeling of something cloudy around Chloe, something not very nice stealthily gathering. She shivered. Maybe a session with the tarot pack was called for. But then again, maybe not. Used by now to her own uncomfortable gift, Cassandra was nevertheless wary of it, and was by no means sure that she *wanted* to know what fate had in store for Chloe Post.

By the time Caro got to London after her encounter with Morgan she felt as though she might be sickening for something. Her temples throbbed and she felt hot. Minerva did not notice any of this, but slouched into the house behind her mother, lost in a surly world of her own.

Patrick was not there and had left a note on the hall table to say that he would be back late, but voices coming from the sitting room indicated that Larch was around. Upon entering the room, Caro found him sprawled on the sofa and in the company of two youths, one of whom was swinging back on one of her chairs, a habit she hated, with his sneakered feet on the seat of another. Nobody took the slightest notice of her.

'Hello,' said Caroline finally.

'Oh, hello,' responded Larch, in a tone which indicated that her arrival was a tiresome interruption. He did not expand on this.

Caro raised her eyebrows in the direction of his guests, neither of whom stood up.

Forced into it, and thinking to himself, Can't she see I'm busy? Larch said with a long-suffering air, 'Ah, yes. This is Nigel, and this is Gary.' He did not, she noticed, introduce her to them.

Doing it for him, Caro said, 'And I am Caroline Barstow, owner of this house, Nigel and Gary.'

Such was her tone that Gary took his feet off the chair.

'Gary and Nigel are protégés of mine,' said Larch, unabashed.

Protégés was Larch language for his juvenile delinquents. Caro was furious. It had been made very clear that Larch was not to bring his work home. She was just debating what her next move should be when Minerva came into the room.

Watching Gary, who was chewing gum and insolently looking her daughter up and down, Caro, whose first instinct had been to lay it on the line later, decided that she wanted them out, and now.

She was opening her mouth to say this when Larch, getting there first, announced, 'Minerva, I want you to meet two young friends of mine, Nigel and Gary. You might find you have a lot in common.'

Behind his back the two of them smirked at each other.

'Hi!' said Minerva, recognizing a bolshie attitude when she saw one, and liking it.

Seething, Caro broke into the introductions. 'If you don't mind, I should like you to reconvene this meeting elsewhere. I have things to do in here.'

'That's all right, Caroline.' Larch was condescending. 'We'll move into the kitchen.'

Caro gave him a level look.

'I have things to do in here *and* in the kitchen.'

'Oh. Oh, I see.' Larch's expression was venomous.

As they were going, Caro asked, 'By the way, where is Emily?'

'Emily has another job,' said Larch. 'Working as a receptionist at an art gallery called, appropriately enough, The Gallery.'

'Oh, really! Oh, terrific.' Caro felt her spirits lift on her sister's behalf.

'Not my sentiments, I'm afraid. It's a fashionable establishment, mainly patronized by the chattering classes and those who have more money than sense. The Haves rather than the Have-Nots. Frivolous! And quite unsuitable for someone as easily led as Emily. However, she seems quite determined to take no notice of my views on the matter!'

Oh, *good*! thought Caro.

'No doubt it will all end in tears.' He turned to the boys. 'Come on, let's go.'

Following Larch to the door, Nigel took out a comb and began to run it through his lank blonde hair. He had a tattoo on the back of his hand, Caro noticed, quite a large one depicting two hearts and bearing the legend *Nigel and Mandy*. Heaven only knew what he had on his chest. How old was he? About fourteen if she guessed right. As they passed through the front door, she heard Larch enquiring, 'What time are you due in court tomorrow, Gary?'

A brief 'Dunno,' was his only answer.

When they had gone, Minerva said censoriously, 'Mum, you shouldn't have done that!'

'Shouldn't have done what?'

'Treated them like that. They probably come from broken homes. It isn't their fault if they've gone wrong. They're probably deprived,' she ended triumphantly.

Deprived? Certainly not materially with two expensive pairs of sneakers, designer jeans and two leather jackets between them.

'I wasn't treating them like anything. Larch was out of order. And while we're on the subject, there are plenty of deprived people who come from broken homes, and worse, who don't end up in front of the juvenile court.'

Her daughter shrugged. 'I just think you should

know what you sound like. You sound like a Conservative. Do you think Dad would let *me* have a tattoo?'

Caro was tart.

'Catch him in the right mood and he'll probably let you have a ring through your nose.'

It was a false move.

'Do you really think so? I might ask him.'

'Right now I suggest you go and unpack. You've got school tomorrow.'

'Bummer!' said Minerva, going.

Caro went to bed early and could not sleep. A Nurofen drove away most of the headache, but left enough behind to make reading impossible. The confusion and misery that had dogged her on and off for years where Morgan and her marriage were concerned, suddenly welled up in her until she could no longer look away from her own distress. A picture of Chloe Post (*'Caroline, this is my fiancée…'*) standing on Newcastle Railway Station rose before her eyes and made her draw in her breath as though she had been stabbed in the heart.

To carry on lying there any longer was insupportable. Such turmoil of spirit demanded movement and probably a therapeutic Munch scream to go with it. Throwing back the sheet, Caro put on a pair of jeans and a T-shirt and went downstairs to the kitchen. The kitchen was large enough to be useful for this sort of exercise, as Emily had found out, and Caro marched endlessly up and down it, sobbing loudly, her arms wrapped around herself as if for protection. And then suddenly, and for no particular reason, grief fell away and rage unexpectedly engulfed her. On impulse she took a glass from the cupboard, filled to the brim with red wine, which she drank at a swallow, and then hurled it at the opposite wall, where it exploded in smithereens, producing a small, scarlet action painting.

'It's not fair,' shouted Caro. 'It's just not fucking well *fair*!'

From her bedroom window Minerva spied Emily coming along the pavement and intercepted her at the door.

'Aunt Emily, I don't think Mum's very well,' said Minerva in a stage whisper. 'She's screaming in the kitchen and I think she's just broken something.'

Emily gave her niece a searching look.

'Where were you when all this was taking place? You haven't upset her, have you?'

'Not at all. I've been getting ready for school tomorrow.' Minerva looked pious.

'Well, you should go back to doing that and leave Mum to me. She's probably just had a bad day, that's all.'

Emily walked along the passage and tentatively knocked on the door.

'Who is it?'

Whatever the agony of spirit that had taken place, Caro sounded quite calm now.

'It's Emily. May I come in?'

'Yes, of course.'

'Caro, are you all right? Minerva says you've been shouting and breaking things.'

'I'm surprised Minerva can hear anything with those earphones on,' was Caro's programmed response. 'Anyway, the answer to your question is that I'm about as all right as I'm ever going to be.'

Unsure how to take this, Emily asked, 'But what's the problem? Is it Morgan?'

'Yes it is, but there's absolutely nothing to be gained by talking about it. He's going to marry the Post heiress, and that's all there is to it.'

That's all there is to it.

Suddenly feeling oddly detached after all the tumult, Caro's eyes rested for a brief appreciative moment on a small glass jug of garden flowers that someone, Emily presumably, had placed on the dresser. The charming sight of their brilliant red and orange and hot yellow velvet faces was to remain in Caro's memory for years, a still life always to be associated with the end of a misfired love affair that in the event had never properly begun.

June

12

After Morgan and Chloe had departed for London, as far as Cassandra was concerned it was as though a light had gone out. At Armitage Lodge the uneventful, repetitive days felt even longer and duller than usual, and in the evenings even the lamps seemed dimmer. Cassandra fretted and stopped arranging the church flowers with Deirdre Ricketts, pleading that she had too much else to do. In so far as she could, she kept clear of her mother, well aware that Leonora could pick out vulnerability at a hundred paces and would show no scruples about ridiculing her if afforded the opportunity.

Leonora's opinion of her future daughter-in-law appeared positive, on the whole, and she did not hesitate to compare her own daughters unfavourably with the elegant new addition to the family. Morgan was a lucky man, said Leonora, not once but several times.

Listening to this, Clara thought sadly that if her mother had only been as positive when she, Clara, had had suitors all those years ago, she too might have married and had children. Even seeing Seth had proved impossible during the Visit, since Leonora had wanted her three daughters constantly on hand to fetch and carry, and had not been prepared to countenance mysterious absences.

If I lose Seth I don't know what I'll do, thought Clara. But something. Something desperate.

Julia, too, was reflective but for different reasons. Julia felt the impending marriage was a mistake. True, Chloe was beautiful and rich, and that was helpful, but there had been no visible signs of the sort of empathy that makes pairings work. She could see how the marriage might just succeed in London, for a while anyway, but the Northumbrian end was a completely different kettle of fish. Here, it would *never* succeed. But, of course, Mother wanted it, and, typically, for all the wrong reasons—looks and money, but mainly money.

It was because of her fears for her future that Clara asked Cassandra to do a tarot sitting for her. Cassandra was reluctant, though she could not really have said why.

'Oh, please, Cassandra,' wheedled Clara. '*Please.*'

The feeling of unease resurfaced.

'Oh, I don't think so, Clara. I have to be in the right frame of mind for it. Otherwise it won't work.'

When she wanted something, Clara had always been very like a dripping tap.

'Oh, go on. Just this once. Say yes.'

Cassandra withstood two days of it before giving in.

'All *right*! But remember, I can't guarantee anything.'

'No, of course not. When shall we do it?'

By now exasperated, Cassandra said snappily, 'Oh,

for heaven's *sake*, Clara! Is tomorrow evening soon enough for you?'

Clara was contrite.

'I'm sorry to be so irritating. Yes, of course it is. Thank you, Cassandra.'

And so it was that ten o'clock the following evening found them both in Cassandra's room, facing each other across a small round rosewood table. They sat within the yellow circle of light projected from the parchment shade of a standard lamp. Around them the room was dark and quite still. A room waiting.

The tarot pack was old and had been given to Cassandra years ago by a governess they had once shared. She had claimed to have the gift of second sight, and having divined the same uncanny ability in her pupil, had taught her what to do. The cards were large and dog-eared, soft and almost furry through years of use, but in spite of the brown bloom the pack had acquired from so much handling, the strong primary colours were still vibrant.

Clara experienced the familiar *frisson* of excitement, potently mixed with dread.

'What do you want me to do?'

'Shuffle!'

Because they lacked the sharp, slippery quality of modern playing cards, this was easier said than done, and Clara, who was nervous anyway, managed to drop almost all of them before she finally succeeded.

'Oh fiddlesticks!' said Clara. 'Does that matter?'

'No, it's all part of it.'

'What now?' She put them down.

'Cut them with your left hand, please.'

Clara did so.

'And choose one of the packs.'

Cassandra bent her head, grey and sleek as that of a seal, over the tarot and began to lay out the cards, cards that might well hold the key to Clara's fate. Long, thin and garnet-ringed, her sister's mobile hands fascinated Clara. The shadows in the bedroom became denser and more oppressive. Silent spectators, they seemed to crowd around the light. Clara resisted the temptation to say, 'What is it? What do you see?' She clasped her own pudgier hands together and tried not to fidget.

Cassandra began to speak very slowly, weighing her words, receiving and transmitting with care.

Disappointingly, her first few observations were of a general nature, and although Clara dutifully wrote these down, she was at a loss as to how they could particularly apply to her.

Cassandra flipped down some more cards, one of which, Clara noticed, was the Lover. There was a very long pause, and Clara was just beginning to suck the end of her pencil when Cassandra said suddenly, 'This is interesting. There's something coming around... It's a man building up. Foreign blood, and I think there's an F in the name. Could be a T, but I think it's more likely an F. You're going to be... Ah! Oh, no, this isn't you! It's Julia. Problems coming up for Julia. She's going to be picking up a thread of the past. Or

maybe the past is going to come to her. Not good, and
when it happens I want to tell her to look away from
it.'

Clara, who did not want to hear about Julia in the
middle of her sitting, shuffled her feet.

'And in an odd sort of way it will affect *you*. All of
us, in fact. I don't like it, whatever it is, and I don't
trust it.'

'Oh!' said Clara.

'And there's strong talk of separation coming into
the home. Followed by a move of house.'

'Is this me?'

'This is very much you, Clara.'

'Oh!' said Clara again, thinking of Seth with a surge
of optimism. 'Perhaps I'm getting married.'

Though she did not say so, Cassandra did not think
this was likely.

'There is going to be a wedding, and it is a member
of the family, but the person I'm getting is a man.
Morgan, perhaps.'

Clara's face fell.

'Doesn't mean to say that there can't be two,' said
Cassandra kindly. 'It may be that it just isn't showing
yet. Take two.'

Clara complied.

'Money! There's going to be a *lot* of money. Somebody's going to hit a jackpot. And very, very good on
that level, but they are also saying be very wary of it.
It will happen suddenly. And when it comes it's associated with an ending.'

By now, Cassandra was well into her stride.

'Might be Mother,' said Clara, trying not to sound too hopeful.

'Maybe,' responded Cassandra, at the same time thinking, But my opinion is that it isn't. 'And there's also going to be *loss* of money, but in a *different* area. Loss of money due to force of circumstances. Recklessness with money.'

Reflecting that she did not like the way it was going and that there was almost something mischievous about the way *nothing* good was showing, or at least almost nothing, Cassandra was silent a moment. Then rather against her better judgement, she continued, 'If you're sure you want to, let's carry on. Take one.'

Clara selected a card.

'Changes, changes, changes!' Settling down to it again, Cassandra's voice sounded far away, almost dreamy. There was a brief silence and then, 'But not all for the better, I fear.'

Really, thought Cassandra, apart from the jackpot, whatever that is, this is getting more and more depressing. I knew we shouldn't have done it.

It was at this point in the reading, as she was refocusing on the cards, that Cassandra received a shock she could have done without. Clara watched her sister grow white and sharply draw in her breath, then put her hand over her mouth.

'Cassandra what is it? What are you getting?'

Cassandra's hands shook.

'Death. There's going to be a death. Death with tremendous shock. *Violent* death! And when it comes he won't be ready for it. Oh! Oh, no! They're saying *she*. *She* won't be ready for it. It's horrible, quite horrible!' An amateur at this sort of thing and therefore unable to arrest its progress or even contain it, Cassandra was aware of the whole sitting sliding out of control. 'Let's stop this now, Clara. I simply can't bear to go on.'

Very agitated she stood up abruptly, tilting the table as she did so, with the result that the tarot pack slid off the polished surface and cascaded over the floor, swords, wands, cups, coins and pentacles all forming a pattern of their own. Right in the middle, lying face up and, from where she was sitting inverted, Clara saw the Devil.

It wasn't until she was back in her own room that Clara realized Cassandra had not told her who it was that had violent death in store. Obviously now was not the time to ask. Clara had never seen Cassandra so rattled. What she did not know was that even if she had asked, she would have been none the wiser, for Cassandra had received the fact but not the detail.

Clara opened her bedroom window. Outside, the June night, which had been so quiet during Cassandra's reading, almost as though it was holding its breath, had come to life again. Because they were so far north, it was still cold. The moon rode high and full but clouded, as though a caul covered its pale face. Owls hooted, and far away Clara could hear the occasional bark of a dog fox.

I wonder what Seth is doing? thought Clara. Perhaps I'll go and see him tomorrow.

Chilled and subdued, she shut the window and turned back to her solitary bedroom.

The next day, knowing nothing of the dramatic events of the night before, Julia decided to go and see Meredith, mainly to find out her view of the projected marriage between Morgan and Chloe. Meredith, former schoolteacher and Justice of the Peace, was always very sensible.

To her relief the Brigadier was not there.

'Where is he?' she asked.

'Playing geriatric bowls,' said Meredith. 'I drove him to the bowling green half an hour ago. I have to say, it's a relief to get him out of the house sometimes.'

Julia could believe it.

'So what's your view of your prospective daughter-in-law?'

'What's yours?'

'Do you want a tactful answer, or what I really think?'

'What you really think, of course, otherwise what's the point of asking you!'

'I think there's no depth to Chloe,' said her friend firmly. 'What you see is what you get. And my view of Morgan is that he needs someone with more bottom.'

Like Caro, perhaps? Oh no, thought Meredith, the last thing I want is that. Briefly she looked into the mess and muddle of the past, and then resolutely turned her face away from it again. Anything but that! Aloud she said, 'But I'm probably completely wrong.'

'No, I don't think you are. My opinion is that apart from a social life, they have absolutely nothing in common.'

'Have you talked to Morgan about it?'

'Morgan never talks to me about the course his life is taking. He talks to Mother.' Julia was aware of sounding as though her nose was very much out of joint.

'Well, all right, but what does she think about it?'

'Oh, she wouldn't tell *me*. What she really thinks, I mean. You know Mother. Invidious comparisons are more her line. She does approve of the looks and the money, because she endlessly tells us so, but I suspect she's not so sure about the breeding. I actually heard her saying to Morgan, "I've heard all about her father's side of the family. American, I gather. Trade, lamentably. Newspapers, I believe. But what about the dam side? *Who* was her mother before she married? I assume that her family is one that we know?"'

Meredith laughed out loud.

'I can see it all in my mind's eye. Leonora really is a class act. Straight out of Ivy Compton-Burnett! What was Morgan's reply?'

'Inaudible,' said Julia, laughing too in spite of herself.

'Talking of breeding, I assume they want children?'

'Whether they want them or not doesn't enter the picture. They've been told to get on with it by Mother.'

'I can imagine Morgan with children.'

'What about Chloe?'

'No, not really. In a curious way, she didn't strike me as physical enough.'

'Ah! Exactly!' exclaimed Julia. 'That's what's been eluding me, and you've put your finger right on it. Not physical enough! That's the problem.'

'Well, it may still fall by the wayside,' said Meredith, fervently hoping, for all sorts of reasons, that it would not. 'Many a slip, and all that.'

'I don't think so. Not now. And the other thing that bothers me is that she has all that money, and Morgan doesn't even have a job.'

'If she's as rich as they all say she is, maybe he won't need one.'

'Yes, he will.' Julia was quite definite. 'Self-respect demands it! In fact, it's more important now than ever.'

She was silent for a moment or two.

'Do you know who I was thinking about the other day?'

'No idea,' said Meredith. 'Tell me.'

'Frederick. Or rather, Frederick and me.'

This was unexpected. Meredith's eyes dilated. Major Fred had been very bad news.

'Oh, really,' she responded neutrally. Was Julia still married to Major Fred? Probably she was. 'Thinking what?'

Julia looked into the middle distance.

'About our marriage, and more particularly Mother's dubious role in the whole débâcle.'

'Do you ever hear from him?'

'Heavens, no. He's dead for all I know.'

The shadow of Major Fred fell between them.

'I should stop thinking about him.' Meredith sounded more robust than she felt. 'After all, what's the point?'

'He's Morgan's father, and Morgan is about to get married.'

For Meredith this was getting uncomfortably close to the bone.

'Has Morgan ever shown any desire to meet his father?'

'None whatever, but then Frederick did decamp before he was born. Probably doesn't even know that he has a son.'

'No, and in my view it's better that way. What about a cup of tea, and then I must go and pick up Father.'

Watching the kettle boil, Meredith let her mind wander back down the years to the era of Major Fred. If I'm honest, she thought, he did seem very dashing to us then, unsophisticated country girls as we were. Nothing like the London girls he must have been used to. I'd never even been to London then, and neither had Julia. And really, there were not that many eligible men around. In her mind's eye she saw him again. The swagger, the superficial charm and the general air of loucheness that had seemed very man-of-the-world to her, and no doubt to Julia too. I wonder what I'd think if I met him now? Not much, I dare say. He had been attractive, though. There had been a certain alluring heedlessness about the Major, later revealed more accurately as selfish irresponsibility and epitomized by the way he had treated Julia. And not just Julia, either. Better for everyone if he never came back.

Meredith took the tray through.

That evening, unaware that Chloe and her daughter had met, Meredith wrote to Caroline.

Darling Caro,
   It was such a pleasure having you and Minerva for a whole week, but a great shame that Patrick was unable to come with you. Fingers crossed for the play, though, and a long and lucrative run! (Some hope, thought Caro, reading this.)

   At this end it has been a veritable hive of activity, with Leonora at the centre as queen bee, very much like the old days. At last we have all been allowed to meet Morgan's fiancée, Chloe Post. I have to say it seems an odd match to me, and Julia thinks the same. On the surface it would appear to be a perfect combination. Two handsome people, and a great deal of money to boot. Even Leonora approves! Imagine that. And yet, and yet…what about love? In a funny way it's all surface and no depth, I suspect, and what will sustain it when they are finally alone together and

*thrown back on each other? All the men are dotty
about her, I may say, including your grandfather,
who keeps repeating that she's the prettiest gal
(sic) that he's seen since he was twenty-one,
which doesn't do much for the memory of your
grandmother, God rest her soul. Anyway, be that
as it may, I'm 99 per cent sure it will all happen.
Whether for better or for worse remains to be
seen.*

*In the meantime, though, Leonora is preparing
to look down on the Posts from a great height,
him because he made the mistake of being born
American (still a colony, according to her), coupled with the fact that the family money was made
in newspapers (trade!), and her because her family is one Leonora has never heard of, which can
only mean that Mrs Post, Veronica I believe her
name is, must be her social inferior. Not One of
Us. That sort of thing.*

*So, as you can see, everything is shaping-up
nicely for a verbal brawl, followed probably by a
general family fallout. Well, that's weddings for
you! We are all going to be invited, according to
Morgan, and I intend to travel to London for it,
and would be grateful for a bed for the night if
you have one spare. I believe the date is yet to
be decided.*

Hopefully by then Larch will have removed himself
back to his own charred kitchen, thought Caro, reading
the last bit. Although I shall miss Emily. She ran her
eye down the rest of the letter, which was inconse-
quential, Meredith ending with the words: *Do you
think my black straw will pass muster for the church?*

Perhaps if I trim it with a new silk rose? I only wear a hat once every ten years, if that, and am very reluctant to buy another!

No, it won't, thought her daughter. With two holes cut in the crown, that hat, new flower notwithstanding, would do very well on a donkey. Her mother was a highly intelligent woman, but utterly clueless when it came to clothes. And anyway, hadn't she worn it to garden in last summer? And wasn't the brim beginning to fray? Folding Meredith's letter in two and putting it in her pocket, she resolved to write and veto any attempts at hat rehabilitation.

But she would buy herself a new one.

If I'm going to watch the love of my life marry someone else, thought Caro, tears in her eyes, I might as well do it in style.

Late that night, putting down *Zen and the Art Of Motorcycle Maintenance*, Larch said to Emily, who was also sitting up in bed reading, 'Would you mind putting down your book please, Emily. I think it's time we had a you/me discussion.'

Emily's heart sank. A you/me discussion usually meant a full and frank appraisal of all her faults, followed by a row.

Reluctantly, she complied.

'Yes?'

He cleared his throat. He must be going to make quite a long speech, she thought. In the event, however, he said only two words, though very portentously.

'The Gallery!'

'Yes?' said Emily again.

'Well?'

'Well, what?'

'What is your decision?'

'You know my decision, Jonathan. I have been offered a lowly job as a receptionist and I have accepted it. That is my decision. Look, do we have to have this discussion now? It's very late.'

They had already had this conversation once, but like a dog with a bone, he seemed determined to dig it up again. Hoping that he would drop the subject, she picked up her book.

'Yes, we do have to have it now. There was a time when you would have asked my advice before taking such a step.'

'Yes, there was, but that was when we first met, years ago. Since then, and with your help, I've grown up a lot and feel able to make my mind up all by myself.'

Mollified, but only slightly, by her admission of his beneficial influence on her, Larch nevertheless felt that the result was not the one he had looked for. In the course of learning how to stand on her own two feet, Emily had over-corrected and become insubordinate.

'After all, it's only a job. I don't understand all the fuss.'

'An unsuitable job that I am asking you to give up. For me.'

'For you? It's nothing to do with you! And anyway, why is it unsuitable?'

'Emily—'

'Look, Jonathan, I've only just started it! I'm enjoying it. What's your objection to The Gallery? It's a business just like any other, and though rather more fun than most, not the endless bacchanalian orgy that you seem to think!' Conscious that her voice had begun to rise, she couldn't resist adding, 'Unfortunately.'

Mystified by her irritability and her inability to see that what he was suggesting was for her own good, and also very unamused by her last remark, Larch said, 'Jack Carey—'

Emily was outraged.

'Oh, so that's it!' She interrupted forcefully. 'Jack Carey has never laid a finger on me! I've only seen him in the distance. I don't think he even knows I exist.'

'Is a lecher,' intoned Larch, as though she had not spoken. 'He has a very unsavoury reputation.'

'But that's nothing to do with me.' Emily shut her book with a bang. 'And what do *you* suggest I do instead?'

Oblivious to her sarcasm, Larch thought for a minute, and then said, 'What about the local library? They might need a secretary.'

'Oh, fuck the local library!'

Emily threw her book on the floor and turned over,

punching her pillow as she did so. She snapped off the light. Because the only bedside lamp was on her side, Larch was left sitting up in the dark. In view of her deplorable mood, he decided not to debate the matter.

Wondering what to do next, he hit upon the generous idea of making love to her to smooth things over. Emily in a temper, with her colour high, was surprisingly fetching. He slipped down the bed and curled himself around what looked like a very intransigent back. But not for long, he though. Larch slid his hand under her white cotton nightdress and up to her thigh.

The response was immediate.

'And fuck you too!' said Emily, brushing it off.

Arriving home at the end of that night's performance, and passing his sister-in-law's bedroom on the way to his, Patrick thought he heard some sort of altercation, although perhaps he was mistaken, since no light was on. On the other hand, there was no earthly reason that he could think of why people shouldn't quarrel in the dark. Dismissing it, he opened his own door.

Caro was in bed reading when he made his entrance. Patrick was glad she was awake. He preferred to share bad news immediately rather than keep it to himself until the morning.

'How was it?' Caro noted the page number and then turned her book over, laying it on the bed beside her. She was reading Henry James's *Portrait of a Lady*, he noticed. 'Full house, I hope?'

'No, nothing like.'

He came and sat on the bed beside her, wondering how to tell her. There was a short, loaded silence until Caro asked, 'What is it? What's the matter?'

'The management called a meeting of the cast at the end of this evening's performance. I'm afraid we close at the end of the month.'

He was clearly dreadfully disappointed.

'Oh, Patrick, what bad luck. Oh, darling, I'm *so* sorry!'

With a spontaneous rush of compassion and tenderness, and tears in her eyes, she took her husband's hands in hers. Tired and defeated Patrick laid his head on her shoulder. He felt like weeping.

'Oh, Caro…'

'It's all right, sweetheart, I'm here!'

That night they made love, gently and circumspectly at first, and then, as pleasure escalated, with the uncomplicated, heady passion of the early years, until finally they came together. And when it was all over they fell asleep in one another's arms.

13

The following morning Emily and Caro shared a minimal breakfast.

'What's happened to Minerva today?' asked Emily. 'No school?'

'She's gone. The Smythes gave her a lift. She wasn't grateful. All smiles to them, but she said to me through gritted teeth that she much preferred being taken to school by her own family. However when I do take her, which as you know is practically all the time, she grumbles every step of the way.'

'It's her age,' said Emily buttering some toast.

'Maybe!' replied Caro absently. 'When does this particular age give way to a better one is what I want to know.'

'I'm told round about eighteen.'

'Eighteen! Christ! So in other words, you're saying I have another five years' hard labour ahead of me.'

'Can be fifteen with a biddable child.'

'No comfort there, then.' Caro sighed.

'Where's Patrick?'

'Still asleep. He got back very late last night. Apparently the management convened a meeting of the cast to tell them that the play has to close at the end of the month.'

'Oh, poor Patrick! And his reviews were so good too.' Thinking as she said it, Well, some of them, anyway.

Loyal Emily!

Caro said it instead.

'Yes, some of them, although there were one or two that were less than ecstatic.'

Quite a few, in fact.

Caro thought of one in particular, which had said: '*The miscasting of Patrick Holland in a key role and his curiously two-dimensional delivery, coupled with a directorial lack of pace, renders a not very witty play moribund.*' The theatre, used to this sort of hiccup, had cannily disregarded most of it and Patrick's photographs outside the Adelphi simply bore the truncated legend: '*Very witty.*'

'Well,' said Emily, eating her cornflakes, 'my good news is that I'm definitely going to leave Jonathan.'

'Oh, *great!*' The words were spoken spontaneously. 'Oh, no! I'm sorry, Em. I don't know what made me say that.'

'The same thing that's making me give him his marching orders, I expect.' Emily appeared philosophical. 'I haven't told him yet.'

'Where is he?'

'He left early in a temper. He really is like a five-year-old when he doesn't get his own way.'

'Emily, you *have* changed!'

'I've come of age, that's all.'

Cradling a cup of black coffee in her hands, Caro walked over to the window. The neighbours' tabby cat dozed on the wall, its nose almost touching the brick. A golden sun, forerunner of the hot summer to come, gilded the weeds in the garden, enriching such humble yellow flowers as dandelions and buttercups. Presiding queenlike over them all was a Genista just coming into bloom, the one shrub that had been tough enough to survive Caro's lack of interest in horticulture. I really must do something about the garden, thought Caro for the hundredth time, recognizing even as she did so that she never ever would.

'When are you going to tell him?'

'When I next see him. Tonight probably. I can't say I'm looking forward to it.'

It looked as though another fraught dinner was in the offing.

'And then what?'

'Well, one of us will have to move back to the burnt offering!'

'*He* will.' Caro was very firm. 'You can stay here. Quite apart from anything else, it's more convenient for The Gallery. How is The Gallery, by the way?'

'It's fun! I mean it's work, but it's fun as well. Going there suddenly put me in touch with how long it's been since I've had any fun.'

Caroline could believe it.

'What are the people who run it like? More to the point, *who* are the people who run it?'

'They're a couple called James and Victoria Harting, and they seem very nice. At the moment they're gearing themselves up for a retrospective of a painter called Jack Carey, whom Jonathan appears to believe is the Devil incarnate.'

Dimly recalling the name, Caro cast her mind back.

'Yes, I remember some scandal a while ago. In fact, hasn't there been scandal on and off for quite a few years? Gossip-column stuff? I think he likes the girls!'

'Lecher was the word Jonathan used. And that's why he's in such a lather. He seems to think my virtue is under siege.'

'And is it?'

'No, alas. God, is that the time? I'm going to be late. Commiserations to Patrick. See you tonight.'

When Emily had gone, Caro sat for some time staring into the middle distance before slowly getting to her feet and preparing to commence her own day.

That afternoon Minerva arrived home from school at four thirty, again courtesy of the Smythes. She did not allow them to see how much this arrangement displeased her, with the result that Mrs Smythe erroneously and endlessly told her own daughters what a helpful girl Minerva Holland was. Instead, Minerva saved up her dissatisfaction as a stick to beat her mother with. It never occurred to her to ask herself why she did this, her uncooperative attitude having insidiously become an almost automatic response to anything that was asked of her. She was, therefore, further put out to discover a note from her mother informing her that today was a teaching day and that her presence was required at some extracurricular activity or other. *Dinner will be late tonight,* wrote Caro, *probably around nine o'clock, so fix yourself an interim snack if you are hungry, and try to get your homework out of the way before we finally eat.*

'I'm a latchkey child, that's what I am,' Minerva announced aloud to no one. 'Neglected!'

Somewhat cheered by the drama of this last utterance, she made her way into the kitchen where she proceeded to make a jam sandwich of heroic proportions. Eating it, she searched the food cupboards, eventually unearthing a square biscuit tin that turned out to be empty of anything but a few stale crumbs.

'*And* I have a mother who never makes cakes like other mothers do.'

She replaced the lid and threw the tin to the back of the shelf, shutting the cupboard door with a bang. Mindful of the house rule that everyone cleared up after themselves, Minerva opened the door of the dishwasher to put her plate and knife away, and made the unwelcome discovery that the machine was full and everything in it clean. Confronted with another house rule, which was that whoever encountered a dishwasher in this particular pristine state emptied it, Minerva shut the door and washed up her utensils in the sink, after which she put them both away. It had to be quicker, she reasoned, and she had her homework to do.

She was in the act of turning her school bag upside down so that a cascade of dog-eared exercise books, pens, pencils and door keys fell on to the kitchen table when there was a knock at the door followed immediately by a ringing of the bell.

'Oh, sod it,' said Minerva, breaking off what she was doing and going to open it.

Two youths with familiar faces stood on the step. At first Minerva could not think who they were. She had forgotten all about Larch's delinquents.

'Is Mr Larch in?' asked one of them.

'No, he isn't, no one is.' And then, 'You're Gary and...' She hesitated.

'Nigel,' said Nigel.

Standing in front of them wearing her school uniform, Minerva felt her street cred to be seriously undermined. She licked her fingers, which were still sticky from the jam sandwich.

'Mr Larch asked us to meet him. Can we come in and wait?'

It seemed odd to Minerva, who knew and disapproved of the fact that her mother had told Larch very bluntly that his problem cases were not to come to the house.

'Course you can,' she said. Disobeying her mother's explicit wish, Minerva's aggression towards Caro began to evaporate.

She led them into the kitchen.

'Nice pad you got.' The speaker was Gary.

'It's all right,' said Minerva, looking at her sur-

roundings, which normally she hardly noticed. 'Can I
get you a Coke?'

'Got any drink?'

'No, I don't think so.' Actually Minerva had no
idea, but would have died rather than admit it.

Nigel opened the fridge.

'Look, Gary. Look what's in 'ere.'

The fact that he did this interested Minerva, who
would never have dreamed of opening somebody
else's fridge unless invited to do so. Without any further reference to her, Nigel extracted a bottle of vodka,
opened it and drank some. He handed it to Gary, who
also drank out of it. Then Nigel said to Minerva,
'What's your name?'

'Minerva,' replied Minerva reluctantly, then added,
'Holland.'

Gary's reaction was scornful. 'Posh!'

'Want some of this?' Nigel indicated the vodka.

After a fractional hesitation, Minerva, who had
never drunk spirits before, said 'Yes, please.'

Nigel gave her the bottle. Watched by both of them,
she swigged deeply. Looking at her, Gary thought she
was a bit of all right, even in school uniform. He wondered how old she was. Probably not old enough.

Minerva thought she was about to be sick. Her first
reaction to the vodka was that it was disgusting. Cold
and fiery at the same time. It burned her mouth and
throat and caused her eyes to fill with water. Determined not to lose face, she took another deep draught,
and then another. Suddenly it seemed as though the

universe lurched to the right and then back to the left again. It was lucky she was sitting down. The sensation of being out of control was unnerving, and then unexpectedly, everything suddenly stabilized again. It was like being on a roller coaster. At this inconvenient moment, the telephone rang. Gary shot a furtive look at Nigel, and tilted his head in the direction of the door.

The caller was Larch.

'Minerva?'

'Yes,' said Minerva, feeling that it was the most she could utter since the room was once again beginning to spin.

'Have either Gary or Nigel rung?'

'No.'

She concentrated on keeping a Staffordshire fairing that stood on the dresser in focus. On the other end of the phone Larch tutted.

'They're here,' she said finally.

'There! But they're supposed to be *here*!'

Where was here and where was there? Minerva fuzzily wondered.

'Could I please speak to one of them?'

'Yes,' was the most Minerva felt she could muster. Nausea was coming and going. Wordlessly she handed the phone to Gary.

'Hello, Jonathan,' said Gary. He put some gum in his mouth.

Like pebbles rattling in a tin, Minerva could faintly hear Larch's agitated voice over the wire, although she could not make out what he was saying. Listening to whatever it was, Gary lounged against the wall, staring out of the window. Every so often he said 'Nah!' or 'Yeah!' or 'Right!' and made a complicitous thumbs-up sign to Nigel. Eventually he hung up.

'He's in a right old strop,' said Gary. 'Too late now, though, so he wants to see us in his office tomorrow instead. He says that's where we were supposed to meet him today. I think there has been a little misunderstanding, Nige my son.'

Both youths laughed.

Gary picked up his jacket and put it on.

'Cheers, Min!'

'Cheers!' said Minerva faintly.

Slim-hipped and broad-shouldered in black leather, and oddly graceful, they loped towards the hall like young panthers. Watching them go, it seemed to Minerva that there was an air of lawlessness and danger about them that would have appealed to her if she had not been feeling as ill as she did. As soon as she heard the front door shut, she ran upstairs and was very sick into the lavatory.

Sitting opposite a very subdued Minerva, Caro wondered where Larch and Emily had got to. Patrick would not be home until after the performance, probably about eleven thirty. Caro dreaded the week following the end of the run, which she knew from experience would be a rough one, mainly devoted to bolstering the wilting ego of a despondent Patrick as he wallowed in a slough of theatrical neglect. And Minerva, she noted, did not look too good either. Her colour was dreadful, and she did not appear to be hungry, which was unusual for her.

The front door slammed.

It was Larch. Without treating them to the nicety of a preliminary greeting, he said, 'Any sign of Emily?'

'I'm afraid not. And I haven't made you any food either, since I had no idea whether you were going to be in this evening.'

'That's all right, I bought myself a takeaway.'

He opened it. Indian. The very strong smell of curry made Minerva's stomach heave. She was halfway through the door when she heard Larch, who must have just opened the fridge, say, 'Who's been drinking my vodka?'

Reflecting that he sounded absurdly like one of the Three Bears, Caro smiled to herself and said, 'No idea.'

She put Emily's cutlets under the grill, intending to put them in the oven until her sister put in an appearance. As she was doing this the telephone rang.

'I'll get it, shall I?' offered Larch, being helpful for once. It must have been Emily, for she heard him ask, 'Where are you?' And then, very peeved, 'At a *party*?'

Caro laughed silently into her cooking.

'Ask my frivolous sister if she wants three lamb cutlets, or has she eaten?'

Larch ignored this. There was a prolonged gap, during the course of which Emily must have explained herself. When she had finished, Larch said in a huffed voice, 'I think you are very inconsiderate these days, Emily! Did it never occur to you that perhaps I would have liked to have gone to the party with you?'

There was another pause. At the end of it, clearly on the defensive, Caro heard him say, 'Well, I know I said that, but—'

Emily must have interrupted him.

'So you're coming home now. And you want to have a what? It's very noisy at your end. I can't hear what you're saying. *A you/me discussion?* But I thought we'd had— Oh, I see, a different one. A what? A one initiated by you, you mean? I see.'

My God, she's really going to do it! thought Caro.

There were a few further words at the other end, and then he put the phone down.

'She's at a cocktail party at The Gallery.'

The disapproval he radiated was practically tangible.

'Come on, Jonathan, it's hardly a capital offence. And she didn't mention it to me this morning, so I think you'll probably find it was something they asked her to attend at the last minute. She may even have been working. After all, entertaining is part of that sort of business.'

'Emily wants to have a private talk when she gets back.'

'Fine,' said Caro. 'Use the sitting room. It's more businesslike than the bedroom. I'll do my marking in here. Did she say she does or doesn't want the lamb cutlets?'

'No idea,' replied Larch. 'I forgot to ask her.'

He seemed very preoccupied.

Emily finally got home at ten, by which time the cutlets, rather like her own kitchen, were shrivelled.

'Never mind,' said Emily, 'I ate a lot of canapés at the party. Oh and by the way, I finally met the wicked Jack Carey. Where's Jonathan?'

Caro pointed in the direction of the sitting room.

'In there. Waiting. *Very* disappointed in your behaviour, Emily, you naughty girl.'

'I dare say, but not for long,' came the prophetic reply.

The new Emily, mistress of her own destiny, auburn curls bouncing, strode off in the direction of the sitting room.

One and a half hours later, when Patrick arrived home, they were still closeted.

'What's going on?' enquired Patrick. 'Why are you sitting in the kitchen?'

'Because', replied Caro, 'Larch and Emily are having a heart-to-heart, or maybe the opposite, in the sitting room. I think she may be in the process of giving him the elbow.'

Her husband's response to this was uncomplicated. 'About time,' said Patrick, and then, looking at his wife, 'but never mind about them.' Caro was wearing a narrow, long-skirted black suit whose jacket was cut like a riding coat, and a white shirt with a jabot. With her gold half-moon spectacles on the end of her nose,

and her candid, searching look, she reminded him of
nothing so much as a young and severe advocate. Por-
tia. On impulse, he came and sat opposite her. Leaning
forward, he took the pen she was still clasping in mid-
tick, and laid it on the table. Taking her hands in his,
he said, 'Stand up,' and when she did so he kissed her.
Kissed her, in fact, the way he had when they first
met, with all the flattering urgency of an overwhelming
physical attraction.

Aroused and at the same time confused, thinking,
Sometimes I think I'm in love with both Morgan and
Patrick. Can one be in love with two people at the
same time? Caro responded and was rewarded by a
treacherously pleasurable resurgence of the old desire.
It would be so much easier to love Patrick, to whom
she was already married, rather than Morgan.

He unbuttoned her shirt, and began to unzip her
skirt.

'Darling, darling Caro.'

'No, not here, Emily and Larch…'

'Then come to bed, Caro, *now*.'

Ascending the stairs after him, the marking abandoned until tomorrow, or maybe some time later that
evening, Caro thought, Morgan is no longer here. I just
have to put him out of my mind. And as the two of
them made love, she did.

Afterwards, exhausted, Patrick fell asleep. There
were still traces of theatrical make-up around his eyes,
Caro noticed, watching him with tenderness and guilt.
She considered her husband handsome. She admired

his face with its sweep of longish blond hair, and decided what a pity it was that he had not become a matinée idol, because he would have enjoyed the fame, and for that sort of person the acting would not be so important. And we really ought to make love more often, she thought. As it is, what with money worries, and Patrick's career in the doldrums, and the fact that I'm bored stiff by my job, we are spread far too thin emotionally. Our marriage is being starved to death.

The feeling that for the first time in months she had at least partially looked her problems in the eye in a positive way gave Caro the impetus to get up and go downstairs to finish the marking. She pulled the bedclothes over Patrick and looked at her watch.

It was very late.

On the way to the kitchen she met Emily. Emily militant. Emily without Larch.

'Where is he?' whispered Caro. 'Has he gone to bed?'

'No, he's on the sofa!'

'Have you sacked him?'

'Yes!'

'How did he take it?'

'He started off by being very aggressive. And patronizing. Telling me what I *ought* to be feeling. And then, suddenly, when he realized that he couldn't intimidate me any more, he broke down and cried.'

Like all bullies.

'So what happens tomorrow?'

'He goes, I suppose. I have to say I did feel rather sorry for him. He looked sort of defeated, somehow.'

'Oh Emily, *don't*!'

'I don't think I can bear to go on talking in whispers. Let's go into the kitchen.'

It was becoming clear to Caro, eyeing it, that the marking was never going to get done, not tonight anyway.

'What was the party like? Any good? Jonathan was very put out about that, you know!'

'Well, the party had been arranged weeks ago, before I went to work there, which is why I didn't know about it until tonight. It was a small private view. Lithographs and etchings mainly. Nobody I'd ever heard of. The Hartings have a split-level arrangement at one end of The Gallery where they exhibit small works of art. Anyway, when Victoria Harting realized I hadn't been asked, she insisted I stay. So I did. Actually, I only meant to have one glass of champagne and then come home, but I found I was enjoying myself so much that I didn't want to leave. And I wasn't looking forward to confronting Jonathan either. So when Jack Carey came up and introduced himself, and started telling me that I have wonderful hair—Pre-Raphaelite hair, he called it—and said he'd like to paint me, the temptation to linger was irresistible.'

'Paint you with or without clothes?'

'We didn't get as far as discussing that.'

'Jonathan would have an apoplectic fit if he could hear you.'

'He already has. I told him! Anyway, to carry on, I was just beginning to think that Jonathan's worst fears were going to be realized, and that the next step really *was* going to be an invitation to go and see his etchings, when Victoria Harting, who had been watching him, came up, smacked him smartly on the wrist, and said, "That's enough of that, Jack. Put Emily down. She's young enough to be your daughter!"'

'He's absolutely right, though. You *are* a Pre-Raphaelite. So what happened then?'

'He laughed and walked off and started talking to someone else, but he kept looking at me across the room. I think he was fairly drunk. But why he should be interested in me, I can't think. His wife is absolutely beautiful!'

Thinking of Morgan, Caro said, 'Take my advice and steer clear of married men. They're bad news. You've got a lot to offer, Emily, and you shouldn't waste it.'

'I've got his card. He gave it to me.'

'Well, throw it in the bin!'

'I'm going to have to look for somewhere to live.'

'You're welcome to stay here while you look, you know that. Sorting out your joint finances is going to be the hardest thing to do. How's the kitchen coming along?'

'Nearly there. And it'll come along much faster with Jonathan *in situ* telling the builder how not to do it.'

'That's certainly true!'

After Emily had finally gone up to bed, Caro

switched off the lights and, on impulse, decided to check her daughter on her way to her own room. Minerva was lying on her back, breathing heavily, her hair spread out around her on the pillow. Bending down to kiss her, Caro was struck by an odd smell. She tried to place it. It couldn't be, of course, but all the same it was very like alcohol.

The next morning, with the exception of Patrick, everyone felt off colour. There was no sign of Larch, who appeared to have left very early. Minerva in particular was *hors de combat* after a comatose but unrefreshing night, and was even more taciturn than usual. Looking for her door keys at Caro's behest, she upended her school bag. There was no sign of them. This was odd, because she remembered putting them in the bag after letting herself into the house the previous afternoon. With an effort, she further recalled turning her bag upside down all over the kitchen table so that she could begin her homework. And the keys had definitely been there then. Lying on the table. In her mind's eye, Minerva could see them. So where were they now? Not on the floor. She crawled around and looked, laddering her tights on the polished floor boards in the process, and then searched the cluttered kitchen dresser.

'I can't find my keys,' she sulkily confessed to her mother.

'Well, have another look when you get home tonight. I don't like the idea of the front-door keys going missing.' Caro was bracing.

'Oh, and I need a letter.'

'A letter! What for?'

By now they were late.

'Saying that you give permission for me to go on the theatre outing.'

'Minerva, couldn't you have told me about this last night? Or', on a note of hope, 'is it a form? Usually all I have to do is sign a form. And, anyway, how long have you had it?'

'Two weeks. I've lost the form. I know I had it, but I haven't got it now.'

'I'll do it tonight. There simply isn't time now.'

'I have to have it today. Today's the last day for handing them in.'

Ye gods! Caro cast her eyes to heaven.

'Mum, everyone makes mistakes!'

Resisting the temptation to point out that this was one Minerva made with relentless regularity, Caro said, very shortly, 'Get in the car would you,' and went off and wrote it. By the time she returned, her daughter had just completed another rummage through her bag.

'I found it,' said Minerva, without the least trace of contrition.

When Caro finally got back to the house after a frustrating crawl through the beginnings of the rush-hour traffic, during which she had wondered if she would ever achieve a gear change above second, the post had arrived. Heart beating fast, she stood stock-still, staring at it where it lay on the doormat. It consisted of one large, stiff, very white envelope, clearly an invitation. Trembling, she picked it up and held it in her hands for a few seconds before turning it over and opening it.

14

The day the wedding invitations arrived at Armitage
Lodge, Leonora gave hers what was known in the family as her lorgnette look. She ran a finger over it to
make sure that it was properly embossed.

'August. St Xavier's. Well, it will do I suppose. We
shall have to decide what to wear. I shall supervise
your choice of gown, Clara!'

But you won't supervise mine, thought Cassandra.
Aloud she said, 'People don't wear gowns to weddings
these days, Mother, they wear suits. And hats.'

Leonora was glacial.

'Thank you, Cassandra, I am well aware of the existence of suits. And hats.' Mentally she took the ruby
earrings away from Cassandra and left them to Julia
instead.

Clara sat holding her invitation in her hand, staring
at it. *Mr John Post and Mrs Veronica Post request the
pleasure of your company at the marriage of their
daughter Chloe*, and so on. It must have been at least
twenty years since anybody had invited her formally
to anything, and she resolved to stand the invitation
on the mantelpiece in her bedroom. She was also conscious of palpitations at the prospect of a fashionable

London wedding attended by fashionable London people. A flutter of the heart such as the young, confident Clara with her string of beaux would never have had.

Watching her sister's face and the various uncertain expressions that crossed it, one after the other, Cassandra divined her anxiety. And when I think what Clara was like as a girl, she reflected. Not very bright, of course, but so pretty and so popular. Now look at her. All that self-assurance gone, eroded by Mother. Mother is a bloodsucker.

'We shall have to buy a present,' ventured Clara, timidly.

'Yes, we shall. I shall tell Julia to buy them one at Robbs department store in Hexham.'

Shuddering at the thought of Mother arriving at a society wedding regally bearing an awful tin tray or something similar from the kitchen department, albeit giftwrapped, Cassandra felt constrained to say, 'I'm sure you'll find that in order to head off sixty toasters, or whatever, there's a wedding list at one of the top London stores. Harrods or the General Trading Company. That sort of thing.'

'I would never dream of buying anyone a toaster,' pronounced Leonora, attempting to close the subject by deliberately missing the point.

'I really think it's a good idea to consult the list because that way we buy them something they actually want,' persisted Cassandra, refusing to let her and thereby unwittingly depriving herself of the ruby brooch that went with the earrings.

'*Whatever* I buy Morgan and Chloe, they will want!'

Suddenly out of patience, Cassandra said, 'I may decide not to come!'

'*Not* to come? Not to *come*! *Of course* you will come!'

And I probably will too, thought Cassandra, for I shall be powerless to resist the temptation of meeting Chloe Post again. She stood up.

'Time I took Jardine out for a run.'

The arrival of the invitations also caused consternation in the Barstow/Fielding household. Dressing up was anathema to Meredith, who had never been very interested in clothes and these days preferred twin sets and tweeds and the inevitable brogues. Holding her black straw hat at arm's length, she dubiously turned it around. Caro was quite right, it was frayed, and after a summer's gardening it was patchily faded as well. Perhaps I can *borrow* a hat, hazarded Meredith. Maybe Julia has one. Although it was entirely likely that Julia, too, only had one, and they couldn't both wear it.

Staring at his daughter staring at her hat, the Brigadier commented. 'Not thinking of wearing that, I hope!'

Offended, Meredith said, 'No, of course not. I was wondering whether to keep it.'

'Throw it out!' said her undiplomatic parent. 'Get rid of it! It never suited you anyway, Meredith old girl. Now it's on its way out, you won't mind me saying that.'

Meredith did mind. What was it about the patrician elderly that made them feel they could be as rude as they pleased?

'Now your mother, your mother couldn't wear hats either!'

He really was relentless.

'There was one I particularly remember...'

He launched into an interminable story about another terrible hat, which when she was alive, he had probably been prone to telling in front of his wife. Appearing to listen, Meredith also remembered her mother, though not in connection with her headgear. Mother had been stately rather than vivacious, and very mannered, a character trait underlined by her conspicuous lack of a sense of humour. Maybe that was why her father had had such a glad eye in his youth. And not just his youth, either, Meredith suspected, thinking of an elderly widow with good ankles who lived at Haltwhistle. She recalled what she always thought of as the Summer of the Steers. That year, the Steers and the Fieldings had done everything together, had been inseparable. And then the intimacy had stopped. Totally and suddenly stopped. Quite a small girl at the time—indeed, such a small girl that she could no longer remember which of her two practically indistinguishable husbands Leonora had been married to at the time—Meredith had asked her mother why, but had never received an answer. Later on the most she had ever been able to discover was that there had been Rumours, although quite what the rumours were had not been spelt out, and Meredith had not cared to ask.

It was the sound of Leonora's name being spoken aloud that brought her out of her reverie.

'Leonora, on the other hand, she could wear hats!' He appeared to be suffering from a hat fixation. 'Large cartwheel hats with feathers! And then, later on, much smaller, sequined hats. Without feathers. Very fetching.'

Hat aggression. Meredith pictured Leonora leading with her hat, and hapless Mother being unfavourably compared, not once, but over and over again, and in public.

In an attempt to change the subject, she said, 'I imagine you won't be attempting the wedding. Long way, ghastly train journey and all that. And very expensive,' she added.

'Quite right!'

Vastly relieved, Meredith said, 'I'm sure that to give it a miss is the right decision. I'm certain they'll all understand.'

'What? By "quite right" I meant long way, *ghastly* journey, and hellishly expensive. All quite right! But it's a party, Meredith. Give it a miss? Never. Not too many more of those before I die.' He lapsed into sombre silence, possibly overcome by intimations of his own mortality.

Panicking, Meredith looked into the middle distance. Hat decisions paled into insignificance before this problem of problems. She decided to leave it for the moment. With luck by tomorrow morning he would have forgotten all about the wedding, never mind the invitation and his determination to accept it.

In London, Joanna Blackstock and Tom Marchant, who were platonically coexisting in the little mews house, received separate invitations to Morgan and Chloe's wedding. Studying hers over breakfast, and then watching Tom do the same, Joanna said, 'You'll be going, of course.'

'I should think so. I'm his best man.'

'And I'm Chloe's maid of honour! Funny expression. I wonder what on earth I'm expected to do.'

'No doubt Veronica Post will tell you.'

'No doubt she will!'

They both laughed.

For the umpteenth time Tom tried to analyse his attraction to this woman. He was honest enough to admit to himself that part of it was money, but also recognized that this was by no means all. So what was it exactly? Taken feature by feature Joanna was unexceptional, but as a whole she worked. Some days he decided that her magnetism must lie more in the force of her personality than in her face and body. Most days, and this was one of them, he would have liked nothing so much as to take her to bed.

'More coffee?' asked Joanna, standing up to make it. She was wearing, probably with nothing underneath it, a narrow, belted, full-length, navy-blue housecoat cut on classic lines with wide shoulders, and as she leant over to execute the mundane act of plugging in the kettle, Tom admired the fluidity of her line from shoulder to waist, and from waist to ankle.

Sensitive to his hungry gaze despite her back being turned, Joanna enquired, 'What are you doing this morning?'

'I'm going to the office.' Tom sounded less than enthusiastic. 'What about you?'

She handed him a cup of coffee.

'I'm not going to the office! I'm due a few days off and this is going to be one of them.'

'So what are you planning to do?'

'I thought I'd lie in bed.'

Immediately interested, for this was very unlike her, he said, 'What, all day?'

'Yes. With you if you like!'

This was so unexpected that Tom nearly dropped his coffee. Having waited so long for the summons, he now wondered for one unnerving moment whether he was up to it.

Joanna drained her cup and, replacing it in its saucer, rose. On her way out of the kitchen she unbelted the housecoat and let it slip off her shoulders to the floor. His surmise that she had been wearing nothing underneath it proved correct. Very plain wedge-heeled velvet slippers emphasized the length of her legs.

Following with alacrity, taking off his tie as he did so, Tom, mindful of the way in which she had kept him waiting thought in a rare burst of virtue: I've really earned this.

Her bedroom contained a graceful four-poster in the Dutch colonial style, hung with curtains of some sort of white gauzy material that billowed slightly in the breeze from the open window. The walls were papered with small, formal climbing roses in rich gradations of red and pink on an ivory background. It was an intimate and pretty room. He noticed with appreciation that facing the end of the bed was an old gilded mirror on top of which sat a fat carved cherub, also golden.

'Why don't you shut the window?'

Joanna took off her watch and placed it on a half-moon table that stood beneath the mirror and was evidently used as a dressing table, judging by the feminine paraphernalia on its surface. Wrestling with his cuff links, but determined not to appear too eager for whatever might be in store, Tom said, 'I think I'd better phone the office before anything else happens.'

He had the feeling that she was amused.

'Of course, Tom, but don't be long. What are you going to say?'

'Oh, that I'm ill or something of that sort,' came the vague reply. Once again, Tom remembered Camilla Vane. Love. The worst disease of all.

By the time he returned Joanna was in the bed and had pulled the curtains across. Through their delicate semitransparence she appeared bridelike, insubstantial and mysterious. And very desirable. Taking her in his arms at last, and feeling the length of her cool, naked body against his own, Tom kissed her with passion.

I've done it, thought Joanna jubilant and responding with abandon, I've got him! He's mine if I want him.

They got up briefly for lunch, and then went back to bed again. The monastic months had done more for Tom than he would ever have expected. Moreover, he thought, I'm in love with Joanna Blackstock, at least I think I am, *and* she's rich. It seemed almost too good to be true.

Eyeing her husband over the breakfast table, it was apparent to Annabel Post that he had been even more out of sorts than usual since Chloe had announced her intention to marry Morgan Steer.

It was strange, agonized Annabel, how much he had changed after their own marriage. Before, he had indulged her, bought her jewellery and clothes, and shown her off, basking in the fact that she was young enough to be his daughter, even on occasion listening to her. Now he frequently complained about her extravagance, never listened to her and seemed to be permanently discontented. Why their wedding day, designed to unite them formally, should have brought about this *froideur* was beyond her. Her other problem was that the person with whom she felt herself to be in competition was not, as might have been expected, Veronica, but Chloe, her newly acquired stepdaughter. I should have liked to have been her friend, thought Annabel, but while Chloe had not been hostile, she had not been the least bit interested in her father's new wife. Pondering the fact that she always felt *de trop* when Chloe was present, Annabel thought, It's the way John flirts with her, there's something perverse about it. Unhealthy. And yet it seemed that he had never taken much notice of his daughter when she had been growing up, except, perhaps, as a trophy child when required, and later as a trophy young woman whose presence by his side enhanced his own image.

She was aware that John had hoped to stop the marriage by ruthlessly exposing their chronic financial imbalance, and denigrating Morgan as a fortune-hunter, a strategy that had been systematically blocked by Chloe, who had made sure that he and her fiancé had never met again without her, Chloe, being present. The fabled job for which Morgan was supposedly on a short list had not as yet materialized, but maybe it soon would, though by then the wedding would have taken place.

Patronized by Veronica, ignored by her husband and only acknowledged by Chloe in the most peripheral way, it was Annabel's heartfelt wish that the whole cutthroat social battle was over.

John Post irritably flapped the *Wall Street Journal*, finally folding it up and looking at his watch as he did so.

This all took place in silence.

Tetchy silence.

Looking at him over the rim of her teacup, Annabel thought that he suddenly looked older. Looked his age, in fact. When he had courted her, the difference had not seemed as great as it did now. Maybe it was the gap between the public and the private. The gap between carefully staged, well-groomed meetings in high-profile restaurants, and seeing him on a daily basis at home. This was particularly evident in the morning, before he had had time to comb his hair, settle down and turn himself into the urbane man she thought she had married. His filthy temper in particular had come as a very unwelcome surprise. Even his suntan, receiving little or no help from the English weather, had faded, and he looked greyer than usual. His hands, she noticed, were liver-spotted. Too many cocktails perhaps. When Chloe and Morgan produced children, as in the fullness of time they no doubt would, he would become a *grandfather*. Annabel did not look forward to the Anno Domini panic that this would surely induce.

Her husband stood up, dropped a kiss on her forehead as though she was five years old, and left for the bank. They had not exchanged one word over breakfast. Lonely, Annabel turned another page of her paper and drank her cold tea.

Veronica was currently residing at Brown's Hotel. Unknown to him, the bill for this comfortable sojourn was being footed by John Post out of the wedding budget. After all, reasoned Veronica, anticipating and rehearsing the spirited debate that would take place when he did find out, I have to stay somewhere, and look at all the work I'm doing. Onerous is the only

word for it, and with no help to speak of from that
vapid girl (the second Mrs Post). Besides which, by
the time John gets around to counting his money I will
be back in Boston, so if he wants to object he'll have
to do it by post.

She rang for room service.

'Lapsang Suchong for one and a very small plate of
langue de chat biscuits,' instructed Veronica. Waiting
for these to arrive, she studied the guest list, which
was a gratifyingly long one, guaranteed to give her ex-
husband a severe pain in his wallet. Acceptances and
refusals, though not too many of the latter, she hoped,
would soon begin to trickle in. Since she had no option
but to relinquish centre stage on this occasion, Veronica looked forward to the next best thing: reigning as
Mother of the Bride of the Year.

The invitations having been sent out, Chloe and
Morgan privately stifled their individual doubts about
the joint course they had allowed their lives to take
and continued their frenetic social round, using the fact
that it was so hectic to prohibit thought. Where the day
itself was concerned, there was very little for them to
do.

'Better to let Mummy have her head with the wedding arrangements,' said Chloe. 'That and bullying
Annabel will keep her quiet.'

Where the dress was concerned, however, she was
obdurate.

'I do not wish to go to Paris for the dress,' said

Chloe. 'I intend to design it myself, and my dress-maker will make it for me.'

This pleased John Post and displeased Veronica.

'Nothing you can say, Mother, will make me change my mind!'

The use of the word *Mother* should have indicated to Veronica that she was about to get nowhere. Nevertheless, she persevered. 'What shall I say when people ask me who made your wedding dress? They are bound to want to know.'

'Are they? Well in that case you can either say that *you* don't know, or, if you would prefer to be strictly accurate, you can say that Mrs Rita Cox of Bayswater ran it up for me.'

Mrs Rita Cox of Bayswater? It did not have quite the same ring as Monsieur Yves St Laurent of Paris. Forced at the end of the day to subside, Veronica decided to be as positive as she could about it and to throw herself heart and soul into costing John as much as she could on other fronts.

It was Morgan who once again raised the idea of a joint family dinner party so that they could all meet each other in advance of the ceremony.

'I think it's a very good idea, Morgan,' responded Veronica graciously, unexpectedly adding, 'But perhaps I could leave that to you. You might like to consider the Gavroche.'

The way she said it, it did not sound as though John Post was about to underwrite this particular soiree. For Morgan, who was having difficulty scraping together the cash to take Chloe abroad for their honeymoon, an expensive restaurant was out of the question. Unless, perhaps, Grandmama…? He dismissed the idea. There was no chance of Leonora, whose natural parsimony had markedly increased as she had got older, taking nine of them out to dinner. No, it would have to be the Prince's Gate flat with *cuisine*, and not very *haute* either, by Mrs Pratt. Wondering why he hadn't had the sense to keep his big mouth shut, Morgan said aloud, 'I'll phone Northumberland tonight and find out when they all intend to travel down.'

August

15

Leonora said to her three daughters, 'There is going to be a dinner party at the Prince's Gate flat the day after we arrive in London, so that we may meet the Posts.' What she really means is so that the Posts may be presented to her, thought Julia, listening to her mother's regal delivery. They don't know what they're in for.

'Oh!' exclaimed Clara. 'It will be a bit of a rush, of course, but would you like me to cook for it?'

Dear God, no! Cassandra froze.

For once a prayer was answered.

'Thank you, Clara, but no, I would not.' Leonora exhibited minimal gratitude for the offer.

Or was it?

'Mrs Pratt will cope with that. I have telephoned her and told her what to do. She will do it. You will simply heat it up.'

Mrs Pratt. Mrs Pratt's cooking was only marginally better than Clara's. What was it about Mother, Cassandra asked herself, that she managed to surround herself with such dire food?

'Why don't we all go to a restaurant?'

'Oh, yes!' Clara, who hadn't been to one for years, clasped her hands in anticipation.

'Dinner for nine? In a restaurant? Forgive me saying so, Cassandra, but that is quite out of the question. The cost of such a thing would be prohibitive. Sometimes I feel you must think I am made of money!'

You certainly ought to be, thought Julia, considering you never spend any.

Unwisely, Cassandra was pushing it. 'I only thought, since the Posts are footing the bill for everything else—'

'The Posts are the parents of the bride and must *expect* to foot the bill. *That* is their unenviable lot. Unlike you, I see no reason to alter the status quo. Now! The arrangements. Julia, you will travel down with me the day before the dinner party. Cassandra, you and Clara will follow the next morning, by which time you will have completed the one or two administrative tasks that need doing before we leave, and will have locked up the house and delegated the dog.'

This was unwelcome news to Julia, who had looked forward to travelling down in relaxed fashion with Meredith.

'I wonder if that's wise, Mother. After all, I'm the only one who can drive, so if I go with you, Cassandra and Clara will be grounded and will have to take a taxi to Hexham Station. But if one of them goes with you, I can drop the two of you off and then the following day leave the car at the station, where it will be waiting for us when we come back. Much less expensive,' she added cannily.

Leonora thought for a moment, and then conceded the point. 'Very well. On the whole that probably does make more sense. So, Cassandra and Clara, which one of you is going to volunteer to come with me?'

Nobody spoke.

I had hoped I might be able to spend a whole night with Seth! thought Clara. What I wouldn't give for one night out of this house and away from Mother's company. She shot a beseeching look at Cassandra.

I don't think I can stand the prospect of five hours on a train with Mother, never mind the ongoing martyrdom at the other end, thought Cassandra, and decided to tough it out. As a result, what should have been a rush to accept began to show signs of becoming an embarrassingly lengthy silence, with the predictable result that it was Clara who cracked first.

'I will.'

'Well, don't look so happy about it.' Leonora was acid. 'And now you may leave, Clara. I wish to talk to Cassandra and Julia about what has to be organized while we are away.'

When Leonora had finally departed for her afternoon rest, Julia said to Cassandra, 'You do realize that Mother is preparing for a field day at this wedding. It will be open season on the Posts.'

'And anybody else who is unwise enough to get in the way.'

'At least we have a day's respite before the battle commences!'

'Yes. Poor old Clara!'

'Poor old Clara!'

Meredith rang Caroline and did not beat about the bush.

'I'm afraid your grandfather is determined to come to the wedding, and I wondered if there was any way you could put both of us up.'

'Are you sure that's wise?'

'I'm sure it isn't, but what can I do? The maddening thing is that usually he forgets decisions he takes from one day to the next, and I've been hoping against hope that this would happen in this case. Unfortunately it appears to be the exception that proves the rule. And what worries me is that while he's very lucid about the past, half the time the present passes him by. I really don't think I'll be able to leave him alone for an instant.'

It had to be said that this did not sound a very relaxing prospect.

'We'll do it in shifts,' said Caro, very practical, 'and that includes Minerva and Patrick. And I'll ask Emily if she can stay with a friend for a couple of nights.'

'What about Jonathan? Where is he?'

'She hasn't told you? They've split up!'

'I have to say, I never thought he was right for her.' Meredith's response was cautious. It would be awful to pronounce publicly and disparagingly on Larch and then discover that Emily had changed her mind and that he was to become her son-in-law after all.

Caro had no such inhibition.

'Well, nor does she now. And since he is an unqualified pill, that can only be a good thing. Anyway, look, don't worry about Grandfather. We'll muddle through somehow.' Maybe I'll cope with him by myself, she thought, let Mother enjoy herself. It will give me something to think about other than the fact that the man with whom I am in love is getting married to someone else.

Encouraged by her elder daughter's support, Meredith said gratefully, 'Thank you, darling. If Father changes his mind, or better still forgets about the wedding entirely, I'll let you know, and in any case we'll be in touch nearer the time.'

Lighter of heart than she had been, she hung up.

On the appointed day, Leonora and Clara travelled to London together.

Clara sat with an unread book in her lap, alternately leafing through it, or, until admonished by her mother, biting her fingernails as she stared out of the window. She thought about Seth. Their last meeting had been unsatisfactory, though the enjoyable improvement in the standard of his lovemaking had continued. In parallel with this, however, went unnerving evidence of the presence of Martha on a far more intimate level than that of cleaner, though probably she was that too. Martha seemed to shower hairgrips wherever she went and on one occasion Clara had found an earring. In between the sheets. It was possible, though unlikely, that this had dropped off while Martha was making the bed as part of her duties, but the lingering, cloying smell of cheap scent made Clara think not. And the tights she had found in the bathroom certainly couldn't have just dropped off. Slut! was Clara's verdict, although she was at a loss as to what to do about the situation. Wounded as she was, she was aware that Seth had a perfect right to bed Martha if he felt like it, and it seemed that he did feel like it. Eating her heart out as Darlington and York flashed by, Clara could see no solution, but was aware that a sizeable inheritance from her mother would probably tip the balance in her favour.

She looked across at Leonora. Leonora's eyes were closed, but Clara did not think she was asleep. Catlike, there was an alertness underpinning the deceptive appearance of relaxation.

In fact, Leonora was reminiscing. Once again she saw in her mind's eye what Meredith referred to as the Summer of the Steers, and what she called the Summer of the Fieldings.

It is amazing to think that I am now ninety! Leonora mused. Or, rather, eighty-five. I don't feel it. And that all those years ago we, Arthur and I... Hardly surprising, though! Celia was so dull, *worthy* even. Those dreadful hats. She really had no idea about clothes.

Going back down the years, Leonora again heard Spencer, mildly aggrieved, saying, 'It's all right for you, old girl, but what about me? I'm stuck with Celia.' And so he was! Stuck with her. For Spencer's seduction of Celia had got nowhere, though not for want of trying.

I don't think she even noticed he was doing it.

Leonora laughed inwardly.

The row when Celia had finally found out what was going on had been memorable, and the intimacy between the Steers and the Fieldings had ceased forthwith. There had been a great deal of gossip, most of which was accurate for once. Leonora, operating on the Wildean principle that bad publicity was better than no publicity, hadn't given tuppence for it, and had actually enjoyed her own notoriety. Eventually, as such things do, it had subsided. Three months after the death of his wife, the Brigadier had once again come to lunch at Armitage Lodge, but things were never quite the same, even though by that time Spencer was dead as well. Leonora had paid Arthur just enough attention to keep him dancing attendance, but that was all.

The train stopped with a jolt. She opened her eyes. They were just outside King's Cross, where they were quite likely to remain for at least twenty minutes. Clara, however, began to panic, heaving luggage down from the rack, and in the process knocking over her open handbag, whose contents spilt all over the grimy floor.

'Oh, blast!' exclaimed Clara, even more exercised, throwing her belongings back into it willy-nilly and once again neglecting to close it. Following the remainder of the luggage, her jacket began to slither towards the floor. Lunging to catch it, Clara capsized her bag again.

By now exasperated, Leonora exclaimed, 'For God's sake, Clara! Sit *down*!'

They eventually took a taxi to Prince's Gate since even her mother could see that there was too much for Clara to manage on her own. As he had said he would, Morgan had vacated the flat. Throwing the windows wide open so that the scented summer air poured in, and with it the soft hum of the Kensington traffic, Leonora said, 'Go and check that Mrs Pratt has bought milk and eggs and bread and butter as I asked her to.'

'Yes, she has,' called Clara from the kitchen, failing to notice as she did so a very small note propped up on the top of the fridge. 'When is she bringing the food for dinner?'

'Tomorrow. At midday. And now I should like a cup of China tea, please.'

The following morning, Clara left early with a list of Leonora's errands. Walking to Knightsbridge, she took a route through the park, and found the freedom of such a commonplace act intoxicating. Nobody knows exactly where I am, thought Clara, and hummed as she travelled.

The day was crystalline, with a sky whose tentative early shimmer would gradually deepen into a vibrant blue the colour of cornflowers as the heat began to rise from the city pavements. Not a leaf stirred and the stillness was emphasized by the muted background roar of urban life. Bearing in mind that this was London, Clara was surprised to see there were not as many people about as she had expected. A rider or two in Rotten Row, quite a few joggers, and a clutch of others like herself, presumably going either to work or to shop. By rising early, Clara had managed to avoid Leonora's inquisition as to her movements and her subsequent strictures to return straight away, and therefore felt under no obligation to do anything of the sort. Instead she looked luxuriously forward to lunch in a King's Road café, preferably sitting outside under a coloured umbrella, the gaudier the better.

Leonora awoke at nine, and made her way to the kitchen. Clara had set out a knife and plate, a cup and saucer with a spoon, and had gone. It was as she opened the fridge door in search of milk for her morning tea that Leonora saw the note. Throughout her life she had received enough of these from domestics to know that they almost always boded no good, usually coming at very short notice and being very inconvenient. This, it turned out, was no exception and, typically, for the genre, was written in Biro on lined paper torn out of a spiral notepad.

Dear Mrs Steer,
  Sorry but NO FOOD, wrote Mrs Pratt, emphasizing the baldness of the statement with block capitals, and then continuing rather more myste-

riously. *In bed. Back has gone. Very painful, doc says disc! About six weeks he thinks and no shopping. I hope you find some somewhere* (food, presumably) *and the housework is to your satisfaction. When Mr Steer next goes to Waitrose we need Mansion polish and Jif.*

Yours faithfully,
N. Pratt (Mrs)

Clicking her tongue with irritation, Leonora screwed up the sheet of paper and threw it in the bin. As Mrs Pratt rightly observed, *No Food*, and a dinner party for nine that evening. And no Clara, either. The list had been a long one, involving several different shops, and taking into account her daughter's inefficiency on top of that, it would no doubt be quite some time before she reappeared.

'Harrods Food Hall,' said Leonora aloud. 'That's the answer.'

Forty-five minutes later, standing on the corner of Kensington Gore and Exhibition Road, Leonora waved down a passing taxi with her stick.

'Harrods!' she commanded very imperiously, getting in as she spoke.

'No chance,' said the cab driver.

She stared at him.

'And pray why not?'

'Bomb scare! There's roadblocks all over the joint. Traffic's solid.'

'I see.' This gave Leonora pause for thought. 'Well, where do you suggest we go instead?'

'Depends what you want, ducky!'

'I want to buy some ready-made food, and don't call me ducky!'

What a battle-axe, he thought as he proposed Marks & Spencer.

'Very well,' replied Leonora, who though she had heard of them had never been inside a Marks & Spencer store. 'Drive on.'

He took her to a branch on Kensington High Street. Slowly alighting with the aid of her stick, she commanded, 'Follow me. I shall need you to carry the parcels.'

Looking at her in amazement, he said, 'I can't do that! I'll get clamped!' He was adamant.

Clamped? It sounded like some medieval torture. A refreshing variation on the thumbscrews, perhaps. Leonora would have liked to have been enlightened, but in the face of his intractability and the fact that time was getting short, decided not to pursue it.

'In that case I will instruct the store to procure a man to help me, and I should like you to meet me here. In half an hour. Do not be late! What is your name?'

'Terry.'

'Do not be late, Terry.'

Watching her stately progress through the swing doors, handbag on arm, Terry restarted the engine and drove around the corner where he parked and opened up that day's *Daily Mirror* at the sports page.

Once inside Marks & Spencer, Leonora had to walk through Lingerie to get to Food. This was interesting.

'Good gracious,' she pronounced, holding up a flimsy, lacy bra. The only part of it she thought she recognized was the whalebone, but that turned out to be rather more modern underwiring. Hanging alongside the bra was the tiniest pair of matching knickers she had ever seen. If this sort of thing had been around when I was younger, I might have been Queen of England! thought Leonora, putting them both back.

The food counters were another revelation, being stocked mainly with ready-made concoctions. In the end she chose smoked-salmon parcels, followed by duck *à l'orange*. The pudding, she decided, natural parsimony reasserting itself, would be fruit salad, which would give Clara, who had got off scot-free so far, something to do. Accordingly she also bought a great many apples, bananas and pears and a pineapple.

After exactly half an hour, Terry saw her emerge followed by a minion with a trolly. With his tip in mind, he decided to underline his own enterprise and commitment to her service. 'You're lucky I'm here, Mrs. Traffic wardens. I've been moved on three times. Very difficult it's been.'

'Mrs Steer. Well you're here now.' And then to the minion, 'Put it down there, would you.' Mrs Steer handed over a coin. Ecstasy, Terry noticed, was not the reaction.

They travelled back to Knightsbridge mainly in silence, though she did quiz him on the subject of clamps. On arrival, she said, 'This is a service road. No clamps here, so I should be grateful if you would carry the shopping upstairs for me.'

He did as he was told. At the front door, having paid him and before going in, she fished around in her purse and pressed a coin into his palm, saying munificently, 'This is for you!'

On his way downstairs, by which time she and her shopping were safely inside, Terry opened up his fist and looked at it.

Five pence.

Clara arrived back at three thirty.

'I hope you got it all,' said Leonora. 'Where have you been?'

Deciding not to mention lunch, Clara said, 'It all took rather a long time, that's all. Did Mrs Pratt turn up with the food?'

'No, she did not.' Leonora was curt. 'She claims to be ill.'

'Oh, so does that mean that I...?'

'No, it does not. I have found some. We are as we were. Telephone Morgan, would you please, Clara, and find out what time he is turning up with the wine. He is purchasing it from the company for which Tom Marchant works, I believe. And then you can make a start on the fruit salad while I have my afternoon rest. Wake me at six, by which time Cassandra and Julia should be here.'

'Yes, Mother,' said Clara dutifully.

16

Their taxi decanted Julia and Cassandra just as Morgan was arriving at Prince's Gate with the wine.

'Aunt Cassandra!' He kissed her on the cheek. 'Mother!' He kissed Julia on the cheek.

Apart from the title, Julia thought, she might as well have been just another aunt. Reciprocating in kind, she asked herself: I wonder if the distance between Morgan and me will ever diminish? Leonora stepped between us at such an early stage and simply took him over. There's something very Jesuitical about Mother. Manipulative. In fact, there are times when I think she's positively dangerous.

They mounted the stairs, Morgan in the lead carrying a case of Hardwick-Smith claret. Clara met them at the door.

'What's for dinner tonight?' asked Morgan, putting the wine on the kitchen table and dreading the reply.

'Smoked salmon and duck *à l'orange*,' came the astonishing answer. 'Followed by fresh fruit salad.'

'Good Lord!' ejaculated Morgan. 'Has Mrs Pratt been taking a secret Cordon Bleu course?'

'Mrs Pratt put her back out. Very inconvenient, to quote Mother, although not half as inconvenient for us as it is for her. No, the whole lot came from Marks & Spencer.'

'What happened to Harrods?'

'She couldn't get there. Bomb scare. Do you want me to wake her up? She did request a call at six.'

'No,' said Morgan hastily. 'I have to leave. I promised Chloe I'd be back not later than six thirty.'

'What's Veronica Post like?' The speaker was Cassandra.

Morgan thought for a moment. 'Very brittle. All surface and no depth, and hellbent on her own way with it.'

'Sounds like one for Mother,' Julia said drily.

'No contest,' said Morgan. 'Grandmama could eat Veronica Post for breakfast. See you later.'

When he had gone, Cassandra said, 'Sounds as if the stage is set for social martyrdom!'

Morgan and Chloe were the first to arrive. Cassandra, sparely tailored in dark green velvet, watched Chloe, svelte in a short black sheath of a skirt and a silver bustier, with desire. Although she was still very slender, it did seem to Cassandra's hungry eye that Chloe had put on a little weight. It had to be admitted that she and Morgan made a very handsome couple.

Followed by Clara, whom she had terrorized into a relatively inoffensive shade of blue, Leonora made her entrance clad in a high-necked, gunmetal grey with a reptilian sheen to it that was perfectly set off by the Steer emeralds. Although these days she relied more and more on her stick outside the house, Leonora was still able to manage without it inside. In memory of her glory days, and with the aid of Julia and a great many hairpins, she had piled her hair, which was still long and normally worn in a loose knot at the nape of her neck, on top of her head, where it emphasized her cheekbones and the length of her (now scraggy) neck. Dressed like this, it was almost as though the challenging ghost of the young, beautiful Leonora stood briefly between the old wrinkled Leonora and Julia herself.

It was unnerving.

The doorbell rang. This time it was Veronica Post. Julia let her in and for a brief, silent moment the two women appraised one another at the door.

Spinsterish! thought Veronica.

Mutton done up as lamb! decided Julia as she introduced herself. Hot on Veronica's heels came John Post and Annabel. This time Veronica performed the introductions. Leading the way along the hall, Julia thought that Annabel Post looked about fourteen. Shades of Humbert Humbert!

'Come and meet Mother,' said Julia.

Beginning with Veronica, Leonora took in the streaked blonde hair, the tightly stretched face and the ultra-chic cocktail dress beneath whose short, hand-stitched designer hem two bony silken knees were visible. How very vulgar, she thought. Impressive pearls, though.

Terrifying! was Veronica's own summing-up as she started to fidget with her necklace.

'How do you do, Mrs Post,' commenced Leonora. 'Now tell me, for I have been wondering, who *were* you before your marriage?'

A profound though baffled silence was all her reply.

We're off, thought Cassandra.

Annabel Post fared no better.

'I was not aware that Chloe had a younger sister,' stated Leonora. And then, turning to Veronica, 'Or perhaps this is *your* much younger sister?'

Finding the impulse to curtsy to this fearsome figure hard to resist, Annabel opened her mouth to frame a reply and sort the matter out, since Veronica seemed to have been uncharacteristically struck dumb, but no words came. Observing this between his own introductions to Clara and Cassandra, John Post suavely stepped in. Propelling Annabel forward, as was his habit, he said, 'This is my wife, Annabel, Mrs Steer.'

'Leonora,' instructed Leonora, an honour she had not as yet bestowed on anyone else.

'Leonora,' he repeated, and was just beginning to preen complacently when she continued with her observations.

'Such a piquant sight, someone of such tender years with someone so much older. Of course, in my day such a difference in age would have been frowned upon as not very…what shall we say? Nice, perhaps. Yes, *nice*. That's the kindest way of putting it. Still I'm all for education. Gather ye rosebuds, eh, John?'

She slanted a flirtatiously insinuating glance in his direction before, to his unutterable relief, turning away to organize Clara organizing the drinks. Mortified and feeling like some venal old baron who had carried off and ravished the fairest flower in the village, Post stepped smartly out of Leonora's immediate orbit. He hoped that he would not be sitting next to her at dinner.

General conversation broke out. Morgan said *sotto voce* to Chloe, 'If it goes on like this there'll be blood on the carpet by the end of the evening.'

Chloe, having been told by her doctor that morning that she was pregnant, although she had not yet passed this on to Morgan, and already feeling sick, did not reply but simply nodded. Handing her a drink, Morgan thought that she looked even paler than usual. Very soon now they would be married. Man and wife. Whichever way you looked at it, and Morgan had viewed the situation from just about every angle, it simply did not feel like a logical progression.

He was brought to himself by Veronica Post's laser-sharp voice saying to him, 'Morgan is such a very unusual name. I wonder what made your mother choose it.'

'She didn't,' said Morgan. 'Grandmama did. It was her maiden name. Both her brothers were killed in the war and she didn't want it to go out of the family.'

'How old is Mrs Steer?'

'Admits to eight-five,' replied Morgan.

'Ah!' said Veronica, very familiar with this sort of

fudge. 'So, ninety. And what about your father? What happened to him?'

'I've never met him. He decamped before I was born. In fact,' added Morgan, 'he may not even know I exist. For all I know, he's dead.'

'Aren't you curious about him?'

Morgan thought for a minute.

'Yes and no. I mean I used to be. These days I hardly ever think about him. He was a military man. According to Grandmama it was a misalliance, and we are all better off without him. He didn't treat Mother very well, either. That's why my name is Steer, not Farrell. She didn't want it.' As far as Morgan was concerned, it was all ancient history. His voice trailed away. 'Will you excuse me. I see Aunt Clara's glass needs topping up.'

'Yes, of course.'

At the other side of the room, John Post's eyes veered away in panic at the approach of his hostess. On she came, inexorably smiling, and when she finally reached him, she said, 'You may take me into dinner, John!' This apparently was a great privilege, though he frankly doubted it. His worst fears were realized when she added, 'You will be sitting on my right. Morgan, would you please escort Veronica.'

They set off along the hall. Temporarily abandoned by her husband in this house of women, Annabel found herself following in their wake with Cassandra. Cassandra unsettled Annabel. There was an intensity about her that the younger woman found interesting and at the same time threatening. Vapid, thought Cassandra of the second Mrs Post, although not so vapid as her dreadful husband. Her eyes rested yearningly on Chloe the unattainable, gliding along just ahead in the company of Julia and Clara. What does Chloe Post think about? wondered Cassandra. To me she's an enigma. What, if anything, makes her tick? Or is she simply just another vacuous member of a vacuous family? In one sense, whatever the answer is, it doesn't really matter, because I am besotted with her!

Unrequited love.

It was not an attractive prospect.

During dinner, to everybody's relief Leonora subsided. She found herself suddenly and unusually, tired. The food was very good. I've practically forgotten what decent food tastes like, she thought, eating with relish. Since he had both supplied and paid for the wine, Morgan felt justified in pouring liberally, and probably as a direct result, although it could still hardly have been described as animated, the conversation more or less held up.

It was towards the end of the meal, while Cassandra on his right was talking to Veronica on her right, that John Post raised the subject of Morgan's career with his hostess.

'There is one thing that troubles me, Leonora.'

'Oh really, and what is that?'

'Chloe is a very wealthy young woman—'

'And apart from a small allowance from me, Morgan does not have independent means!' Giving him a sardonic look, she finished his sentence for him, deciding as she did so that he was a boor. Definitely not a gentleman. There was nothing wrong with *thinking* about money, of course, she did that all the time, but *talking* about it, and over dinner, was quite beyond the pale.

Impervious, Post was continuing. 'Plus he is presently unemployed. Although I gather he is, or was, on the short list for quite an impressive job.'

Job? *Impressive* job? Conversationally very quick on her feet, Leonora, who had heard nothing of any of this and who furthermore found it inherently unlikely, replied without hesitation. 'Yes, that is the case. A very lucrative job.'

He waited.

She let him.

Just as he thought she must have forgotten what they were talking about and was about to ask another leading question, she resumed. 'But all the details are confidential. Morgan has, of course, confided in me, but I am not allowed to confide in you, much as you would no doubt like me to.' He was still reeling from this snub, when she went on, looking down her thin, straight nose; 'And while I am bound to say that I find the whole process of discussing money *extremely* distasteful, since you seem determined to pursue the subject, John, what I will divulge is that when I die, Morgan *will* have some.' Here she raised her hand forbiddingly. 'And before you ask me, I do not wish to disclose how much. Until then I fail to see that it matters who has it, so long as one of them does.'

Having delivered this broadside, she stood up.

So complete was her authority that silence fell and they all followed suit.

'I suggest we adjourn to the drawing room. In the fullness of time Clara will bring the coffee through, aided by Morgan in order to prevent the sort of spectacular Minton crash to which we have all become accustomed. Come!'

17

Chloe and Morgan did not spend the night before their wedding together, although in the interests of keeping his nerve, Morgan felt it might have been better if they had. In the event he spent the evening with Tom Marchant, and Chloe with Joanna Blackstock.

She really shouldn't be doing this, thought Joanna, watching her friend narrowly. Chloe was preoccupied and jumpy. Restlessly she wandered around Joanna's small sitting room, straightening pictures and picking up ornaments and then putting them down again.

'Where is Morgan taking you on your honeymoon?' asked Joanna, more to break the silence than for any other reason.

'We're going to Paris and staying at the Crillon. It's what I want.'

'Good heavens! Can Morgan afford...?'

'No, he can't. Morgan wanted to go to Rome. To a small hotel he knows in Trastevere.'

'Sounds charming.'

'Apparently it is.'

'So why didn't you? And won't he be embarrassed when it comes to the bill?'

'I'm paying the difference,' said Chloe. 'I can't see

that it matters who foots the bill so long as it's a success.'

The lack of sensitivity shown by those who had a great deal of money to those who did not had often been noted by Joanna, but not quite as tellingly as in this particular instance. And if Chloe was unable to hack an unpretentious though pretty Roman hotel for the two weeks of her honeymoon, how was she going to measure up to the rigours of Northumberland? Perhaps, even at this late date, it was not too late to call the whole thing off. After all, such things did happen. Joanna remembered one spectacular occasion when the bride had refused at the altar, had been asked again and had refused again, and that had been that. The guests, with the groom but minus the bride, had all gone to the reception afterwards, which in the light of the preceding events had turned into something very like a wake.

It was Chloe who put an end to all this speculation, saying, 'I'm pregnant!'

Ah! Swinging without hesitation into damage limitation, Joanna said, 'Chloe, what a surprise! You must be delighted! And so must Morgan!'

Chloe's voice trembled.

'Morgan doesn't know yet. And I'm not delighted. I don't *want* it.' Leaning against the mantelpiece, she began to weep, silent, convulsive weeping that shook the whole of her slight frame. Eventually she calmed down enough to say, 'I'm frightened. Frightened of having a child. Oh, Joanna, what am I going to do?'

This is disaster! thought Joanna as she said, 'Lots of women are afraid of childbirth. You aren't the first and you certainly won't be the last.' She put an arm around her friend's shoulders. 'Come on, *courage*, Chloe! You're obviously in a highly emotional state. Pre-wedding nerves coupled with hormones in uproar. It'll all be all right, you'll see.'

Anodyne, meaningless words, for it was plain to Joanna that it was never going to be all right. Standing looking over Chloe's bowed head, she wondered whether there was time to talk to Morgan, and even if there was, which she doubted, whether she *should* talk to Morgan.

'Do you have any idea where Tom and Morgan intended to go tonight?'

'I'm afraid not.' Chloe was fishing around in her small shoulder bag for a handkerchief.

'Where are you staying?'

'With Annabel and Daddy. I didn't want to spend the night before my wedding in bed with Morgan.'

To Joanna this was incomprehensible. She wondered what Morgan thought about it.

'Well, that's your privilege, I suppose. After all, you've got the rest of your lives together.'

'Yes.' Chloe sounded bleak. 'Look, I'd better go. Apart from anything else, I don't want to look a fright in the morning.'

'You never look a fright!'

Joanna saw Chloe to the door and watched her as far as her car, which was parked at the end of the mews, listening to the light tap of her high-heeled shoes on the cobbles. Afterwards she went upstairs and sat in the button-backed chair by the open window, breathing in the jasmine-scented night air and thinking.

She was still there at half-past twelve when Tom returned.

'Where have you been?' asked Joanna.

He kissed her.

'We had dinner at the Brasserie St Quentin. Why, have you been missing me? And why are you sitting here in the dark?'

'No special reason.' Joanna decided to pick Tom's brains first. 'How did you find Morgan?'

Tom poured himself a whisky.

'Do you know, he hasn't exactly come right out and said it, but I don't think Morgan's heart is in this marriage. Whether he admits it to himself or not, I'd bet money on the fact that he's still in love with Caroline Barstow.'

'Chloe's pregnant, and very unhappy about it.'

Tom was astonished.

'Morgan never mentioned it to me!'

'Morgan doesn't know. And for what it's worth, I think she'd pull out too if she could.'

'It's gone too far to duck out now. They're on parade tomorrow in front of hordes of grisly relations, hers and his, and even some of mine.'

'It's never too late to duck out of that sort of mistake.'

Joanna took Tom's glass, had a sip of whisky and handed it back to him.

'Nothing to be done about it. After all, they're both grown-up. If it doesn't work, they'll just have to get unmarried again,' said Tom easily, thinking without regret of the imminent finalization of his own uncontested divorce. 'Busy day tomorrow. Let's go to bed!'

The next morning Chloe opened her eyes to a shining day. She remained where she was without moving, dazzled by the diffuse light that flowed through the pale curtains and over the bed on which she lay.

Today, at eleven o'clock, I am getting married.

It seemed hard to believe. And so did the fact that she was pregnant. She ran her hands over her breasts, which felt heavy and tender and not like hers at all, and then over her stomach, which, as yet, seemed unchanged. For the first time in my life, thought Chloe, I do not like my own body. It feels alien to me. Thoughts of escape ran through her head and were overtaken by the old familiar passivity that elected to let what had started finish.

She looked at her watch.

In our hour, Joanna would be coming, ostensibly to help her dress, but in fact to bolster morale. Better have her shower and fortify herself for the ordeal ahead with a great deal of black coffee.

Joanna arrived a few minutes earlier than they had arranged, bracing herself for tears and lamentations and prepared to suggest, despite the eleventh hour, that Chloe should call the whole thing off. To her relief, she found her friend composed and already dressed.

Perhaps the outburst of the night before had been nothing more than pre-wedding nerves, thought Joanna, observing aloud, 'Chloe, you look absolutely stunning!'

They embraced.

'Thank you,' replied Chloe. 'Well, it's do or die. No going back now.' The fatalistic way in which she delivered this short speech caused Joanna to give her a long look. There was something about Chloe's mien that put her in mind of Tennyson Maud. '*Icily regular, spendidly null.*' Wasn't that how it went?

'How late should I be at the church do you think?'

Joanna concentrated on the practical. 'Oh, five minutes. Ten at the most. Otherwise the older guests will start having palpitations. What jewellery are you going to wear?'

'I thought pearls with this.'

For tears, perhaps?

In the absence of any invitation to express her own opinion of the course Chloe was embarking upon, Joanna felt that she had no alternative but to keep her own counsel, and as a result was to wonder remorsefully on and off for years afterwards whether if she had spoken, a tragedy might have been averted.

'Is your father coming here, or are we picking him up *en route*?'

'Picking him up *en route*. Without Annabel, though.

She will have gone on ahead to the church. I just hope Mummy behaves herself.'

How very complicated extended families make this sort of occasion, thought Joanna, listening to her. A veritable social minefield, in fact. She wondered how John Post felt about giving his daughter away to Morgan.

Chloe put pearl studs in her ears. 'Such a shame your father won't be there.' She had always had a soft spot for Harry Blackstock, who seemed to possess the sort of reassuring normality so conspicuously lacking in her own parents.

'Yes, it is a shame,' agreed Joanna. 'I had rather hoped to smooth the path of his first meeting with Tom amid crowds of wedding guests all cheerily tanked up with champagne. As it is we're all having lunch together in a week's time, once he gets back. It promises to be a sticky occasion.'

'Why is he so resolutely against Tom?'

'Because he thinks Tom is a waster. Which is a difficult one to refute as things stand because Tom *is* a waster, but he won't be by the time I've finished with him. That's what I have to get across to Daddy.'

'Sounds like a tough one, but I expect you'll succeed.' For the first time Chloe smiled. 'Where are the flowers? Did you succeed in getting lilies?'

'I did.'

'Shall we go?'

Standing beside Tom Marchant, Morgan turned his head as the music began. Watching his bride walk

down the aisle on the arm of her father, he felt his
heart miss a beat. Chloe was wearing a narrow, long-
skirted suit made of some sort of heavy cream silk that
was substantial enough to hold and even emphasize
the simply elegant statement of its classic lines. The
neckline of the fitted jacket was low at the front but
contrived to rise dramatically at the back into a collar
that stood crisply and unexpectedly high, her slender
and sleek dark head framed against it like the stamen
in the heart of a lily. There was a murmur of appreciation. Even Veronica had to admit that Mrs Rita Cox
of Bayswater had pulled it off.

Twenty minutes later they were man and wife.

As she signed the register, Chloe Steer was assailed
by a feeling of unreality and the knowledge that, with
the pregnancy and the very public nature of the ceremony, an irrevocable step had been taken down a road
which she was by no means certain she wished to
travel.

Congratulations.

Kisses.

Laughter.

Photographs.

More photographs.

Thank God, no time to think.

On to the reception. Still more photographs. The
Family Group. Leonora and Veronica vying for pole
position. Veronica vanquished. Leonora the clear win-

ner. Much looking down the aristocratic Steer nose at the parvenue.

'Smile, please.'

Click.

'Again, please. And again. And again.'

Click, click, click.

'One more.' Click. 'Thank you, ladies and gentlemen. And now just the bride and groom.'

Click.

And finally, the bride alone.

I just can't believe this is my wedding day, thought Chloe, inwardly desperate, outwardly smiling at the camera. I just can't believe it.

Afterwards, at the reception, Morgan inevitably came face to face with Caro. They confronted one another for a moment in silence. He remembered her wedding to Patrick years ago and the anguish it had caused him. Disconcertingly, he still experienced the magnetic pull she had always exercised where he was concerned.

Unable to stop himself, he said in a low voice, 'I have always loved you, and I always will.'

In turmoil, and unable to meet his intense gaze in case she should give herself away, she looked down, and because of the wide brim of her very becoming hat, he could not see her reaction to this statement. When she finally did look up again, he saw that her eyes were full of tears.

'Goodbye, Morgan,' said Caro.

Seeing out of the corner of his eye the daunting

figure of Leonora bearing down on them both, Morgan whispered urgently, 'I mean it! You think I don't, but I do!'

He watched her walk away from him yet again. Conscious of his shameful betrayal of Chloe, he exclaimed, 'Oh, *fuck* it!' under his breath, before turning to greet his grandmother.

Across the room, Meredith Barstow, who had been watching Caro and Morgan's tête-à-tête with a certain degree of concern, was relieved to see them part company. Thank *God* Morgan is safely married at last, she thought. Hopefully, that is now that.

Caro found Patrick talking to Annabel Post. Or rather, at Annabel Post, who seemed to be making no contribution whatever. On Caro's arrival, Annabel took the opportunity to slip away.

'Patrick I want to leave,' stated Caro, without any preamble.

Startled he exclaimed, 'But we've only just got here! What's the matter? Are you ill or something?'

'Ill? Oh, *ill*! Yes, that's it. Ill! Or rather, I think I may be sickening for something. I feel one degree under, that sort of thing.'

'Have another glass of champagne! It's the best medicine in the world, especially when it's Krug.' He drained his glass and held it out to the waiter for a refill. It was obvious to Caro that dislodging Patrick was not going to be easy.

'Besides, you promised Meredith you would help her look after the Brig.'

This was true. She had. Maybe that was the answer. Tank up with champagne and make sure Grandfather never left her side so that it would be impossible for Morgan to corner her again. Taking a canapé and another glass of Krug, she went in search of him.

In another part of the room, John Post was saying to his daughter, 'Say, honey, when does Morgan start his new job?'

'He doesn't.' The wedding over, Chloe felt she could afford to set the record straight. 'It all fell through, I'm afraid, so he hasn't got one.'

Post was divided between malicious pleasure at this news and the urge to express disapproval.

'So what's he going to live off?'

'Me, I should think. Until he does get one, that is.'

She smiled seductively up at him, and not for the first time he caught himself thinking what a pity it was that Chloe was his daughter and, as such, out of bounds. He looked across the room without affection at his new son-in-law, who was currently in conversation with the terrifying Leonora Steer. As though her social antennae picked up his gaze even though she had her back to him, Leonora suddenly turned and stared in his direction. Anxious to avoid eye contact, Post's attention veered back to Chloe. He gave her sixty seconds of pure concentration, by which time he hoped the coast would be clear for another furtive look at the Steers. Oh Christ, she was coming over. And not only that, there was no time for escape, for she was nearly upon him.

Monitoring Leonora's imperious progress with interest, the Brigadier, who was sitting down with Caro on one side and Meredith on the other, said, 'She's a fine woman. A fine woman! I've always said so...' His voice trailed away.

'Quite,' said Meredith. He's beginning to maunder, she reflected. Too much champagne.

'Wonder if I should get married again.'

Meredith was not sure she had heard aright. As one, mother and daughter turned in his direction.

'Who to, Father?'

'Leonora, of course!'

Meredith's eyes glazed at the prospect of having both of them on her hands. Though maybe both of them would be on Julia's hands. Whoever drew the short straw, it did not bear thinking about.

He pursued it. 'We could have another party. Like this one. Pretty girls. Champagne. And while we're on the subject, I'd like a refill.' He tapped his glass with his signet ring.

'Don't you think you've had—'

Too late. The waiter had done it.

Drinking deeply, the Brigadier frowned. 'What was I talking about?'

'Parties, pretty girls, that sort of thing,' offered Meredith with something of a sigh.

Her father brightened up immediately. 'Yes, that's right. Wine, women and song.' He cracked his knuckles, a habit that got on Meredith's nerves, and then lapsed into silence, remembering one party in particular where he had danced the night away with Leonora and Celia had been unaccountably upset.

'After all,' he suddenly announced aloud, 'one doesn't go to parties to dance with one's wife. One can dance with one's wife any bloody day of the week!'

'What are you talking about, Grandfather?'

The speaker was Caro.

'Dancing, of course.' He peered at her as though she was very dense. 'Wake up girl!' He paused. 'Of course,' he resumed, 'she was no fun!'

Frankly mystified as to his drift. Meredith asked, '*Who* wasn't?'

'Another one who isn't listening!' proclaimed the Brigadier to the world at large. 'Your mother!' He sounded irascible.

'If Mother was so dreary, I wonder why you ever married her.' Meredith was snappy, reflecting that having made her mother's life a misery while she was alive, the least he could do now that she was dead was stop sniping.

He was incorrigible. 'I thought I could cheer her up. But, no dice!' He fell into another reverie, leaning forward, hands on his silver knobbed cane. Behind her father's back, Meredith said *sotto voce* to Caro, 'I think we'd better get him back before he actually *does* propose, but before that I'm going to have another glass of Krug. I feel I need one. What about you?'

'I feel I need one too!'

On her way to collect them, Meredith ran into Julia.

Wanting to talk to her friend, she buttonholed a waiter, indicated Caro and said, 'Could you please give another glass of champagne to the lady over there. Thank you so much.' When he had departed, she said, 'I won't beat about the bush. Father is threatening to propose to Leonora.'

Julia was unfazed. 'Don't panic, Meredith. The question you have to ask yourself where Mother is concerned is what would she have to gain? And the answer is, nothing. After all, it's not as though she even likes men very much. They've always been a means to an end for her. Unless...' Julia hesitated. 'I hope you don't mind me asking you this, but has your father got any money?'

'Not so far as I'm aware,' said Meredith.

'Then you're home and dry. Mother may not be romantic but she is grasping, and if there's nothing *to* grasp, she won't be interested. Although be that as it may, she's not above leading him on before telling him no.'

The prospect of such geriatric flirtation made Meredith wince as a commotion at the other end of the room caused them both to turn round.

'It looks as though Morgan and Chloe may be leaving.'

'What, before the cake?'

'There isn't a cake. Veronica Post vetoed it. She says wedding cakes are vulgar!'

'Well, she would know all about that, of course.'

Meredith eyed the Mother of the Bride with distaste. 'She must be my age, and look at her!'

They moved to join the gathering by the door. Standing by Morgan, shortly to be left alone with him for the greater part of the rest of her life, Chloe experienced desperation. She searched for Joanna and finally located her at the back of the crowd in the company of Tom Marchant, who had his arm around her friend's waist. On impulse, Chloe tossed her bouquet high in the air so that it soared over the heads of those in front. Cream and apricot ribbons trailing like the tail feathers of some exotic bird, it rose and fell, and to universal disapproval it was Tom, with the advantage of his height, who caught it.

'*You're* not supposed to do that!' Joanna was half amused and half irritated.

'You don't know what I'm going to do next!' Presenting her with the lilies, he said, with a courtly half-bow, 'I'm going to ask you to marry me!'

It was obvious that he expected her to accept gratefully.

And of course, it *was* what she wanted.

Nevertheless, thought Joanna, receiving the flowers, Tom doesn't appreciate anything he gets without a struggle. Easy come, easy go. In the end, she answered, after a short silence, 'I'm very flattered, Tom, but let's see how we go. Besides, you're still married!'

As responses went, it was less than ecstatic. Tom suddenly became aware that the two of them were subject to the interested attention of a semicircle of wedding guests mutely mesmerized by the whole exchange. Feeling something of a fool but also relieved (did he really want to subject himself to the yoke of marriage again quite so soon?) Tom, unable to think of an answer to her last observation, decided to give them all something to look at as well as listen to, and kissed Joanna instead.

The sight of the two of them embracing was Chloe's last poignant impression of her own wedding as she and Morgan left for their honeymoon.

It was with a heart as leaden as Chloe's that Caro went home afterwards with her grandfather, her mother and her husband. No amount of Krug could compensate for what I've just gone through, thought Caro. Unaware of her despair, and equally full of Krug, Patrick was cheerful, and therefore irritating. Propped up by his cane and filled with more Krug than both of them put together, the Brigadier walked unsteadily behind them with Meredith, sunk in a sombre introspection that he suddenly rose above for just long enough to state, 'I completely forgot to propose. That's your fault, Meredith, you should have reminded me!'

'Am I my father's keeper?' Meredith, who had had enough, was tart.

Clearly suddenly miles away again, the Brigadier did not respond to this, but as they descended the steps into Bond Street tube station, she heard him inexplicably say to himself, 'A conservatory is what I need. That's it! A conservatory,' after which, to her enormous relief, he fell into a reverie again. With Patrick talking incessantly, and Caro and Meredith and Sir Arthur each locked away in personally unsatisfactory worlds of their own, the four of them travelled back to Clapham.

September

18

The mugging of Larch came as a shock to everyone. Recognizing the general increase of random urban violence was one thing, but a brutal manifestation of it involving someone one knew was quite another. It was for this reason and no other that Caro went to visit her sister's ex-lover in hospital.

Larch was in the main ward, wearing unfortunate striped pyjamas several sizes too big for him. Lying on the narrow white bed he looked curiously diminished. Trying to put her finger on what the difference was, apart from a spectacular black eye and several broken ribs, she finally came to the conclusion that it was the aura of sanctimonious superiority that was missing.

Caro pulled up a chair and prepared to minister.

'So sorry to hear about this. How are you, Jonathan?'

He pulled himself up the bed so that he was half sitting, wincing as he did so. 'OK, thanks, Caroline.'

'Do they have any idea who did it?'

An oddly fugitive look crossed his face. After a prolonged pause, he said, 'No. No, they don't.'

'What about you?' Caro studied him closely as she asked this.

Larch looked obliquely across the room. The impression conveyed was one of both shiftiness and anxiety. Still not meeting her candid gaze, he said, 'They came up behind me. I never saw them.' He closed his eyes. For a moment Caro thought he might have gone to sleep, and then he opened them again. 'Is Emily coming to see me? I miss Emily.'

Dreading that he might be about to weep, Caro replied, 'I'm sure she'll come and visit. But how long are they going to keep you in?'

'*I* don't know.' He was so dispirited that Caro, who had troubles of her own, felt her heart plummet still further just watching him. Unnervingly, he took her hand. His felt narrow and cold, and at the same time curiously limp. Repressing a desire to take hers away, Caro let it lie uneasily where it was. She felt embarrassed.

Larch said, 'Caro, I have a favour to ask. Will you intervene for me with Emily? Please?'

Oh no! Caro thought. I wish he wasn't asking me this, lying here with a black eye and four broken ribs. It just isn't *fair*.

Caro gave his hand a reassuring squeeze prior to repossessing her own, and then said, 'Look, Jonathan, I'd like to help, but I really think it would be inappropriate for me to interfere between you and Emily. Why don't you talk to her about it when she comes to see you?'

Uttering these words she felt very hard-hearted.

Clearly in decline, he let his head fall back on the pillow and watching him, it was impossible for Caroline to decide which she disliked more, Larch in the ascendant or Larch languishing.

Without directly responding to her last statement, he said, 'I'm tired. I think I'd like to go to sleep now.'

When she was finally gone, he lay where he was, reviewing the events of the past twenty-four hours. He remembered the heady smell of late roses infusing the warm, amaranthine September night as he walked from Notting Hill Gate down Kensington Park Road to Elgin Crescent, and the sound of his own footsteps ringing on the grey London flags. It had been peaceful, nobody much about, the sort of balmy late-summer night that induced a heightened sense of self as part of the whole. As he made his way, he had thought of Emily. Surely Emily would come to her senses, would see that in spite of their recent contretemps, the way forward was together. Stopping in order to change the carrier bag of groceries he was carrying from one hand to the other, it was at this moment that his assailants, who must have crept up on him on sneakered feet, struck. Larch found himself yanked backwards by his ponytail. His carrier bag exploded on contact with the pavement, sending health food shooting down the hill, and as it hit the stone with a crack, his head felt as though it might be about to do the same.

Someone laughed.

He felt a hand going through his pockets. Consciousness painfully coming and going, he tried to lever himself off the ground until a punch in the face put an end to any further ambitions he might have nurtured in that direction. Unable to protect himself, he felt a series of painful thuds to the side of his body. They must be kicking him, Larch groaned. The last thing he heard before mercifully blacking out were the words, 'Give 'im another one Nige!' spoken in a voice he recognized.

A large nurse came into view.

'Time for your painkillers, Mr Larch, and do you need a bedpan?'

This humiliating enquiry was broadcast to the ward at large. For the first time in his life, Larch found himself on the receiving end of the sort of officious, insensitive treatment that he was wont to dole out to those less fortunate than himself. When she had finally taken both herself and the bedpan off, Larch, his ribs throbbing despite a liberal dose of pills, visualized Nigel and Gary in his mind's eye. Gary was the stupid one, and looked it. A lumpen youth with a chip on his shoulder but not the mental equipment to deal with it. Violence took the place of thought for Gary. But Nigel was something else again. Though largely uneducated, Nigel was not stupid, and had the dangerous good looks of a Luciferian angel. And Nigel was vicious. Larch knew this from his record. But, Larch mused, I thought I was forging some sort of relationship with him. Had his respect, even his...his what? Hot tears took Larch by surprise, and as he lay there, it suddenly came to him with devastating clarity that he was not in love with Emily. Loved Emily, yes, though not, apparently, in the way she wanted, but had never been *in* love with Emily. No, he, Jonathan Larch, was sexually attracted to Nigel Moult.

The new, liberated Emily, who had just promised Jack Carey that she would pose for him in the nude, went with lagging steps to visit Larch. Before setting out she had taken the decision that under no circumstances would she relent, not even when she came face to face with her former lover in such sorry circumstances. For her the affair was over.

Standing at the end of his bed, she wondered how she had ever found him attractive. Larch, serene in his new enlightenment, even though such recognition probably raised more problems than it solved, felt he could afford to be generous.

Listening to what he had to say and without knowing any of the reasons for such an abrupt change of heart, Emily was startled. His lofty discourse still reminded her of Mr Casaubon, but at least, for once, he was telling her something she wanted to hear. When he paused for breath, Emily said, 'I'll put the house on the market tomorrow if you like.' Time was of the essence. She experienced an overwhelming urge to get out of this relationship as soon as possible, before he changed his mind again.

'You must put the house on the market,' instructed

Larch as though she had not already said it, 'and the way to do that is to—'

'I know how to put a house on the market,' interrupted Emily, who actually had no idea.

Once again pursuing his own line of thought as though she had not spoken, he intoned, 'And you will have to supervise the rehabilitation of the kitchen while I am confined to this hospital bed.'

'No need to supervise anything. It's down to decoration now, and I'm willing to bet that whoever buys it will want to choose the paint themselves, especially when they find they can have it on our insurance.'

Thinking how intransigent Emily was these days, really not the girl he used to know at all, Larch said, 'Well, that's about it. I hope, Emily, that when all our affairs are sorted out we shall keep in touch, and that you will always come to me when you need guidance.'

Emily, who had no intention whatever of keeping in touch, said perfidiously, 'Yes, I'm sure I shall.'

Out of the corner of his eye Larch saw his tormentor the stout nurse rolling tanklike down the ward. Anxious to avoid another discussion of his more intimate functions at top decibels, he said, 'I should like to rest now.'

'Yes, of course.'

They shook hands. What a very odd thing to do, reflected Emily. We used to share a bed, and now we're shaking hands.

'Goodbye, Jonathan.'

'Goodbye, Emily.'

* * *

Joanna decided to meet her father for a drink in advance of their lunch, more in order to prepare the ground than for any other reason. She arrived at the Savoy ten minutes late and finally ran him to earth in a wing armchair, leafing through *The Economist* and smoking a cigar the size of a small canoe. His joy on seeing her was unfeigned. Harry Blackstock doted on his daughter, and felt as protective of her now as he had when she was a very small girl.

He signalled to a waiter.

'Glass of Chablis do for you, Joanna love?'

'Yes, please!'

'And a whisky sour for me,' ordered Harry. When the drinks arrived, they touched glasses and said together, 'Here's to you!', a Blackstock ritual.

Eating a salted peanut and then following this with a crisp, Harry observed grudgingly, 'You're looking well. That ne'er-do-well Marchant must be looking after you.'

'Daddy, tell me exactly what it is you have against Tom.'

Harry, who was not a hypocrite, and who had done some fly City deals in his time, was not tempted to moralize. 'Silly ass got caught! That's his real crime. Incompetence, not insider dealing! Everyone does *that.*'

'He won't do it again.'

'No, he won't, because with the City currently trying to turn itself into a whited sepulchre he won't be allowed to!'

'He's currently working in the wine business.'

'Sounds about right to me,' rejoined the tycoon, pulling on his cigar. 'Don't tell me. He's gone into partnership with another member of the old-boy network.'

Not for the first time, Joanna was struck by her father's perspicacity.

'Daddy, you must have met Tom,' she accused.

'No, I never have, but that hasn't prevented the reverberations of what was quite a scandal from reaching me. The rest of it's predictable. Including the fact that he's in the process of being divorced by one well-heeled wife while in hot pursuit of another one, namely my daughter!'

Well aware that there was no point in being anything other than frank, Joanna said, 'I think money was the main attraction at first. He certainly wasn't all that interested until he found out about it. But now that's not the case. And of course, if we ever did marry, there would have to be a monetary agreement drawn up by the lawyers and signed by Tom, at your insistence naturally. I couldn't do it. You would have to make it clear that this was a precondition *whoever* I married. Otherwise no cash.'

Harry looked at his daughter with undisguised admiration. She really was a chip off the old block.

'Just a precaution,' said Joanna. 'You know.'

'*That's* my girl,' said Harry. 'But why marry Marchant? Why not keep him for amusement only?'

'Time I settled down. Besides, I'm in love with him.'

'That means you're one down before you even start! Being in love warps the judgement.'

'No, because firstly I haven't told him, and secondly, *he's* in love with me.'

And who wouldn't be? thought Harry fondly, eyeing his practical only child with approval.

'Well,' he conceded, finishing his whisky sour, 'it sounds to me as if you've got everything under control. Mind you keep your eye on the ball. Just remind me, when are you going to wheel Marchant out for my inspection?'

'Still to be decided, but when it does happen Tom will be inspecting you, too, don't forget, so you're not to put him off. Best behaviour, Daddy.'

'Anything you want, I want too. You know that, Joanna. But mind, if he lets you down, I'll kill him.'

'If he lets me down you won't have to. I'll do it myself. Shall we get the bill?'

Chloe and Morgan had a very sybaritic time in the Crillon, and on that level they both enjoyed the honeymoon. But without the diversion of a party every night, conversation was oddly stilted, and silence often fell like a dead hand between them. Still, Morgan thought, determined to stifle all reservations and almost succeeding, it's a well-known fact that honeymoons can be sticky. It was also his view, though he did not say so to Chloe, that the pretty hotel in Rome which had been his first choice would probably have been a lot more fun than the Crillon, which Morgan found lacking in intimacy.

At the end of one particularly uncommunicative day, travelling by taxi from the Musée de Chasse to the Left Bank, where they intended to have a drink, Chloe finally decided to pass on her news.

'Darling, isn't it wonderful.' There was an almost imperceptible hesitation. 'I'm pregnant.'

'What! Are you sure?' Morgan was first incredulous and then ecstatic. Misgivings evaporated.

'How long have you known?'

How long had she known?

'Since the day before the wedding.'

'But why ever didn't you tell me before?' As he said it, Morgan remembered with guilt his exchange with Caro. Would he have said those things if he had known then what he knew now? Probably not. Filled with remorse and tenderness, he took Chloe in his arms and kissed her.

Chloe knew why she had not told him. Not telling him allowed her to indulge in the fantasy that it was all a bad dream that would eventually go away. Now that Morgan knew, she would have to confront her fear.

She stared out of the window. Paris in the evening was a little cooler and purple-shadowed, as though preparing for autumn, but at the same time it retained the benign milkiness of late summer. As they drove along, the fiery sun seemed to move with them, bowling along the misty tops of the trees in the park.

'I don't know why I didn't tell you,' fibbed Chloe.

19

Proceeding very stately down Battle Hill on her way
from the solicitor's office where she had been tinkering
with her will, Leonora Steer suddenly stopped dead.
So abruptly did she stop that the person behind her
walked straight into her. Watching the person on the
other side of the road like a hawk, she nevertheless
took time off to admonish.

'Kindly look where you are going,' said Leonora,
very starchy, still keeping her eyes fixed on the real
object of her attention, who was hovering on the edge
of the kerb, apparently irresolute about which direction
to take. I'm sure it's him, thought Leonora, shading
her eyes. Looks shabby, but it *is* him. Must have fallen
on hard times.

Still he stood there. Moving slowly with the aid of
the stick, she finally caught up with him.

'Major Farrell, I believe!'

He jumped. There was a furtive air about him, Leonora decided. After a short pause, during the course of
which he peered at her, he gathered his wits.

'Good Lord, if it isn't Mrs Steer!'

'It is! And by coming across you like this, I have

no doubt saved you the trouble of finding *me*. Where can we go and talk? Are you staying at an hotel?'

The Major, who had a room in a very seedy lodging house, was reluctant to divulge where this was. He found himself longing for a drink.

'I am, but it's quite a long walk. What about the pub?'

'A public house?' She looked down her nose. 'Very well, if you insist.'

The one he chose was very old and oak-beamed, and had been extensively used by farmers in the days when hirings used to take place at the beginning of every new farming season. Down the years, smoke from the fire had turned the walls the colour of burnt sienna. Picking up an overflowing ashtray, and uttering the word 'Disgusting!' as she did so, Leonora summoned a minion.

'Take that away would you please,' Turning to the Major, 'and my companion would like to order when you have done that.'

'A double gin and tonic, lemon, no ice,' instructed Leonora. 'And I prefer to pour my own tonic.'

'A double gin and tonic, lemon, no ice, and the lady prefers to pour her own tonic, plus a half of your best bitter for me,' said the Major, who was down to his last twenty pounds.

Aware of the years between this meeting and their last, they sat and studied one another.

Dilapidated! decided Leonora, taking on board her companion's thinning grey hair, which still retained an

evocative hint of its original sandy colour. Drinks too
much as well, I dare say. And the eyes. Rheumy, with
that unfortunate yellow film... In sum total, the dashing Major has become old. Old and addled. Just about
ready for putting down, I should say.

Christ, she's ancient, Major Fred was thinking at the
same time. On the other hand, she must be ninety if
she's a day. Still aggressive, though. He remembered
the very gritty negotiations concerning his payoff that
he and Mrs Steer had had over the inevitable cucumber
sandwiches, at the end of which he had not succeeded
in taking away nearly as much as he would have liked.

Leonora smiled dangerously at him over the rim of
her glass. It took him back decades and he was suddenly aware all over again of her ageless sexual appeal, which could even surmount her four score years
and ten, no trouble at all, when she chose to let it.

'Cheers!' said the Major uneasily.

'So why *are* you here?' enquired Leonora, without
responding to his toast. Then, answering herself, very
wintrily, 'Money, I expect!'

Uncomfortably, he recalled that frontal assault had
always been her way. Since her expectation was perfectly correct, he found himself at an uncharacteristic
loss for words.

Watching him narrowly, Leonora registered the fact
that he had not once mentioned Morgan. Or Julia, for
that matter. Well, we both know about Julia, but I suspect we don't both know about Morgan. She assessed
the implications of this, finishing her gin and tonic and

indicating at the same time that a refill would be appreciated.

Doing some mental arithmetic, Major Fred wondered how many she was capable of inbibing at a sitting. Clearly, since he intended to stay in Hexham for a little while, it would not be wise to bounce a cheque in The Grapes. To his relief, she announced, 'This will have to be my last. I am meeting Julia, who is doing some shopping for me, outside the Moot Hall. Perhaps you would care to come with me and become reacquainted with your wife? I suppose she is still your wife?'

Yes, he supposed she was. He certainly had not done anything about dissolving the marriage.

'Ah, yes, dear Julia!' He was aware of his false bonhomie and of Leonora's sardonic look indicating that she had registered it too. 'Another time. Today I have some business I need to attend to.' His voice trailed away. He hoped she would not ask him what it was.

Leonora did not enquire any further. 'Ah, yes, of course you have.' And then, very unexpectedly, 'We shall, of course, expect you for luncheon on Sunday. Twelve thirty for one. Please do not be late.'

She picked up her stick.

The thought of Julia's reproachful gaze even after, or maybe because of, all these years made Major Fred's blood freeze.

'Well, I'm not sure—'

Leonora cut him off in mid-sentence.

'Excellent, then that's settled. Goodbye, Frederick.'

Escorting her to the door, he decided that when he had seen her off he would go back and have another drink, a very stiff one this time.

Leonora found Julia packing the boot of the Ford.

'The only think I couldn't get was a cob loaf,' she said. 'Sold out, I'm afraid.'

Lost in thought, Leonora did not immediately answer.

'Mother? Did you hear what I said?'

'Yes, I did. Don't be tiresome, Julia. The existence or nonexistence of cob loaves is your department. Something much more important is preoccupying my mind at the moment. Would you please open the car door for me?'

Julia complied, saying as she did so, 'Really? What?'

Leonora dickered, undisclosed knowledge usually being the most potentially powerful kind, and then, mindful of the fact that Julia's errant husband was coming to visit them at the weekend anyway, at which time the secret would be a secret no longer, she decided to tantalize until they reached Armitage Lodge, and then to divulge what had happened.

Accordingly, all she would say was, 'We have an unexpected guest coming to lunch on Sunday. Perhaps we should stop off at the butcher on our way back.'

Cassandra, entering the house with Jardine at her heels, was astonished to hear what sounded like a furious quarrel taking place in the drawing room. Standing stock-still in the act of taking off her mac, she wondered who it was. The appearance of Clara from the direction of the kitchen sorted that out. It must be Mother and Julia.

'What's going on?' asked Cassandra, *sotto voce*.

'I don't know, but they've been going at it hammer and tongs for at least half an hour. Julia keeps shouting, "How could you, Mother!" There she goes again! She sounds demented.'

'It's a fairly consistent refrain where Mother is concerned.'

'Do you think we should interfere?' quavered Clara.

'Not unless you are prepared to sustain a flesh wound.'

A loud report coupled with the sound of breaking glass caused them both to fall silent. Jardine, ears back, began to whine.

'What on earth do you think that was?'

'That', stated Cassandra, 'could only have been the domed stuffed bird! One of them must have knocked it for six. Have you noticed that Mother doesn't appear to have lost her temper at all? It's all Julia. Look, let's make ourselves scarce. We can go and collect the body when Mother has left the field.'

Creeping past the drawing-room door, the last thing they heard before achieving the beginning of the kitchen corridor was Leonora saying in what Cassandra called bombazine tones, 'This is a *disgraceful* exhibition, Julia. Pray compose yourself!' The predictable upshot of this rebuke was an audible escalation of Julia's anguish. After another 'How could you,

Mother?' came more hysterical screaming and crying, followed by a smart slap, followed by silence. Cassandra and Clara stood transfixed, and then the sound of somebody, Leonora presumably, making her way to the door caused them both to scurry for the kitchen.

By dint of leaving the kitchen door ajar, they heard her slowly ascend the stairs, and then the bell from her bedroom began to jangle.

'You go,' said Cassandra. 'I'll go and mop up the blood.'

'Must I?'

'Yes, you must. Otherwise she'll come down here again, and we don't want that. There might be a murder.'

Dragging her feet, Clara went.

Cassandra quietly opened the drawing-room door. Julia was half sitting, half lying on the sofa with her head thrown back, but she appeared calmer. One of her cheeks was streaked with red.

'It was Mother's ringed hand,' said Julia.

Released from its glass prison, the stuffed bird lay on its back in a tangle of fruit and leaves, both legs in the air and its little clawlike feet still curled around a now non-existent branch. Large, thick chunks of dome covered a surprisingly large area and among them, Cassandra noticed, were fragments of an entirely different kind. She picked one up. Oh no, surely it couldn't be? Apparently it was.

'Yes! I threw the Meissen figurine at it,' said Julia in response to Cassandra's unspoken question. 'The one the Prince of Wales gave her. Mother's lucky I didn't throw it at her. Has she gone?'

'Having created even more mayhem than usual, yes, she has. She's currently bullying Clara. What on earth happened?'

'You'll never guess who she met in Hexham.'

'No, I probably never will. Who was it?'

'Major Frederick Farrell.'

'Good God!' exclaimed Cassandra, who was not in fact as surprised as she sounded.

'Yes, it seems I have a husband in the offing, and what's more, Mother has invited him to lunch on Sunday. When I think of the humiliation I suffered at the hands of that man, and Mother, *Mother*, asks him here, to Armitage Lodge, without even bothering to consult me!'

'Well, you have to admit consultation never was Mother's style,' observed Cassandra. 'But why do you think he's come back?'

'Oh, I don't know.' Julia closed her eyes. 'We all know there's nothing altruistic about Frederick. So he must want something.'

A thought struck Cassandra. 'I'll bet he's here because he knows about Morgan's advantageous marriage!'

'So far as I'm aware, he never even knew about Morgan, never mind Morgan's advantageous marriage.'

'No, but he would only have had to read about the nuptials in a gossip column to put two and two together. I wonder where he's been all this time?'

'Wouldn't surprise me if the answer to that wasn't: in prison. What surprises me is Mother. Mother always loathed Frederick. It was the one thing she was absolutely right about. So what's going on?'

'I think two things may be going on. Firstly, Mother is bored, which always makes her lethal, and secondly, she believes in staying close to the enemy, so that if he is up to something, such as extortion, she will be the first to know about it and will be well placed to see him off. When are Morgan and Chloe next coming here?'

Chloe! Cassandra's heart lifted at the prospect of a visit.

'End of October, I think, unless they bring it forward. Hopefully he'll have gone by then.'

Separately, but without saying so, they both doubted it.

'Fetch me the inkpot and pen,' commanded Leonora, who had never acknowledged the arrival of the Biro on the writing scene, and who preferred this antediluvian method of writing to her own slim gold fountain pen for the task she was about to undertake. 'And kindly pass me the large buff envelope from the bottom drawer.'

Eyeing this with apprehension, for she knew what it was, Clara complied.

'And now, Clara, you may withdraw, for I intend to alter my will.'

20

Julia declined to attend the lunch. Because she and Leonora were not on speaking terms, Clara was given the unwelcome task of passing on this piece of information. Faced with it, Leonora said, 'Frederick is Julia's husband. It is her duty to be present!'

Listening to this, Cassandra entered the lists with, 'Well, be that as it may, she seems quite determined. And after all, Frederick did treat her very badly.'

'Her duty to *me*, I mean,' said Leonora, clearing up the matter. 'And of course he did!' She was scornful. 'I advised Julia against marrying him and she defied me. She is now reaping what she has sown.'

'Yes, but you've been doing some sowing for her this time around.' Cassandra was not prepared to let Leonora get away with this. 'You didn't have to invite him to Armitage Lodge.'

'I shall invite whomsoever I please to my own house.' Aware of insubordination and choosing to miss the point, Leonora was glacial.

'But *why* have you done so?' Clara was frankly mystified.

Leonora spoke very slowly, as to a bear of very small brain. 'Frederick is a loose cannon. He needs tying down and then neutralizing. Only when I know what he wants can I see him off.'

Clara frowned. 'Maybe he doesn't *want* anything.'

'Clara, if you believe that, you'll believe anything. Frederick is plainly down on his luck. Ergo, he is here for one of two reasons. Either he thinks that it can't be long until I die, and he wants to be around when that happens in case there is something in it for him, or he has latched on to the fact that he has a son who has married a very wealthy woman, and the same thing applies. It is my unenviable lot to inform him that there is nothing in it for him anywhere. I had hoped that Julia might have helped me perform this task, might have *enjoyed* helping me perform this task, but it seems not.'

It occurred to Cassandra, not for the first time, that while Mother was quite often right, the *way* she handled being right was almost always wrong.

Later, in the privacy of Julia's room, Cassandra said, 'She wants to get rid of him.'

'That may be,' replied Julia, 'but I don't want to be there while she does it. Quite simply, I never want to see Frederick again, and especially not old, sad, down-at-heel Frederick.'

Understanding, Cassandra was silent.

'Well, if you won't do the dance of the seven veils, Mother as Herodias won't get half as much pleasure out of securing the Major's head on a platter.'

Julia laughed.

'No. I know.'

'Where will you go while we are subjected to this grisly performance?'

'I shall go and visit Meredith.'

Meredith. Something stirred in Cassandra's memory. What was it? Julia, the Major and Meredith. Something about all three of them. Cassandra tried to remember and failed. It was all such a long time ago now.

'Does she know that Frederick has come back?'

'It would be hard not to know in a town like Hexham. *I* haven't told her yet, if that's what you mean.'

Meredith, it transpired, did not know, and when Julia relayed the fact of the Major's return on the telephone, there was an audible intake of breath.

'So I wondered if I might come and lurk with you at Tyne Green until he's gone.'

'Of course!' said Meredith, rallying in the face of what was catastrophic news. 'But no need just to lurk, come and have lunch as well.'

And so it was that bumping down the hill in the old Ford, Julia passed Major Fred bumping up the hill in an equally old taxi. Thank God that's the closest he'll get to me today, thought Julia with a shudder, resolutely looking straight ahead.

The Major paid off the taxi without bestowing a tip, and as it reversed out of the drive, he stood back and surveyed Armitage Lodge. It hadn't changed at all, probably hadn't even been painted since he had last seen it, all those years ago. He half expected to see the face of the young Julia at one of the upstairs windows, anticipating his arrival.

In the event it was Leonora herself who answered the door to him.

'I'm afraid your wife declined to have lunch with you today,' was her opening salvo. 'Still, no doubt three women as opposed to four will suffice, or,' with a flash of malice and alluding to his reputation as a womanizer, 'perhaps they won't. Now,' she said, leading the way into the drawing room, 'you remember, Clara, don't you?'

He should have thought he would, but this person bore no resemblance to the girl he once had known. Clara had been one of the belles of the county, with a string of beaux. Not as intelligent as Julia, but with a fine figure and a good seat on a horse. He had lusted after Clara but in the end had decided that her sister was more attainable. Rightly, though unproductively, as it had later unfortunately turned out. Faded and timorous, Clara greeted her sister's husband with restraint and one eye on her formidable parent.

'And Cassandra?'

Cassandra, on the other hand, had turned into very much what he would have expected, probably because she had always had a more independent spirit than Clara. Without ever having been a beauty, there was a spareness and elegance about Cassandra that had endured and even been enhanced by the years. However, Cassandra, he intuited, had never liked men and perhaps it was the absence of disappointment in this regard that had, in an odd sort of way, preserved her. He wondered what Julia looked like now, but was clearly destined not to find out. Not today at any rate.

Lunch was both unappetizing and unstimulating. Chewing his way through some particularly fibrous pork, the Major got the impression that the meal was not the point of the exercise, and this was reinforced when, at the end of it, Leonora said, 'Frederick and I will now retire to the drawing room. Cassandra, you and Clara will do the clearing away. In the fullness of time, but not until I ring the bell, we should like some coffee. Cassandra, you had better bring it.'

Following Leonora out of the room, Major Fred saw Cassandra shoot her mother's retreating back a look of such venomous dislike that he was momentarily stopped in his tracks. Possibly conscious of the fact that he had seen it, she lowered her eyes and gathered up a plate and some cutlery.

'Very well, Mother,' said Cassandra in a neutral tone of voice.

The drawing room had the tiniest fire he had ever seen. Apparently he was not the only one who was being forced to economize. 'Hah!' he said, standing uneasily in front of the minuscule flicker, feet apart, hands clasped behind his back. 'Hah!'

Leonora did not respond, but simply watched his discomfiture, basilisk-like, from her armchair.

Silence fell.

'Hah, indeed!' said Leonora finally. 'Now tell me, Frederick, for I should like us to be perfectly frank with one another, what you are really here for. Not a trip down Memory Lane, I shouldn't have thought.'

With the gauntlet lying on the ground in front of him, the Major stared out of the window. A fine gauzy drizzle that looked as though it could go on for the rest of the day was falling, throwing a grey veil over the garden, which glistened damply. Christ, I hate the Northumbrian weather, he thought. He cleared his throat.

'I have only just found out that I have a son. I presume Morgan Steer *is* my son?'

She was ready for it.

'Well, you presume too much,' Leonora lied, 'though Morgan *is* Julia's son. After you left, there was, shall we say, an indiscretion, the upshot of which was Morgan. Which is why his name is Steer, not Farrell. If pressed I can, no doubt, unearth the birth certificate, which states "Father Unknown". It was pointed out to Julia that it would be much easier all round if the child was given her married name, but in the light of the way in which you had treated her, she was obdurate, saying that she wanted nothing more to do with you. Julia was very headstrong in those days, alas.'

The Major was suspicious. 'But the dates tally.'

'I dare say they look as though they do, but Morgan was, in fact, very premature. Lucky to survive. I am sorry to deprive you of the chance to prove yourself the perfect father, but there it is.'

Disregarding this sarcastic shaft, he was still not convinced.

'I would like to talk to Julia!'

'You can only talk to Julia if Julia wishes to talk to you, and I'm afraid she does not.'

All in all, Julia's absence was turning out to more potent than her presence.

He decided to abandon all pretence.

'Look, Mrs Steer—Leonora!—to be perfectly honest with you, I'm on my uppers. Business deal that went wrong, you know the sort of thing, and I wondered whether you could see your way to advancing me a small sum. Just until I'm back on my feet again. And when I am, but not until then, I'd like to talk to Julia about a reconciliation!'

Really! His effrontery knew no bounds!

Without immediately deigning to give a direct answer, thereby giving him cause to hope that she might come through with something, Leonora enquired, 'May I ask about the nature of the business you have been engaged in? And where you conduct it?'

Since he had been a guest, albeit unwillingly, of one of Her Majesty's prisons for the last four years because of the nature of his business, Major Fred was reluctant to be too specific.

'Oh, wholesale…abroad…' He groped for words, or the word, and came up with, 'Export…you know!'

Leonora said that she did not know, and then suddenly became animated. 'Not gunrunning? I'm told that's very lucrative!'

Startled, and wondering who she could possibly know in that sort of business, he replied, 'No, not gun-running.'

'Drug smuggling then?' She sounded very excited, even hopeful. 'Lot of money to be made there too, I gather.'

'No, not that either.'

'What a shame!'

She made him jump through several more hoops, most of which were almost too small to negotiate successfully, before finally demolishing all hope by saying, 'I'm afraid I can't oblige you. I have no capital. Nobody does these days, you know! However, I expect an astute businessman like yourself will find some somewhere.'

Leonora rang the bell.

'As to a *rapprochement* with Julia, you will have to ask her about that, although I have to say that I wouldn't hold out much hope. What you have to ask yourself, Frederick, is what could possibly be in it for her?'

Half an hour later as he was leaving, having been comprehensively trounced, he said, 'What about Meredith Barstow? Does she still live around here?'

In Meredith's pleasant sitting room, Julia looked at her watch.

'Three o'clock. I wonder if it's safe to return yet. It probably is.'

'You may find it's safer than you know. Forget

about Leonora's offensive—he may not have survived Clara's cooking.'

Julia was amused. 'Oh, well, that's certainly true!'

'What are you going to do if he turns up on the doorstep again?' Never mind Julia, she thought, what am *I* going to do if he turns up on *my* doorstep?

Driving away from Tyne Green along the side of the burn prior to mounting Gilesgate Bank up into the town, Julia once again passed her husband on the road. This time, however, Major Fred, who had bounced a cheque a safe distance outside Hexham and was once more travelling in a taxi, was hidden from view.

Meredith heard a car draw up and looked out of the window. She knew immediately who it was, and for once wished her difficult parent was at home and not playing bowls. Major Fred was paying the fare. It occurred to Meredith to dodge out of sight and pretend to be out. Too late. He had seen her. A dreadful jaunty wave followed the sighting. She opened the door.

'I have seen off the Major, no thanks to you,' Leonora informed Julia. Although technically they were still not speaking, it had been necessary to call a halt to hostilities in order to brief Julia on what had been said. Listening to it, it was Julia's view that when it came to deception, you certainly had to hand it to Mother.

'So as a result of what you've told him, the whole of Hexham will shortly think that I'm a scarlet woman'

(the prospect was not unalluring) 'and that Morgan is
illegitimate!'

'The whole of Hexham won't think anything. *He*
won't tell anyone. He'll look a fool if he does. And
anyway, what does it matter? He went off saying that
he intended to look up Meredith Barstow, no doubt in
order to extort money from her, though what Meredith
could have to hide I have no idea.'

Nor had Julia.

'He's probably just going to see her for old times'
sake.'

'I doubt it. That isn't the way that kind of person
operates.'

Whatever did take place between Major Fred and
Meredith, Julia was never to know for Meredith never
mentioned that a visit had taken place. Which was odd.
And because she never so much as mentioned it, Julia
found herself unable to bring the subject up, so it lay
between them, an unexplained omission that created a
hairline crack in their relationship. And it was interesting, Julia mused, that the only other hiccup during
the course of her long friendship with Meredith had
also been caused by Frederick. I accused her of setting
her cap at him, remembered Julia, and the ensuing row
was really quite nasty. Water under the bridge now, of
course, though at the time it had all been very unpleasant.

When the Major had finally taken his leave, Meredith sank down trembling on the couch. It was so many

years since Frederick had left that she had allowed herself to relax into the illusion that he would never ever come back. And now here he was, his capacity to make mischief exacerbated by a desperation probably born out of his plainly reduced circumstances.

Unsurprisingly he had failed to get any change whatever out of Leonora Steer, and when he related to Meredith what she had told him concerning Morgan's parentage, though amazed, Meredith kept her own counsel, only saying, 'Oh, she told you that did she!' Clearly Leonora had thought on her feet very quickly, or maybe the strategy had been previously worked out. She, Meredith, who had not been expecting him, was not so lucky,

'I wouldn't have come to you, Meredith old girl,' apologized Major Fred, 'if the old trout had coughed up. But if you could see your way to giving me, let's say, a hundred, it would tide me over, you know.'

His wheedling tone revolted her. Where on earth was Father, who was supposed to have been given a lift home? He must have stayed on at the club for tea and buns.

'A hundred! I don't keep that sort of money in the house. Twenty-five's more like it.'

He looked disappointed, and then decided to be magnanimous.

'Never mind, you can send it to me. On a regular basis. Let's say once a month, shall we?'

He wrote down his address.

'There you are.'

This was an even more nightmarish scenario than Meredith's worst dreams. She saw that like the old man of the sea, dislodging him would be practically impossible.

'Frederick, I can't *afford* that sort of money every month.'

It fell on deaf ears. Unabashed and stuffing the twenty-five pounds into his wallet, he said, 'I expect you'll find a way! By the way, how's the family?'

'Father's just arriving. I think you'd better go!'

As she opened the door for him, she said, 'What made you come back after all these years?'

Major Fred, who, like Meredith, had his own secrets and also wanted to keep them, said, 'Force of circumstance, Meredith, force of circumstance.' Passing the Brigadier on his way out, he touched his hat, a soft brown trilby that in palmier days had accompanied him to the races.

Looking after him, the Brigadier said, 'Who was that, Meredith? Looked familiar!'

Hastily, she said, 'No, Father, I don't think he could have done.' And then adroitly changing the subject, she asked, 'How did you get on at the bowling green today?'

In London, unaware of the little drama currently unfolding in Northumberland, Caro said to Patrick, 'So what *are* the chances of you travelling to Northumberland with us at half-term?'

'Minimal, I'm afraid,' said Patrick. 'Smollet's got

another part lined up for me. It's only more spear-carrying, but all the same I can't afford to turn it down.'

No, he certainly couldn't afford to turn it down. After a prolonged period of no money except Social Security coming in from Patrick, selling the house and trading down to something smaller was on the way to becoming a necessity. Meanwhile, the distance between them seemed to be increasing by the day. Wrapped up in his own disappointment, Patrick had become introspective and morose. These days they hardly ever made love. Even Emily noticed the general impasse.

'Caro, you're going to have to do something about Patrick. I honestly think he's clinically depressed.'

'What can I do? I can't get him a job, and apparently neither can Smollet most of the time.'

'Perhaps he needs a new agent.'

'Possibly, but more than that he needs a new attitude. It's no good palely loitering, generally feeling sorry for himself. Other people when they are resting go out and get another job until something turns up for them, but Patrick just moons about. He doesn't even help in the house anymore!' Caro was aware of sounding very impatient, even tart.

'You *do* sound fed up.'

'That's because I am!' It was a relief to say it. 'In fact, I don't know how long I can go on like this. And Minerva's very stroppy just now too. She probably senses the atmosphere.'

Hard not to, thought Emily.

'Have you tried talking to him?'

'Yes of course I have, but it gets me nowhere. In fact the last time I tried, it got me a lot of eyewash about the Artistic Temperament, after which he sulked for a week. You may have noticed.'

Emily had, and even though the urge to defend her embattled brother-in-law was strong, she had to concede that Caro had a case. It's such a pity, thought Emily. Here I am enjoying my job, absolutely revelling in the Artistic Temperament, in fact, even being painted by the famous Jack Carey ('Emily's getting quite *rackety* these days,' Patrick had said, admiringly), and here's Caro, usually so positive, more disillusioned than I've ever seen her. It doesn't sound temporary either. If this goes on, she may leave Patrick. And life's timing being what it is, Morgan is now married to somebody else, of course.

Aloud she said, 'Look, are you still going to Hexham at half-term? Supposing you are and Patrick isn't, perhaps, if the opportunity arises, I should talk to him? If you think it would help, that is.'

Sadness engulfed Caro. She no longer felt militant. 'Oh, Emily, please do! He's very fond of you and he might listen, whereas I just make him irritable. It never used to be like this, did it? Honestly, things have been going downhill for so long that I find it hard to remember what my marriage was really like at the beginning. Was I ever in love with Patrick? Was he in love with me?'

Emily could remember the early days when Patrick had been optimistic and Caro hopeful and both had been full of plans for their joint future. She, Emily, had envied them and wished for something similar for herself, and now the whole thing appeared to be falling apart. It was clearly the time to speak.

'Yes, you were. In spite of Morgan, you both were. Oh Caro, don't give up on it. It would be such a shame!'

'I was intending to take a decision about staying or going during the Northumbrian trip, but perhaps I should defer it until I get back.'

October

21

Sometime after Morgan and Chloe got back from their honeymoon, Morgan reminded Chloe that they had agreed to go to Northumberland during October.

'Just to keep Grandmama happy,' he said. 'Oh, and Mother, of course!'

Chloe balked. What about keeping me happy? she thought. However, it did not seem politic to put it quite so baldly as that, so in the event she said, 'I really think that perhaps in the early stages I should stay within the orbit of my gynaecologist. Maybe I'll come up for a week later on.'

Startled, and at the same time recognizing that a marker was being put down, Morgan observed coolly, 'Children are born in Northumberland too, you know! And there are doctors and even hospitals.'

'Don't be angry, Morgan.'

She put a beseeching hand on his arm.

'I'm not angry, just disappointed. And anyway, what are you going to do all by yourself while I'm away?'

'Well…rest, I should think.' Chloe vaguely remembered hearing her mother telling someone that when she, Veronica, had been pregnant she had rested every morning and every afternoon. On the other hand, Veronica never did do much during the day, pregnant or not, except possibly a little light shopping.

In the end, Morgan went north on his own, but he was not happy about it, and he let Chloe know that he was not. And that was not all that disquieted him either, for the sexual side of their very young marriage looked as though it might be about to run into the sand as well.

'I'm so terribly tired all the time,' said Chloe, taking her mother's way out and blaming this shortfall on her condition. Sex was important to Morgan, and without it the threadbare patches in the fabric of their relationship, some of which he had already recognized but had succeeded in looking away from, seemed to become even more apparent, until he could no longer ignore them.

When he had gone, Chloe rang Joanna. Joanna said, 'Believe it or not, I don't have one single free lunch this week, except for Thursday, and I've earmarked that for an exhibition of French paintings at the National Gallery because it closes on Saturday, and I don't want to miss it. Why don't you come with me?'

Chloe noticed that she said 'me' not 'us'.

'What about Tom?'

'It isn't really Tom's cup of tea, but that doesn't mean that I should pass it up, so what about it?'

'I'd love to.'

'Excellent. Does twelve forty-five at the Gallery shop suit? We'll have a sandwich afterwards. See you then.'

She rang off.

For the first time ever Chloe envied Joanna her job. Joanna sounded fulfilled and busy and, more importantly, happy. And what did she, Chloe, have at the end of the day?

The exhibition was uplifting and temporarily took Chloe's mind off her own situation. Joanna particularly liked the work of Claude Lorrain. Crystalline skies took the eye to far horizons, at the same time illuminating the pastoral foreground, where mythical figures disported themselves watched by interested shepherds and uninterested sheep and goats.

Joanna's favourite was *Perseus and the Origin of Coral*. Eyeing the severed Gorgon's head, which, beneath yet another translucent sky, was surrounded by a bevy of graceful sea-nymphs all marvelling as the blood of the monster caused seaweed to harden into coral, Joanna observed, 'I have to say that I had completely forgotten that Pegasus sprang from the blood of the Gorgon, but I love the idea of something so graceful and strange coming from something so hideous. It's heartening. It makes one feel that good can come out of almost anything.'

They looked at the painting in silence for a few moments. The silver disc of the moon was reflected in the sea, and far away, across the water, a classical temple could be seen. From it emanated a sense of timelessness and peace that, in different ways, reached out to both women.

Chloe said, 'You're right. It is wonderful, though I think I prefer *Narcissus and Echo*.'

Inspecting this, Joanna could quite see why. Almost naked and asleep in one corner lay a water-nymph whose small, high breasts and slender body were reminiscent of Chloe's own. By the pool, immune to this charming sight, was Narcissus, mesmerized by his own handsome reflection. In an odd sort of way, it was all imperviousness and self-regard, all Chloe.

'I'm not so sure about that,' said Joanna. 'After all, Narcissus ended up dying of love for himself. All rather sterile, really.'

'Mmm, I suppose so, though he did turn into a particularly graceful flower at the end of the day.'

'Yes, but what sort of consolation is that? Let's go and have some lunch.'

Sitting on high stools at a sandwich bar round the corner, Chloe aired her troubles and dissatisfactions to Joanna.

Sympathy was not forthcoming.

After listening to it all, Joanna, practical daughter of a self-made, entrepreneurial father, said, 'Look, Chloe, I don't want to seem too bracing' (Chloe braced herself) 'but I really don't think you're giving it your best shot. Sure you weren't expecting the pregnancy quite so soon, but you did know having children was in the cards. And you did know all about the Northumbrian scenario. And now you're married, Morgan should be your first consideration, not your last. Plus

I honestly think that since millions of people do it, having a baby can't be that big an ordeal.'

At the end of this speech, Chloe was crestfallen and Joanna, watching her, was sorry.

Nevertheless.

'It's my strong feeling that if you don't take a more positive'—she was tempted to say less selfish—'outlook, and resolve to get on with things as they are, and not always as you want them to be, you'll lose Morgan. Especially if you insist on sending him up on his own to what is, to all intents and purposes, Barstow country!'

Joanna remembered Caroline Barstow from the wedding. Both the women in Morgan's life were beautiful, but it had not escaped her that Caroline had an added dimension, a spiritual dimension perhaps, that Chloe did not. And though she had not, of course, been able to hear what was said, she had witnessed the odd, intense little scene that had taken place between Morgan and Caroline from across the room. Watching it, she had received an emotional reverberation that had been powerful enough to convince her that the other woman still posed a major threat.

Silence.

Joanna had one more go at it.

'Marriage is a long haul, but it could be rewarding if you take the decision to *make* it work. Unless you do, you and Morgan have had it. He can't do it by himself.'

It was plainly not what her friend wanted to hear.

In the face of such a barrage of common sense, Chloe drooped.

'Oh, Chloe, I don't mean to upset you, and if your friendship wasn't so important to me, I shouldn't care enough about you to say these things. Don't you see?'

Embattled, Chloe tried to smile bravely, and then, apparently still unable to rise above her own desires, or, more specifically, the lack of them, said, 'The trouble is that *none* of it is what I want. Not even Morgan these days.'

All the same, back in her flat she mulled over what Joanna had said. After all, thought Chloe, she's right. What *would* I do if Morgan left? Or if I left Morgan? The old arid feeling of rootlessness briefly resurfaced. That had not provided much joy either. And now I'm pregnant, my wings well and truly clipped. Perhaps Joanna is right and I should be more positive. After all, what else is there? Uncertainly she saw in her mind's eye the beckoning finger of selfless, marital endeavour, and decided to give it a go.

That night she rang Morgan at Armitage Lodge, and offered to travel to Northumberland.

'Darling, I should leave it this time,' said Morgan, generous in the face of the fact that his wife was now prepared to come, and even sounded as though she wanted to come. 'We'll be coming here again for Christmas anyway.'

He did not mention Leonora's raised eyebrows

when she had been informed that Chloe had not come
with him, and why.

'I was still riding practically until the day before
Julia was born,' she had said.

'It's probably why I feel perpetually battered,' Julia
had said, *sotto voce*, to Cassandra as they listened to
this.

On the other end of the line, Chloe tried to imagine
a festival as joyous as Christmas at Armitage Lodge,
and failed.

'Oh, I will look forward to that,' she lied, 'and hopefully by then I won't be feeling sick all the time.'

It was from Julia that Morgan learned of the impending arrival of Caro and Minerva.

'We are invited over to the Barstows for lunch on
Sunday, and I'm sure that since you're here Meredith
will include you. By we I mean Clara, Cassandra and
myself. The Brig has invited himself here for lunch
with Mother for, I quote, "a chinwag about old
times".'

Although it was the last thing she wanted, when
faced with the request that Morgan should join them
all for lunch, Meredith could think of no way in which
she could refuse.

Major Fred had now left Hexham, and hoping
against hope that the attempt on his part to extort
money had been at best her own imagination and at
worst a bad joke, she had neglected to send the first
monthly instalment. Any optimism she might have

nurtured on this front was dissipated by a very businesslike reminder. Meredith dipped into her savings and sent the money.

Atypically for the North of England, this October was clement. Under a bronze sun and a darkly blue sky, the trees flared yellow and scarlet and burnt orange, and drifts of tinder-dry leaves the colour of caramelized peel blew along the ground.

'What a perfect day,' remarked Julia, as she drove them all to Tyne Green. 'It's so mild one could almost have drinks in the garden.'

Seeing Caro for the first time since the wedding, Morgan was struck by the change in her. It was partly a physical refinement, in that she appeared to be thinner, with the result that the narrowness of her face further emphasized the languorousness of her extraordinary eyes. But more than that, perhaps because she was in the country and temporarily away from the uncertainty and friction of her marriage, there was a quality of repose about her that appealed to Morgan's own troubled spirit, and caused him to want to reach out to her.

Watching him watch her daughter, Meredith felt defeated. Whatever she did, it was as though a mischievous fate kept intervening to throw these two together. Giving up on it for the time being, she said, 'Who feels up to drinks in the garden?'

With the exception of Meredith and Minerva, they all enjoyed lunch. When it was over, his eyes on his beloved, Morgan said, 'Why don't we go for a walk? There won't be many more days like this before winter sets in. What about you, Caro?'

She pushed back her hair.

'I'd love to!'

Meredith, who would have given a great deal to put her feet up for five minutes, found herself saying with simulated enthusiasm, 'What a brilliant idea. I think we should all go.'

'Not me!' Minerva, who was leafing through a book on dowsing she had found on one of the chairs, loathed physical exercise of the variety being proposed and was quite decided. 'Whose book is this?'

'It's a library book,' said Cassandra. 'I discovered years ago that I can dowse, but have no idea how or why it works, so I thought I'd do some reading on the subject. If you like, while the others are away on their tramp, I'll show you what to do. You never know, you may find it's one of your more useless talents too.'

Minerva was interested. 'Would you, Miss Steer?'

Wishing that with the exception of Caro, they all wanted to stay behind and dowse, Morgan said, 'So, apart from Caro and myself, the walkers are Mother, Aunt Clara and Meredith.'

Clara began to flap.

'I should very much like to come but I'm afraid I shall have to get my brogues out of the car.'

'Well, instead of talking about it, Clara, why don't you just *do* it?' Listening to herself, Julia thought: God help me, I sound just like Mother.

Clara went.

'Oh, Meredith', said Julia, 'while she's doing that, there's something I want to ask you about.'

Seizing his opportunity, Morgan said, 'Look, Caro and I are ready, so why don't we go on ahead? We'll go towards the river, and then along it in the St John Lee direction.'

St John Lee was a small, pretty church a mile or two from the little village of Acomb on the opposite side of the Tyne, and could be seen across the water.

'Good idea,' said Julia, 'Now, Meredith...'

Once out of the house, Morgan walked very fast. They crossed the green and then passed under a narrow railway line by means of a curious little tunnel locals called the Cattle Creep. When they were through it and out of sight of the house, Morgan struck off to the left.

'Hey, this isn't the way to St John Lee!'

Morgan took Caro's arm and put it through his own.

'Who said anything about St John Lee?'

'*You* did! Just now. They'll all go in the wrong direction!'

'Yes, they will.'

The river flowed past them. In parts it was shallow, and where this happened clusters of large brown stones worn smooth by centuries of moving water rose out of it. Here, during the course of an idyllic country childhood, Morgan, Caro and Emily, both the girls with their dresses tucked into their knickers to avoid getting wet, had picnicked and fished and bounced small round stones across the top of the water while either Julia or Meredith looked on.

'Do you remember—'

Caro stopped him. 'Yes, I do. As though it were yesterday. It's hard to believe so many years have passed between then and now.'

She drew her cloak around her. Shortly the sun would go down, and when it did the temperature would drop. Standing beside her, and without needing to touch her, Morgan felt at one with Caro and knew that she felt the same. The urgency and panic of the last few years receded to be replaced by a sense of inevitability. I am married, thought Morgan, and she is married, so right now there is nothing to be done, but in the final scheme of things, I will spend what's left of my life with this woman. It has to be.

'Let's move on.'

Eventually, as the light began to dim, they stopped. As they did so, Morgan turned Caro towards him, took her face in both hands and gently kissed her on the lips.

'I love you,' said Morgan.

Caro kissed him back, and then sighed. She suddenly felt both fatigued and exultant, as though the end of a very long journey was in sight.

The way she kissed him told Morgan everything he needed to know.

'Yes, but for the time being there is nothing to be done.' *Nothing to be done.*

The telepathic echo of his own thoughts made him

aware beyond all doubt that they finally understood one another.

'We should return. They'll be wondering what's happened to us.'

Hand in hand, under a darkening evening sky whose far horizon was shot with crimson, Caro and Morgan, two lovers who had never consummated their love, made their way slowly back to the house through the dusk.

When the others had gone, Cassandra said to Minerva, 'If you're still interested in learning how to dowse, I'll show you how to do it.'

'Don't we need a twig, Miss Steer?' asked Minerva, who had got that far in the book.

'Yes, we do, and the one I cut for myself is in the boot of the car. Would you mind getting it? Here's the key.'

The twig was quite large, forked and—Minerva tested it—very springy. Hazel, Miss Steer said.

'Where shall we do it?'

'I suggest the orchard at the back of the house,' said Cassandra.

Standing among the fruit trees, Cassandra noticed that the breeze had dropped. It was very still, almost unnaturally so, and the atmosphere was all at once charged with...what? Cassandra was not sure, but had had enough experience of this sort of psychic impression to know that in the fullness of time, the point of it would become clear. She decided to get on with the tutorial.

'Before we start, Minerva, I should warn you that not everyone can do this. It's a gift, and you mustn't be disappointed if it's one you don't possess. Now, watch me. First, this is how you hold it.'

With the palms of her hands uppermost, Cassandra held both sides of the forked end of the hazel lightly securing them with her thumbs. The stem pointed straight ahead of her.

'The next thing you do is to tension the twig, but sensitively, nothing heavy-handed.' She spread the fork slightly as she did so. 'Lastly, you hold it steady, not in a vicelike grip, but steady, so that if and when the pull comes you can feel it. OK, let's see what happens.'

With Minerva moving alongside her, Cassandra walked forward between the trees. For a while nothing happened, and then the rod began to dip.

'Here it comes. I'm going to try to resist the pull.'

Cassandra's knuckles were white with the effort, Minerva noticed, but nevertheless the downward sweep continued inexorably, slowly at first as Cassandra apparently succeeded in impeding its progress, and then abruptly finishing in a violent and apparently irresistible rotational movement, so that the stem was pointing straight down.

It was eerie! Minerva was intrigued.

'Can I have a go?'

Striding out with the twig, she was disappointed to experience no sensation of any kind.

'There's nothing happening.'

'Give it a chance,' responded Cassandra.

Still nothing happened. In spite of Cassandra's instructions to the contrary, Minerva felt inordinately disappointed.

'I think I must be one of those people who just can't do it.'

'Well, I wouldn't let it get you down,' said Cassandra. 'I did tell you that there are millions who can't, and very few who can.' Words that were of no consolation to Minerva, who desperately wanted to be one of the very few.

The sound of the front door slamming indicated that someone had returned. Grandfather, probably.

'I'd like to have another try, but not now,' said Minerva. 'Would you mind very much if I borrowed the rod? I promise I'll give it back to you!'

Sensitive to Minerva's dejection, Cassandra said, 'Not at all. In fact, you can keep it. Plenty more where that came from. Do you want to borrow the book as well?'

Minerva's face was transfigured by her smile. And I've always thought her such a sulky child, thought Cassandra.

'No, just the twig please. Thank you, Miss Steer! By the way, is it only water that one can dowse for, or anything?'

'Well, I don't know about anything, but not just water, anyway.'

The next day, whilst the adults were in town, Minerva decided to have another try. Once again she paraded up and down to no avail, glad that no one could see her, when suddenly, by the dry-stone wall at the back of the orchard, she felt a tremor in the rod and the faintest tug. Amazed, Minerva stood still, and then walked on a few steps. Under the branches of an old cherry whose autumn leaves flamed vermilion, the pull grew stronger and stronger, and with surprising force the twig flipped over so that she dropped it. Picking it up, she walked forward and was interested to discover that, as she moved on, the pull significantly lessened until it ceased altogether. Minerva retraced her steps and the reverse occurred. Finally, in the same place as before, the rod moved down in a strong arc.

For a moment, Minerva stood irresolute, and then, on impulse, fell to her knees and began to scrape at the soil with her fingertips. She did not have far to go, and cracked two nails on what she encountered.

'Major bummer!' exclaimed Minerva, stopping work to tear both off before resuming her labours. Eventually, and not without some difficulty, she managed to dislodge an object that appeared to be roughly eight inches in length and quite heavy. When she had broken off the clods of earth that encrusted it, Minerva found herself inspecting a figurine which, unbeknown to her, was a Roman effigy of the goddess who was her namesake. Dazzled by the spectacular success of this, only her second dowsing experiment, Minerva carefully gathered up both the little figure, which she hoped to have time to clean up before the shoppers returned, and Miss Steer's forked hazel twig, and took them into the house, where she intended to hide them in her bedroom. Both would remain her secret.

22

That night Minerva took the little deity from the drawer in which she had concealed it and stood it on her bedroom mantelpiece. Even though she had no idea what it was, she was instinctively aware that it was powerful and regarded it with awe.

'Who are you?' enquired Minerva of the goddess.

Haughty and mysterious, though, she sensed, benevolent, the statue kept its own counsel. It was wearing a loose robe with a girdle, and Minerva had paid enough attention during history lessons to associate such clothes with Classical times. In this case, presumably, it was from Rome, since Hadrian's Wall was so close. The idea that her find might be that old fascinated Minerva. She lifted the figurine off the mantelpiece in order to inspect it more closely, and in doing so received what felt like a mild electrical charge. Disconcerted, Minerva quickly put it down, but replacing it did not appear to cut off the energy that flowed between them. Intrigued, she picked it up again, and then, sitting cross-legged on her bed with the deity in both hands, Minerva, lonely only child of a faltering marriage, began to talk.

She talked and talked.

She told it things she had not told even her best friend at school, including something she had barely admitted to herself, namely her fear that her parents might separate, and that she, Minerva, who loved them both, might be forced to choose between them.

'I *know* Dad's difficult,' she said in conclusion, 'but all he wants to do is act. Nothing else.' Since the prospect of having to do anything she did not want to do appalled Minerva, she perfectly understood her father's point of view, and it did not occur to her that in order to sustain this ostrichlike attitude and keep some money coming in, her mother was carrying not only her own load of dissatisfaction, but also her husband's.

The bronze was mute but, in Minerva's view, definitely listening.

To Minerva, Quintus, architect, pays a vow.

With sudden, certain insight, she said, 'You can help me. I know you can. Please, *please* get Dad a job. And then Mum would cheer up and things would go back to where they used to be. I want them to love each other again!'

Scalding tears that had been repressed for a very long time welled and spilled over. Hugging the little goddess to her chest, and rocking backwards and forwards as she did so, Minerva wept.

The London weather was also unseasonably mild for October. Letting himself into the house at the end of that night's performance, Patrick noticed that someone must have forgotten to double-lock the door.

He switched on the light.

The hall looked the same as usual except for the fact that a chair appeared to have been knocked over. Very odd! On closer inspection Patrick recognized it as one of the kitchen chairs, which should not have been there at all. With a feeling of foreboding, he stood it upright and passed on into the sitting room.

He was standing surveying the wreckage when there was the sound of another key trying first the mortice and then the Chubb. Emily must have thought that she had double-locked the door.

'Patrick,' called Emily. 'Is that you? Where are you?'

'I'm in the sitting room. I'm afraid we've been burgled!'

The sight of it caused Emily to suck in her breath. One of Caro's carving knives had been used to slash the sofas, whose stuffing had disgorged itself all over the floor. Obscenities were daubed over the walls, and books, many of whose pages had been torn out, were scattered everywhere. Worst of all, all Patrick's theatrical memorabilia had been vandalized, even the prep-school robin photograph, on which someone had used a thick black felt-tipped pen to decorate Patrick with two horns and a devil's tail with a barb on the end.

'Oh, Patrick, I'm so sorry. Is it just this room or everywhere?'

'I've no idea.' Patrick sounded inexpressibly weary.

'I got back literally five minutes before you did. Why don't you ring the police, and I'll take a look round.'

He, or maybe they, had been everywhere. Upstairs was a similar scene of devastation. Drawers had been pulled out and upended, and the words *Snooty Bitch* had been written on the dressing-table mirror with one of Caro's own lipsticks.

'Bastards!' shouted Patrick. 'Bastards!'

He ran downstairs and into the kitchen, where it looked as though a plate-throwing contest had taken place. The criminals had apparently had the confidence to sit down and split a bottle of wine between them in the middle of it all. Two glasses, Patrick noticed, so two of them.

The police, not very hopeful about apprehending anyone, came and went. They did notice that there appeared to be no sign of a break-in, and inferred to an outraged Patrick that they thought it might be an inside job. When they had finally departed, he and Emily dispiritedly began to clear up the mess. Clearly it was going to involve an endless insurance claim. Christ, I hope I renewed the policy! thought Patrick.

Finally, having done all they could, they balanced beside one another on one of the disembowelled sofas.

'What do you think I should do about Caro?' enquired Patrick. 'Do you think I should ring and tell her or leave it until she gets back?'

'Leave it!' Emily was quite decided. 'What's the point of spoiling the time she has left? She'll just get into a flap, and there's nothing she can do from up there anyway, is there?'

'No. No, there isn't.'

One o'clock in the morning.

Patrick put his arm around Emily.

Emily, who was exhausted, let her red-gold Pre-Raphaelite head fall on to her brother-in-law's shoulder.

'So tired,' murmured Emily.

Patrick looked around the room. He felt bereft, a victim of paper rape and pillage. First-night photographs, reviews, family snapshots, the entire record of his life to date, trashed.

'Stay with me tonight, Emily. I don't want to sleep alone.'

Being beseeched like this put her on the spot, especially since if Caro had definitively bowed out, the new emancipated Emily would not have been at all averse to taking over Patrick herself.

But the way things are, I couldn't do that to Caro.

Fending off an importunate Jack Carey had given Emily a great deal of useful practice in the art of tactful but firm refusal. Mindful of Siegfried and Brunnhilde, who had slept with a sword between them, she said, 'If it will help, I'll sleep alongside you. Why don't you go on up? I'll follow.'

If Patrick was disappointed in the shortfall implicit in this offer, he did not say so. In the event, by the time she got upstairs, he was on his back, unconscious, one arm flung wide, putting her in mind of the painting of the *Death of Chatterton*. Too exhausted to take her clothes off, which anyway might have been misunderstood, Emily virtuously rolled herself up in her own duvet, modern equivalent of the sword, and lay down beside him.

Although she was very tired, she did not immediately go to sleep, but lay awake into the small hours thinking. She had much to think about, for whoever had vandalized Caro's bedroom and scrawled all over her mirror had the distinctive habit of topping each 'I' with a circle rather than a dot, and the only person Emily knew who did this was Nigel Moult.

November

23

A letter from London arrived for Leonora. It was not from Coutts—wrong postmark—but had a very official and, to Cassandra's sensitive antennae, portentous look to it. Holding it up to the light produced no further illumination concerning its contents, and in the end she went back to assembling her mother's breakfast tray. Cassandra checked the tray against her list, and having propped the letter up against the pot of tea, took it upstairs.

Leonora was sitting up in bed.

'Good morning, Mother,' said Cassandra, settling the tray in front of her parent. 'There is a letter for you today.'

She crossed the room and drew back the curtains.

Leonora eyed the envelope without very much interest. Though not the dreary buff variety with a window that signified a bill, it did not look as though it would be very amusing. It was probably from the bank, or possibly from her stockbroker. Either way it could wait. She extracted it from its position on the tray and put it on her bedside table, intending to open it later.

'Thank you, Cassandra,' she said in dismissal, breaking into her boiled egg with a smart report.

Cassandra went.

She cleared up the kitchen, fed Jardine and then took some tea and toast to Clara, who was ailing. Once again downstairs, she consulted her watch. It was forty-five minutes since she had taken up her mother's tray, and although there had been no summons to come and take it away, Cassandra decided to risk a reproof and go in search of it. Approaching Leonora's bedroom door, she was electrified by a thud and a jangling crash followed by silence, a dead silence more alarming than screams and cries would have been.

Heart pounding, Cassandra opened the door.

Both Leonora and the telephone were on the Turkish rug, together with the shattered remains of the breakfast tray. Automatically, Cassandra picked up the receiver. It still appeared to be working, but whoever Mother had been talking to had gone. Probably deafened by the explosion when the whole lot had hit the floor. A large piece had broken right off the telephone, which was one of the old-fashioned, black Bakelite sort with a dial. She turned her attention to Leonora, who on first inspection appeared to have fainted. Attempting to lift her mother onto the bed, Cassandra was suddenly aware that Leonora's eyes were open, and that although Leonora was attempting to speak, she could not.

My God, thought Cassandra, I do believe Mother's had a stroke!

It was Julia who rang Morgan and Chloe.

'The outlook is not good, I'm afraid. Mother's brain appears to be all right, but she's paralysed and unable to speak, though this may improve. As things stand, it's a full-time nursing job. She can't do anything for herself. It looks like the beginning of the end, and although it could be protracted, I think you would be wise to travel north as soon as you can.'

'Christ!' Morgan was shocked. 'Did anything specific bring it on?'

'We don't know. She appeared to have been speaking on the telephone when it happened, but who to we have no idea. Could just be Anno Domini, after all she is very ancient.'

Reflecting that his mother did not sound very sorry about what had happened, Morgan said, 'We'll come up by train as soon as possible. I'll let you know when immediately I've booked it.'

In the event, leaving London for an indeterminate stay was more difficult to achieve than he expected, and there were moments when he wondered if Chloe wasn't deliberately dragging her feet. In the end, fed up with negotiating about it, Morgan booked two seats and informed his wife when they were going, and that was that. He rang Julia and gave her the details.

'I'll be there to pick you up,' said Julia. 'Meanwhile, I'm afraid that there has been no improvement. Mother is as she was, and the prognosis is not good.'

They stayed for two weeks, which to Chloe felt like two years. In particular she found the sight of a *compos mentis* but speechless Leonora Steer unnerving. The stroke had affected the right side more than the left, and rather as though a thread had been pulled, had given that side of her face a gathered look. Chloe shuddered at the prospect of old age almost as much as she feared childbirth. The days dragged by, and she and Morgan seemed to have less and less to say to each other. This house is like a morgue, thought Chloe.

Her pregnancy was now apparent, and Morgan found himself in the odd cleft stick of experiencing overwhelming tenderness for this, his first child, while at the same time recognizing the extent of the gulf between its mother and himself. It was at this stage of his growing disenchantment, that he learnt from Julia of Caro's arrival.

'It's the Brig,' announced Julia. 'Mother's stroke upset him dreadfully. As you know, he's always carried a torch for Mother. But quite apart from that, according to Meredith he's getting dottier by the day. In an effort to spread the load, Caro has travelled up to give her mother a few days off and to devote some time to her grandfather. Did you know, by the way, that the Hollands were burgled? Apparently the whole house was wrecked.' He hadn't, and was not all that interested. In Morgan's experience almost everyone in London was burgled sooner or later.

'Anyway,' continued Julia, 'apparently the thinking behind it is that Sir Arthur won't be there for ever.

Caroline has always been very good like that. She cares!'

She cares.

Listening to this, and thinking of his beloved with longing and desire, Morgan made up his mind to go and see her. Certain that she would decline his invitation, he proposed a walk to Chloe, and in return received the convenient reply, 'What! A country hike in my condition!'

Chloe was uncomfortably aware that she was in danger of parodying her own mother on the pregnancy front, and she was also aware that all the good resolutions she had made at Joanna's suggestion seemed to have evaporated. But it's no good, she thought. The country and I just have nothing to contribute to one another. Nothing! Once we're back in London I'll try harder.

Morgan pursued it far enough to observe, 'The exercise would do you good. And the fresh air! Don't you get bored just sitting in the house all day?'

'No,' replied Chloe, who was not impressed by the idea of either exercise or fresh air, 'I don't!'

So he went with only Jardine for company, and on his way telephoned the Barstow household.

Caro answered.

'Morgan! Yes, I'd love to come with you,' said Caro, 'but I can't get away until Grandfather gets picked up. It's his club afternoon. Where had you thought of going?'

'I thought we might drive to the Wall. Like in the old days!'

Knowing that she should not be doing it, and conscious at the same time of an anticipatory leap of the heart, Caro said, 'Come at two.'

And it *was* just like the old days. They leant into a biting wind that had more than a hint of early snow in it and whipped their clothes hard against them, causing Caro's purple cloak to stream behind her. Ahead of them bounded Jardine. There is something exhilarating about the sheer aggression of Northumbrian weather, though Caro, born and bred in the county. Perhaps one day I shall come and live up here again.

Aware that they were approaching a part of the Wall that fell steeply away, Morgan shouted for his dog. It was a struggle to make himself heard above the escalating noise.

Intent on pursuing something, and probably overexcited by the high wind, Jardine took no notice. Perhaps, after all, he could not hear his master.

'Bloody animal!' exclaimed Morgan, who disliked nothing so much as a badly trained dog and was vastly put out to discover that it looked as though he owned one. 'Aunt Cassandra said he was getting very disobedient. Jardine!'

Veering dangerously close to the edge of the Wall, Jardine rushed on. Swearing, Morgan set off in pursuit.

'Jardine! Fuck that dog! Heel! JARDINE!'

Running after Morgan, Caro was almost lifted off

her feet by a freak gust of wind. Shaking her hair out
of her eyes, she watched Jardine *disappear*! Disbeliev-
ing, she saw Morgan abruptly stop. Ironically, at this
moment there was a brief lull in the gale. Breathing
hard, Caro caught Morgan up.

She hardly dared speak.

'Morgan?'

Morgan looked dazed.

'He's gone. He either ran off the Wall or was blown
off. I'm not sure which. Either way, he's gone!'

In a sympathetic keening lament, the wind began to
rise again.

Standing with Caro on Hadrian's Wall, Morgan
wept for the loss of his dog.

Caro let him grieve. Eventually, she said gently,
'Let's get back to the car and try to organize a search
party. He just may have survived it.'

Privately both doubted this.

Going back to the car, his unattainable sweetheart
by his side, Morgan suddenly understood with great
clarity the transitoriness of all he had previously taken
for granted. He halted suddenly, turned Caro to face
him, and took her by the shoulders.

'Look,' said Morgan, 'let's cut through everything.
I'll tell Chloe, you tell Patrick. I want you to be with
me, not in some distant future, but now.'

To Caro, Morgan pays a vow.

Caro opened her mouth to say 'But what about Minerva? And Chloe! Chloe is pregnant!' And said instead, 'I'll do it. I'll come away with you!' She trem-

bled at the sound of her own words, and the importance of what she had just said made her feel suddenly faint. Underlining her decision, more for her own benefit than his, she reiterated, 'I will do it! I promise,' thinking as she did so of Patrick and Minerva and what this would do to them. Racked with doubt now that push had finally come to shove, and suddenly aware that the self-indulgence of entertaining a dream was quite different from the reality, with all its consequences, Caro realized that she might be about to make the worst mistake of her life. Silently panicking, she got into the car.

24

In the days that followed Caro endlessly rehearsed to herself the pros and cons of staying and going. She could think of nothing else and her confusion was absolute. Surely if eloping with Morgan is right, I wouldn't be tormented by these awful misgivings? she thought. Intrigue and betrayal did not come naturally, but she now found herself in a situation where, whatever she did, she would be guilty of an act of treachery against people she loved. In desperation she wrote down the arguments for and against, with the result that whichever list she read last carried the day. Thus, in the wake of sleepless nights, there were mornings when she clearly saw her way forward with Morgan, but these were interspersed with other mornings, also preceded by sleepless nights, where she saw nothing clearly. Taking the veil in the nearest nunnery seemed the only honourable course left.

Meredith, looking refreshed after a brief stay with an old friend, came back on one of Caro's Run Away With Morgan days. Had it been the Tough It Out With Patrick variety, things might have turned out differently. In the event, Caro, who felt she could no longer shoulder the burden of her own indecision by herself, decided that as soon as she could get Meredith on her own, she would tell her mother what was going on.

'I feel a different person,' said Meredith on her return, unaware of what was in store for her and proposing a walk into town to buy one or two things she had run out of. The day was cold and dank. Shades of the weather to come. They set off along the side of the burn, which was separated from the street by a low stone wall along the top of which Caro had sometimes used to walk when a small girl.

'You're very quiet!' Meredith looked keenly at her daughter. 'Father been a trial, has he?'

'No, not really. Though I think constant proximity of the sort you have to cope with might get me down after a while. He's very forgetful, isn't he? And seems to be getting more cantankerous.'

'Father's always been cantankerous,' said Meredith with feeling. 'Sometimes I used to ask myself how Mother ever put up with it.' By now they were climbing Gilesgate. Passing the abbey and the bowling green on their right gave Caro an idea.

'Look, I really don't have any shopping to do as such, so why don't you go and do yours and I'll meet you in the abbey.'

'In the abbey?' Meredith was surprised. 'Yes, all right, if that's what you want. I shan't be very long.'

Caro entered the church. Unusually, nobody else was there. So complete was the silence that it seemed almost tangible and Caro felt enveloped by it, peaceful at last. She crossed the nave and went and sat on the bottom steps of the Night Stair, its stone treads worn by the generations of monks who had passed up and down it. Caro hugged her knees to her chest, and reviewed her life.

She had not spoken to Morgan since Jardine's accident because she had not dared to telephone Armitage Lodge in case Chloe answered. Caro wondered whether Morgan had told his wife that she had been with him that day on the Wall. On the whole she doubted it, unless he had done straight away what she was about to do, and told Chloe the truth. At one remove, as though in a trance, she felt an intense, scented stillness insulating her from the serious decision she was about to take, and its consequences. For the moment her troubles seemed insubstantial, even transient.

The door opened and, preceded by a wedge of light, someone entered. Caro took a deep breath, and then said, 'I'm over here. Let's sit down for a while. There is something I have to tell you.'

When Caro had finished, Meredith sat in silence for a moment or two, and clearly saw that there was no hope for it.

'And I', said Meredith, 'have something to tell you.'

At the end of it, Caro sat, stunned in silence. My life has been based on a false premise, thought Caro, and will never be the same again.

'But why didn't you tell me this before? Oh Mother,

you should have. You should never have let things get this far!' She was aware of sounding accusatory.

Meredith bowed her head.

'Forgive me, but I hoped that there would be no need, that sleeping dogs could just be left to lie.'

Distraught, Caro got to her feet. She stood for a moment trying to marshal her thoughts, twisting her hands, one around the other, and pulling at her wedding ring.

'This changes everything. I have to get to Morgan. I have to stop him saying anything to Chloe. It will be calamitous if I don't.'

With no further reference to her mother, she turned and ran out of the abbey.

After her daughter had gone and the echo of her tempestuous going had died away, Meredith sat on in the darkening church with the one secret she still had left. But I shall never reveal that, thought Meredith. There really is no need this time. It wouldn't help. Let sleeping dogs lie.

Clara voiced what they all were thinking. 'I wonder', she said, 'whether there's a copy of her latest will in the house.'

'Bound to be,' said Julia. 'Although the day she met Frederick in Hexham, she had just been to the solicitor. It was the main reason for going in.'

'I know where she keeps them,' announced Clara.

'So do I,' said Cassandra. 'And I know where she keeps the key.'

'Oh, really! Where?'

'Usually on a thin gold chain around her neck.'

'Are you sure? What an extraordinary place to keep a key.'

'Well, I've been in charge of bathing her since the stroke, so I should know.' Cassandra was short, the more so because nursing Leonora was not a task she enjoyed. 'When Mother is asleep, I'll remove the key and extract the will. Then I'll replace the key. At another time, when we've all read it, I'll replace the will. She'll never know.'

There was an uncertain silence. All were tempted. The independence they craved seemed so close.

'Knowing now would enable us to plan ahead,' said Cassandra.

'Yes, but I wonder whether... Well, shouldn't we, perhaps, ask?'

'Ask! Ask what? Ask Mother if we may please know what is in her will?' Slicing through Clara's timid murmurings, Cassandra was scathing.

Her sister's unemotional intention sent a chill creeping down Julia's spine. All the same, she thought, like the other two, I do want to know the potential quality of whatever life I have left. Aloud, and quelling her misgivings, she said, 'I think that's a good idea. And as you say she'll never know.'

The same day, Cassandra put her plan into operation. Leonora lay on her back breathing stertorously. Very carefully, she undid the top two buttons of her mother's high-necked blouse.

Leonora stirred.

Cassandra stopped.

Then, reflecting that in any case even if she did wake up there was not very much Leonora could do about what was happening, Cassandra continued. Being weightier than the chain itself, the catch had moved round and was hanging down along with the key. Hardly daring to breathe, Cassandra undid it and slipped off the key. This she inserted into one of the drawers of the chest, and then turned it.

There was nothing resembling a will there at all.

The drawer was filled with gloves. Cassandra had never seen so many. Short and buttoned, long and buttoned, white kid, black silk, even some still wrapped in tissue. All probably dating from Leonora's heyday. Why, Cassandra asked herself, should her mother secrete a key around her neck when the only things it protected were gloves and, she opened one out, two fans? She began to sift through the layers, taking pairs out one by one. Nothing. It was not until she was replacing them that the weight of one of the pairs caught her attention. Examining the glove in question she found a small brass key tucked into its silken thumb. There was only one candidate for this particular sort, and that was the *bonheur du jour* that stood opposite the window, and there Cassandra found what she sought. It was a certified copy. The original must be with the solicitor.

Very quietly, she eased the drawer shut and locked it, retaining the key. Then she finished reinstating the gloves in the drawer of the chest, and having shut and locked it, replaced the key on the gold chain and re-buttoned the blouse.

Once downstairs again, she went in search of the other two.

'I've got it!' said Cassandra, holding the will aloft. She placed it on the table. Like cats with a bowl of cream, they clustered avidly around it.

'I've done my bit. Who's going to read it?'

'I will,' said Julia.

Trying to keep her hands steady, she opened it up.

When she left Meredith, Caro ran blindly across the marketplace and along Fore Street in such a turmoil of spirit that she neither saw nor, indeed, cared where she was going, and it was in this distressed state that she turned the corner into Battle Hill and collided with Morgan.

'Oh, Morgan! Oh, thank heavens!'

She looked close to collapse.

'Where's Chloe? Is Chloe with you? Have you told her?'

Morgan looked at her in astonishment and said, 'No, she isn't. She's resting,' reflecting as he said it that Chloe always seemed to be resting these days.

'But have you told her? About us? Have you?'

'Darling, what on earth's the matter?' It was the first time he had ever called her that, she registered. Conscious of the fact that they were attracting a certain amount of attention, Morgan took Caro by the elbow

and said, 'Look, you're very upset. Let's find somewhere quiet to sit down and talk, and you can tell me
what on earth's the matter.'

'Not inside. I couldn't bear to sit inside!'

'Sweetheart, do calm down. Well, where then?'

'The bowling green. Let's go and sit on one of those
seats by the bowling green.'

'Yes, all right, but won't you get very cold?'

'It really doesn't matter if I do.'

The bowling green and the seats surrounding it were
quite empty. Hardly surprising, thought Morgan, considering the temperature.

After a moment's pause to compose herself, Caro
said, 'Morgan, you are the son of Major Farrell, aren't
you?'

'Yes, you know I am.' Morgan was mystified.

Sweetly, the abbey clock chimed the hour. He
waited for what was to come.

'I have just learnt from Mother that I am the illegitimate daughter of Major Farrell.'

25

When Julia had finished reading Leonora's will, they stared at one another, aghast.

'How could she do that?' Clara was close to crying.

'Oh well, you know Mother!' Though equally disappointed, Cassandra was dry. 'Never has been into philanthropy, or even fairness come to that, has she.' She looked forward into a depressing future of salmon-pink church gladioli, she and Deirdre Ricketts arranging them in the vestry.

'I still don't understand why,' said Julia at last, her own dream of world travel as a solitary, mysterious woman of private means in tatters. 'Chloe has more money than she knows what to do with. And what does Mother do? She gives her some more. *Our* money!'

'She hasn't exactly left it to Chloe. She's left some to Morgan, presumably so that he can keep his end up financially with his wife, and the rest in trust for the child. If the child and Chloe both predecease Morgan, then we get it back. Whatever happens, we are allowed to live in the house.'

'Yes, but on what?' Julia was caustic. 'And anyway, who *wants* to go on living in the house?'

'I do!' Clara sounded and looked beaten. 'Where else would I go?'

'We live on whatever Morgan is prepared to dole out. Same scenario as with Mother. Which reminds me, I'd better go and check her.'

Leonora was lying where Cassandra had left her, but this time her eyes were open. Cassandra plumped up the pillows, and hauled her mother into a sitting position. Too late she saw the key to the *bonheur du jour* lying on the bedspread where she had put it down in order to refasten Leonora's blouse, and knew that her mother had seen it too.

Until now well preserved for her age, the severity of her illness had tipped Leonora into looking all of her ninety years. Suddenly, huddled in the middle of the huge bed, she seemed much smaller. Her face looked as though a dark cobweb had been spun all over it.

Who would have thought Cassandra would have the nerve to do that! Leonora might have been speechless but she was still mentally articulate. Maybe I've underestimated her all these years, she conceded to herself. And Julia? Perhaps. Not Clara, though. No, nobody could underestimate Clara. She continued staring at her daughter.

Caught out, Cassandra became defensive and then, as years of resentment and dislike welled to the surface, offensive.

'Well, Mother, what did you expect?' Cassandra clenched her fists. 'All those years of manipulation and

oppression and sheer bloody-mindedness. Clara could
have married. *Should* have married! But oh no! Clara
must be at Armitage Lodge to dance attendance, and
any suggestion that someone else might enjoy the
limelight for a change must be ruthlessly crushed. And
Julia. Julia had a good brain which, thanks to your
possessiveness, has never been used. Julia is a misfired
person with nothing to show for her life except an
inappropriate marriage to the Major. And do you know
why she did that, Mother? Do you? She did it to get
away from *you*! You are an evil old woman whose
spite has even extended to denying all three of us any
quality of life after your death. You still want to rule
from beyond the grave, and it looks as though you've
succeeded!'

I *have* underestimated Cassandra, thought Leonora,
impressed rather than abashed or angered by her
daughter's tirade. Now, having changed my mind so
often, I cannot remember who I left the emeralds to.
Nothing to be done about it now, of course, but clearly,
as the only one of those three with any backbone, Cassandra should have had them.

Emeralds. Of what use are emeralds to me like this?

She closed her eyes, and when she opened them
again, Cassandra had gone. Dusk had filtered into the
room. Lying there helplessly, Leonora felt her heart
miss a beat, and then another. And then, after a short
interval, another. She tried to call out, and could not.
Slipping in and out of consciousness, she was dimly
aware of a darkness more profound than she had ever

known. It coiled around her and then slid, snakelike, over her, obliterating all light as it came.

No need for emeralds now.

Morgan stared at Caro for a long time without speaking.

At this moment certain things suddenly became very clear. He recalled his own voice saying to Tom Marchant, 'It's an affinity. I can't explain it any other way. I feel as though I'm part of her and Caro's part of me.'

Too true, if what Meredith Barstow had said was to be believed.

'No disrespect, but are you sure your mother has got it right?'

With a flash of sombre humour, Caro said, 'Why would Mother lie about it? There's nothing in it but grief for her. And if she doesn't know who my father is, then who does?'

'It's just that I've always felt she didn't like me very much!'

'Morgan, I don't think it's anything to do with you in that sort of way. She could see the mutual attraction and was afraid of it, and when I married Patrick she hoped the danger was past. No need to say anything. Don't forget, Mother has been a pillar of the community for years. Not a hint of scandal, only good works and a distinguished local career. And then, when you married Chloe, what a sigh of relief she must have breathed. That was that. Home and dry.'

It's extraordinary, reflected Caro, listening to her

own detached voice, that here we are, Morgan and I, rationally, even calmly, discussing the biggest upset that either of us is ever likely to face.

'But you still haven't answered my question. Have you told Chloe?'

'No,' replied Morgan. 'I was going to do that this evening.'

Caro shivered, and then stood up.

'I think we shouldn't meet for a while. I shall always love you, but it has to be different now.'

Tears began to stream down her face, tears that felt as though they were in danger of freezing, so cold had it suddenly become.

Unable to stop himself, and for the last time, Morgan kissed her like a lover and then they went their separate ways.

To the goddess Minerva, Minerva Holland pays a vow.

Waiting for her daughter to come home, Meredith decided to write a letter. Accordingly she opened up the bureau and was just pulling out a sheet of unheaded writing paper and an envelope, when the Brigadier entered.

'Who are you writing to, Meredith old girl?'

Reflecting that he had never had any conception of other people's privacy, and hating to be called old girl, Meredith replied very shortly, 'It's a personal matter, Father.'

'Personal? At your age? Oh well, don't let me interrupt you.' Obviously miffed, he sat down and opened up the day's *Telegraph*. Feeling it was safe to carry on while he invisibly tutted over the day's news behind it, Meredith wrote to the Major.

> *Dear Major Farrell,*
>
> *The secret is out. So no cheque this month, or any other month come to that. I should be grateful for the postal return of the letters in your possession. Since there is no longer any reason not to, should you ever turn up here again I shall feel free immediately to inform the police of your activities.*
>
> *Yours sincerely,*
> *M.B.*

Mindful of the Major's propensity for blackmail, she did not sign this note as she had so naively signed the love letters all those years ago.

'Finished already? Not a very long letter, was it,' announced the intrusive voice from behind the newspaper. 'Lot of fuss about nothing, Meredith, I should say!'

'Yes, Father,' said Meredith through gritted teeth. She addressed the envelope and inserted the letter. Tomorrow she would post it.

They both heard Caro come in. She did not enter the drawing room but went straight upstairs. Meredith stood up. This was the interview she had been dreading, but which had to be faced.

'Come in,' said Caro when she knocked.

Caro was sitting on her bed. Her pallor was startling, but otherwise she appeared calm, the only indication of the tumult within a damp handkerchief she was twisting between her fingers.

'Caro, I'm so sorry.'

'I ran into Morgan in the town, literally ran into him, so now he knows.' Her daughter's voice was toneless. 'Fortunately he had not yet told Chloe about us. And Morgan and I have agreed that we won't tell a soul what you told me, not even Emily.' The mention of her sister's name brought more tears to Caro's eyes.

Although she longed to take her daughter in her arms, Meredith, fearing rejection, dared not do it. She sat down on the window seat.

'Oh, Caro…'

'It's all right, Mother, really it's all right!'

'Will you ever forgive me?'

The irony of it is, Meredith thought, speaking these words, that there may be nothing to forgive, for, at the end of the day, I do not know if Caro is my husband's daughter or Frederick's. The last shameful secret.

'I have forgiven you. In an odd sort of way, telling me when you did has reordered my own priorities. Although I thought I was in love with Morgan, if I had gone away with him I don't think I could ever have been at ease with the knowledge of what I had done to Minerva. And to Patrick. And to Chloe, come to that. I shall never stop loving Morgan, it's just that from now on it's a different sort of love. But at least it's one where we can meet without guilt.'

Because she felt too ashamed to talk about it, Caro did not tell her mother of the relief that had flooded through her after the initial shock, relief that the ultimate responsibility for a decision which might have wrecked the lives of others as well as her own had been taken from her.

Guilt.

Meredith was silent. There was a kind of stoical dignity, even nobility, about Caro that left nothing further to be said. She would go back to Patrick, and maybe now that Morgan had been revealed as (possibly) a blood relation, the two of them would be able to enter a new phase together. How it would affect Morgan and Chloe, she could not begin to guess. Nevertheless, it's a mess, thought Meredith. And it's all my fault. I should have told Caro years ago.

Downstairs the telephone began to ring.

'Meredith! Telephone!' shouted her father, who never answered it when she was in the house.

Wearily, Meredith got up. Caro rose too. Stepping forward, she wordlessly embraced her mother, and the two women stood for a few moments together in healing silence.

'Meredith!'

'All *right*, Father!' Meredith knew her rejoinder was unnecessarily forceful. 'I'd better go. Oh, it's stopped.'

Caro was mystified. 'Why doesn't Grandfather pick it up?'

'*I* don't know. Making some sort of point, I think, though what it is I can't imagine.'

The telephone started up again.

'MEREDITH!'

'COMING!'

When her mother had gone, Caro lay down on her bed. I am so tired, she thought, so very tired. I feel as though I could sleep for a hundred years. She was aware, just, of the rise and fall of Meredith's voice on the phone, and the almost imperceptible vibration which indicated that the receiver had been replaced on its cradle, then Meredith reappeared at the door.

'That was Julia. Leonora Steer has died.'

In London Harry Blackstock took Tom Marchant out to dinner, though without his daughter present. He did not tell Joanna he was going to do this, and chose a time when he knew she was away visiting friends in the country, the reason for this being that he wanted to assess his future son-in-law for himself.

Tom arrived at the appointed hour to find his host already there. Harry was ensconced at a table for two with a glass of champagne. Apparently impervious to the pained looks of other diners, he was wreathed in blue curlicues of smoke emanating from a cigar of truly Churchillian proportions.

He greeted Tom expansively.

'Ah, Tom, good to meet you at last.' They shook hands. 'Sit down.' Then, to the waiter, 'A glass of champagne for my guest, please, and another menu.'

While they both decided what to order, Harry sat for a few minutes in silence, peacefully puffing. Sipping his drink, Tom covertly studied him. Harry was of medium height, thickset but not fat, rather compactly muscular, and expensively suited. His very compactness exuded success and aggression. Searching for some likeness to Joanna, Tom found it in his host's direct delivery, but there was no physical resemblance. Joanna's looks must have come from her mother.

Harry leant back in his chair.

'Now, Tom, let's talk turkey.'

Here it came.

Alerted and wary, Tom said nothing.

'My daughter, Joanna, who is the apple of my eye, says you have asked her to marry you.'

Tom attempted to speak.

'Well, sir, I—'

Harry held up his hand.

'No! Don't say a word! You can have your say when I've finished. Now, where was I? Marriage! I'm all for it. Joanna's mother was a wonderful woman. A wonderful woman, Tom. I was a devoted husband. Not faithful, of course, but devoted. Marriage', Harry extemporized, 'is a great institution. Where would we all be without it?'

His discourse had all the hallmarks of becoming an endless stream of consciousness. Like many powerful men he clearly had no interest in anything anybody else might have to say. Listening to it, Tom wondered how consoling Mrs Blackstock had found faithless devotion.

'Cigar?'

Watching the waiter approaching with their first courses, Tom declined. Undeterred, Harry lit his second, causing the tables to their right and left to visibly wilt, and one of the diners to vigorously beat the air with a menu. The waiter arrived and was sent away again with an instruction to come back in ten minutes.

Harry resumed. 'Now you can't deny, Tom, that you are a waster. You like money and you like spending it. Not too hot at making it, though.'

Tom blinked. It was clear where Joanna got her candour from. Such forthrightness almost eclipsed Leonora Steer.

He refocused on Harry. The accuracy of Harry's statement was such that there seemed no point in denying it.

'I'm from Yorkshire,' Harry was saying now, 'where we call a spade a spade.'

Certainly do, thought Tom, wincing.

'Where's that waiter?' Harry was suddenly irritable. 'Must be half an hour since we ordered!'

He signalled.

'Now, being a waster doesn't mean you can't be rehabilitated. Joanna says she can do it, and it's quite possible she's right. She's a very strong-minded young lady, my daughter. But I have a duty to protect her interests, and as one of the trustees of her money, originally *my* money, I'm not prepared to let her marry

anybody—wouldn't matter if it was the Archbishop of
Canterbury himself, by the way, Tom, so don't take
offence—without the signing of a prenuptial agreement. If she does, no cash.'

He waved his cigar about to emphasize his point,
causing a pungent violet cloud to collect above each
adjacent table.

'Right, now we understand one another, let's eat!
What do you say to a bottle of Sancerre to start with?'

'So how did you get on with Daddy?' enquired
Joanna on her return. 'I rang him about something
quite else while I was away, and he told me that you'd
had dinner the night before. He didn't want me to
come. Said he wanted to meet you without any dis-
tractions.'

'He seemed to think we are on the point of getting
married. So, when I could get a word in, I told him
that I'd asked you and been turned down.'

'Oh really!' Joanna ran a comb through her hair.
'And what did he say to that?'

'He said, "Then we don't have a problem. Sensible
girl, my daughter, you know. Have another glass of
Sancerre, Tom"?'

She laughed.

'Yes, I can just hear him! And of course, unless you
ask me again, he doesn't have a problem.'

'And what if I do?'

'Then, as he sees it, he does! He's worried about
my money, or rather, his money. Having pulled him-

self up by his bootstraps and made it all himself, he's not about to give it away to an undeserving cause, not even to the person I marry.'

She did not specifically mention the prenuptial agreement and neither did Tom.

'Actually, I thought we got on very well,' said Tom, which, once the financial markers had been put down, had been true. 'But mainly he talked, I listened.'

'Sounds like Daddy!' She laughed again.

Oh, fuck the prenuptial agreement, thought Tom. I love this woman!

He took her in his arms.

'Well?' said Tom.

'Well what?'

'*Will* you marry me?'

Without immediately answering, Joanna said, 'Did he rabbit on about prenuptial agreements?' Better to get it out of the way and make sure they understood one another before things went any further.

'He did!'

'And you didn't mind?'

'You couldn't have exactly called it a vote of confidence. Any chance he'll relent do you think?'

Since frankness seemed to be the mode, Tom thought he might as well ask.

'No chance. He's much too foxy for that.'

'Too bad. But it's you I want.'

He kissed her.

'I love you. So will you?'

Apart from one thing, the way appeared to be open.

'Yes, I will! When does your divorce come through?'

'It's imminent. Any day. I'll ring my solicitor. Spring wedding?'

'Spring wedding.'

'Let's go to bed.'

The following morning a letter arrived for Caro. It was from Patrick, which in itself was unusual for normally they communicated by telephone when she was in Northumberland. From the general tenor of it, although he did not say so, she divined that Emily had kept her promise and had talked to him. Beginning by mending fences, it finished as a love letter. Right at the end, Patrick wrote: *Caro, you are my life. There would no longer be any point to my existence if you left me. Come home soon, darling, and believe me when I say that things will be different from now on. Minerva and I love you and miss you.*

Gratitude welling up for this second chance, she read it a second time.

If you left me…

Emily must really have laid it on the line. God bless Emily. For the first time in weeks, Caro, exhausted, slept through the night. She dreamt that she and Morgan, wearing long, loose robes, were dancing side by side, a strange, ritualistic dance, very slow and measured, during the course of which their eyes did not meet and they did not touch one another. And when, exhilarated, she finally turned to her partner, it was to find that she had been dancing with Patrick all the time and not Morgan at all.

As always happens in a town the size of Hexham, news travelled quickly, and Seth heard about the death of old Mrs Steer from Martha, who had overheard someone else talking about it while standing in a queue at the butcher's.

Sitting cleaning his Sunday shoes, even though he never went to church, Seth sang 'Cushie Butterfield' while he mulled it over.

'Ye'll oft see hor doon at Sangit when the fresh harrin cums in,'

sang Seth, in broadest Tyneside.

'She's like a bagful o' saadust tied roon wiv a string;
She weers big golashes tee, an' hor stockins once was white,
  An' hor bedgoon it's laelock, an' hor hat's niv- ver strite.
  She's a big lass an' a bonnie lass an' she likes hor beor,
An' they caall hor Cushie Butterfield an' Aa wish she was heor.'

Clara was a big lass, and Martha was a bonny lass. On the other hand, while Martha had the body, Clara looked like having the money. At last. It was time he settled down, Seth recognized. Ideally he would have liked both women, since each had something different to contribute, but he doubted whether even Clara would put up with that. In the end he decided to settle for the money.

> 'When Aa axed hor te marry us, she started te laff:
> "Noo, nwen o' yor munkey tricks, for Aa like nee sic chaff";
> Then she started a' bubblin' an' roared like a bull,
> An' the cheps on the Keel ses Aa's nowt but a fyeul.'

Out of respect for her mother, Clara did not go and see Seth straight away, although she would have liked to. In spite of Leonora's demise, nothing much had changed, and presumably nothing would until the will was sorted out. Cassandra, resigned to the fact that Chloe was out of reach, resumed her friendship with Deirdre Ricketts, whose sensible shoes acquired an extra spring in their step as a result.

Once the funeral was over, Morgan promised Chloe that they would go back to London.

'But we shall have to return in January,' warned Morgan, 'to sort out Grandmother's affairs. And I say "we", Chloe, because I want you to come with me.'

Bowing to force majeure, Morgan had decided to

give his best to his marriage. Given the mental distance that already existed between them, any sort of geographical distance as well would only exacerbate their problem. All too pleased to get out of spending Christmas at Armitage Lodge, Chloe put a good face on this. Her pregnancy emphasized the childlike thinness of her arms and legs and this brought out a tenderness in Morgan that took him by surprise. Maybe we can make a go of it, he thought, resolutely putting Caro to the back of his mind, although there was little he could do about her at night, when her image haunted his dreams and he woke up feeling a sense of loss that was almost insupportable.

The funeral was a frigid affair. The Northumbrian winter suddenly asserted itself with a strong, icy blast and a heavy snowfall. Lowering clouds the colour of pewter massed and surged and the far horizon was tinged with ochre, indicating that there was more still to come. Outside the church, the freezing atmosphere had a loaded denseness about it and the smell of impending snow was in the air. Within the church, which was full of a mixture of family, friends and the curious, it was, if anything, even colder. Singing the last hymn, Morgan had difficulty stopping his teeth from chattering. Leonora would have approved of the economical attitude to heating, though.

Afterwards they all followed the coffin to the family grave where his grandmother was to be buried. In death she would lie beside a husband she had never been all that keen on in life. I hope they don't reserve a slot for me, Morgan reflected gloomily. I'd rather be incinerated and scattered than interred. Nobody wept. They all looked suitably dismal, as befitted a family funeral, but nobody wept.

He took Chloe's arm. Well wrapped up in a spectacular fur, she was, presumably, warm enough, which was more than Morgan could say for himself. He noticed that nobody had mentioned the will, though what it contained was obviously of great importance to them all. He supposed that it must be lodged with the solicitor. Time enough to sort that out after Christmas, which was nearly on top of them anyway.

Ashes to ashes, dust to dust.

When it was all over they adjourned to Armitage Lodge. Watching Sir Arthur lose a filling on one of Clara's rock cakes, Cassandra thought: *Plus ça change.* Mother has died, Clara's cooking goes on wreaking havoc. She wondered what would happen to herself and her sisters. The depressing answer was probably that nothing would. *Plus ça change.*

That evening the snow arrived in force. It fell all night, so that in the morning, by which time the wind had dropped, the world looked bridal. Swathes of un-sullied white glittered as far as the eye could see. A new incarnation. And, Julia recognized, its complete transformation of the landscape the evening after her funeral set the seal on the end of Mother and her reign.

26

Patrick went to King's Cross to meet Caro's train. As she walked down the platform, she saw his tall figure at the barrier. Finally freed from the ambivalence of the past, she wanted nothing so much as to take him in her arms.

Seizing her case, he kissed her and simply said, 'Welcome back!'

He steered her in the direction of the taxi rank.

'A cab? Oh, but Patrick, can we afford—?'

He cut into her misgivings. 'We can now! The good news is that I've got a job. Or rather Smollet got me a job. It's a TV series with the expectation of more if it proves popular. It's all signed.'

He was very excited.

'Surely this can't all have happened since I've been away!'

'No, it hasn't. The whole thing was mooted some time ago, with quite a strong element of now you see it, now you don't, but it suddenly firmed into a decision to go ahead, since when there have been protracted negotiations. I didn't want to raise your hopes after all those folding plays!'

Patrick shot Caro a droll look. It was the first time for months he had been able to joke about such things.

'It's the chance I've been waiting for. It could be the most wonderful opening for me.'

Caro saw it, and also saw television and the tactful editing that went with it would be the perfect medium for Patrick's talent.

She put her arm through his. 'Darling, I'm absolutely thrilled for you. It's brilliant news. You deserve a break. *We* deserve a break! Does Minerva know?'

'No, not yet. I wanted you to be the first. But I thought I might take both the women in my life out to dinner tonight, and we'd tell her then. Caro, I want this to be a new beginning for us.' Apart from the letter, which Minerva was to find years later among her mother's papers after her death, it was the closest he was ever going to get to telling her that he knew he had nearly lost her. When they were both finally installed in the back of a taxi, he kissed her again and again, eventually saying as they drew up outside the house, 'Oh Caro, I love you. Tell me that you forgive me.'

'Nothing to forgive.' She kissed him back with passion.

'Second honeymoon, is it?' commented the taxi driver, pocketing a generous tip and secretly romantically stirred by this manifestation of comparatively mature love.

'Yes, that's exactly what it is,' said Caro.

Watching them both over dinner that evening, Minerva was aware that the alteration in their attitude to one another was not just the result of Dad's new job, but was at a loss to explain what else could have wrought such a spectacular change. There was a bloom about her mother that had been absent for months, maybe years. The light from the candle on the table encircled the three of them. We are a family again, thought Minerva.

There could only be one explanation for such an unlooked-for turn of events.

Later that evening, before going to bed, she fished the figurine out of the drawer in which she had concealed it, and stood it on top of the trestle table she normally used for doing her homework.

'Thank you,' said Minerva fervently. 'Oh, thank you!'

Clara at last went to see Seth. As usual, Julia dropped her at the end of the lane. Trudging through the snow, Clara was aware that part of her allure for Seth had been the prospect of her money. Now that there wasn't going to be any, she wasn't hopeful about the happy outcome of this, their first meeting since Leonora's death.

Seth listened in silence to what Clara had to say.

When she had finished he did not utter a word, but simply knocked his pipe out and sat back, apparently ruminating.

'So, well, that's it,' said Clara lamely, more to break the silence than for any other reason.

Seth stood up.

'I have to get back to work now! I'll be writing to you.'

Writing to her? In all the history of their association, Seth had never so much as committed one word to paper.

Left on her own in the kitchen, Clara felt as though she might faint. Two mugs were standing on the draining board, she noticed. One of them had a lipstick imprint. Do I really want to marry somebody who only wants me for my money? Clara asked herself. She was so desperate that the answer appeared to be yes.

The distant sound of Julia's car horn brought her to herself. With a heavy sigh, Clara gathered herself together, and set off again through the snow.

'Mission accomplished?' enquired Julia, one eye on a very deflated Clara.

'Depends what you mean by accomplished,' answered Clara, but did not vouchsafe any more information. Her depression was palpable.

No letter ever arrived, and it was Cassandra who saw the announcement of the engagement between Seth Murgatroyd and Martha in the *Hexham Courant*. A proclamation of this sort would not have occurred to Seth, so it must have been Martha's idea. Going public straight away so that he couldn't go back on it, perhaps. She debated whether to draw Clara's attention to the notice or not, and in the end decided to do so. On receiving this news, Clara exuded depression, though not, Cassandra thought, surprise, saying only,

'Thank you, Cassandra. I told him there was no money, you know.' After which the matter was not mentioned again.

All the same, after the defection of Seth, both her sisters noticed a change in Clara. Disappointment hardened into a withdrawn, bitter moroseness, and when Clara did speak she was snappy.

'She'll get over it in time,' observed Julia to Cassandra. 'Hopefully.'

Without actually saying so, Cassandra was of the opinion that Clara would never get over it. The iron had entered too deep into Clara's soul for that sort of recovery.

Though there was no letter from Seth, a card with a letter inside arrived for Julia.

'Would you believe it, it's from Frederick!'

'Yes, I would believe it,' said Cassandra. 'What does he want?' Julia scanned the letter, and then read it out loud to her sister.

Dearest Julia, ('The nerve of the man!' said Julia)
It was with great sorrow that I learnt of the sad demise of your mother. ('Nauseating!' said Cassandra. 'Yes, isn't it,' said Julia.) *Sadly, during my recent visit to Armitage Lodge you and I did not encounter one another (a prior luncheon engagement, I think your mother said), so my trip down Memory Lane did not include you, my dear wife.* ('I never think of you as his wife,' said Cassandra. 'Nor do I,' said Julia, 'and, if the truth be

told, neither does he.') *However, I did broach the possibility of a rapprochement between you and me with Mrs Steer, and received the distinct impression that she would have given her blessing to such a development.* ('Huh!' said Julia. 'Are we sure it was Mother he was talking to?' said Cassandra. 'It doesn't sound like her.') *Perhaps in the fullness of time, dear Julia, we could meet again. I should like to make amends for the wrong I did you. Will you give me permission to pay my addresses? I look forward to your early reply. Meanwhile, please accept my sincere condolences.*

Yours ever,
Frederick

'He smells money. He thinks I'm now the part possessor of Mother's riches. Little does he know!'

'What shall you do?'

'I shall write to him as he requests, though not as he expects.'

In the event she wrote: *Dear Frederick*, and then, pithily and in his own gambling vernacular, *No dice. Yours never, Julia.*

December/January

27

As he had said they would, as soon as Christmas was over, Morgan and Chloe travelled to Northumberland. Christmas Day itself had been spent in stilted fashion with John and Annabel Post. To everybody's relief, Veronica had decided to remain in Boston for the festivities.

'So how are things shaping up on the job front, Morgan?' Post enquired, carving the turkey as he said it. Chloe's pregnancy seemed to have exacerbated his enmity rather than the opposite. Perhaps his obsession with the youthful look prevented him from savouring the prospect of becoming a grandfather. Whatever it was, he seemed very out of sorts, and as usual, though for reasons she could not define, Annabel received the impression that it was all her fault.

Reflecting that his father-in-law was very like a dog with a bone in that he kept digging the subject up, Morgan got as far as, 'The job front? Ah, yes, well…' when Chloe interrupted him.

'Now, Daddy, we don't want to talk about business on Christmas Day. Do we, Annabel?'

It was clear that Annabel did not appreciate being drawn into the conversation at this point, since agreeing with Chloe would amount to insubordination. In the event she made a noncommittal sound.

'There you are. Annabel agrees with me,' resumed Chloe unhelpfully.

By now very irritable, Post shot his wife a disenchanted look. 'Who prefers leg?'

The day rumbled on. Sitting in the Posts' very modern and very soulless flat, where even the Christmas tree was of the designer sort, Morgan fervently wished it was over. What was it about Christmas that brought out the worst in everyone?

Now, as the train pulled out of Peterborough on its way north, Morgan thought, Thank God it's over for one more year.

As might have been expected, there had been some changes at Armitage Lodge. The first was an improvement not so much in the cooking, which was still performed by Clara, but in the ingredients. A decent joint of beef, for instance. The second was that the heating had been turned on. All in all, it was almost cheerful.

Morgan had earmarked the following day for a trawl through Leonora's affairs. A certain amount of post had arrived since her death, and had been placed unopened on her desk by Cassandra. He telephoned the family solicitor and was informed that a letter had been sent a while before. Morgan hung up, having arranged to be back in touch once he had read it. The next morning he rose very early, leaving Chloe behind in bed. Armed with Leonora's keys, which Cassandra had given him, he started work.

* * *

Chloe woke up at ten o'clock. Morgan was nowhere to be seen. Leisurely, she prepared for the day. The existence of hot water in the mornings was another of the benefits that had attended Leonora's passing, and Chloe treated herself to a long and self-indulgent bath. An hour later, attired in a short, dark grey flannel dress whose white collar made her look like a chorister, and red tights, she walked along the landing and paused at the head of the stairs to put on her watch.

She was so engrossed in coping with the catch that she did not notice there was someone behind her. When Chloe stopped, the other stopped too. And then padded forward again, footsteps muffled by fluffy old-fashioned bedroom slippers. Close, closer, closer still. The catch done up, Chloe adjusted the watch on her wrist, and then, one hand on the banister to steady herself, she prepared to descend the polished stairs.

If the child and Chloe both predecease Morgan, then we get it back.

Fluttery and lethal, a death's-head moth, Clara succumbed to a sudden overwhelming impulse.

And pushed.

And watched Chloe fall.

28

Meredith rang Caro.

'Have you heard? You probably haven't. There has been the most awful tragedy at Armitage Lodge! Chloe and the baby. Chloe fell downstairs, right from the top, and broke her neck. Clara was there and saw it happen. It seems she slipped.'

'Oh poor Chloe! And poor, *poor* Morgan!' Caro was horrified. 'When did it happen?'

'Yesterday morning, and so soon after Leonora too! They're all shattered.'

'I'm sure! What a dreadful thing.' Caro suddenly felt shaky.

'But that's not all.'

'What do you mean?'

'Well, you know how Leonora cracked the whip of the money over all of them. Apparently, according to Julia, there isn't any. Morgan discovered by dint of going through her papers and copious telephone calls both to the bank and to the solicitor, that most of it was spent decades ago. Leonora has been living on her share income, plus a very large overdraft at the bank. Even the jewellery may be paste.'

'What about the value of the shares?'

As she spoke the words, Caro knew what was coming next.

'That's gone too. Wiped out in the stockmarket crash. So it's woe all round. But, interestingly, the letter from her stockbroker refers to a telephone call on the day of her death informing Leonora of the scale of the losses. It looks as though the house will have to go as well, by the way.'

'So you think that may have brought on…?'

'Possibly. Though, after all, she was ninety. We'll probably never know. Anyway, I'm so sorry to be the bearer of such bad tidings.'

'Mother, is Emily still up there with you?'

'Yes, she is. Going back in two days' time.'

'Do you think I could speak to her?'

'Of course! I'll get her.'

Emily came to the phone.

'Caro?'

'Oh Em, I want to ask you to do something for me. Would you go and see Morgan? From down here I can't do anything to help, but maybe you could. Just by being there, if you know what I mean.'

'Yes, of course I will. I wonder if I shouldn't phone first.'

'No, if you do that he'll tell you not to come. Just go.'

In the immediate aftermath of the death of his wife, Morgan plumbed such depths of despair that at times he thought he might be going mad. Tormented beyond measure by what he considered to be his responsibility for Chloe's fatal fall, he swung painfully between overwhelming grief for the loss of his child and bitter, guilty regret. Caro had been right when she had said that if he was still in love with her, regardless of whether she was available or not, he should not marry Chloe, or anyone else. And yet, knowing in his heart of hearts that she was right, he had still gone ahead and done the dishonourable thing. And that exactly sums it up, thought Morgan, head in hands. I am a man without honour, and do not deserve to be alive when my wife and child are dead.

Clara appeared to be in even worse shape than he was, weeping noisily most of the time. Unable to deal with his own desperation, which if anything was exacerbated by hers, Morgan took to eating in his room, picking at food that was silently and sympathetically brought up on trays by either Julia or Cassandra. At night, unable to sleep, he frequently let himself out of the house and walked and walked. There was a cold purity about freshly fallen snow that suited his penitent mood, and, in an odd sort of way, hinted at the possibility of absolution. Although, Morgan realized, without a dispassionate assessment of what had gone wrong and a candid admission of his own part in it, there could be no hope of any such thing.

Cassandra, who was also often still up at one in the morning, saw him from her bedroom window, a lonely figure setting off across the frozen garden under a sharp sickle moon. Watching her nephew until he disappeared from view, her thoughts turned to Clara. Clara had been diagnosed as suffering from a nervous breakdown, and on the doctor's advice, Cassandra had returned that day from installing her sister in the local hospital. Clara had not wanted to go, had pleaded not to go. Cassandra remembered with a shiver the reading she had done, a reading that unnervingly had come full circle in more ways than one. Apart from the dreadful accident and the reappearance of Major Farrell, a move of house had been forecast for Clara. *Not good*, it had said. And here it was, and, as prophesied, not what Clara had hoped for. Witnessing her sister's increasingly tenuous grasp of reality Cassandra's opinion was that the relocation might prove permanent. I may well decide to throw that tarot pack away, Cassandra decided. I'm beginning to wonder if it isn't positively dangerous.

In their different ways and from their different standpoints, the whole household took stock after the tragedy. Where her son was concerned, it was Julia's view that because he had been brought face to face with himself so brutally, by the time he had worked through the ensuing self-hatred and grief, Morgan would have acquired a new dimension of self-knowledge. All the same, it was baptism by fire. Observing his chronic unhappiness with compassion, Julia would have liked to offer succour, but found herself at a loss as to how to go about it, probably because her mother, the usurper, had stepped in all those years ago, thereby ensuring from the very beginning that she and her son would never be close in that sort of way.

It *all* went back to Mother!

Mother ruled this house and us with a rod of iron, thought Julia, and we let her get away with it. One of the reasons for this mess is that everyone in Armitage Lodge, Morgan included, accepted Mother's deplorable values. He never should have married Chloe. The tyranny of family money, I used to call it. Impossible to escape, I used to say, and now I see there was no tyranny except the one I imposed upon myself. The whole thing was an illusion. I incarcerated myself in this house all these years in anticipation of something that did not exist on any level, and as soon as I decently can, I shall leave. Though heaven knows where I shall go. I've been the worst kind of fool.

In self-flagellating mode, Julia passed this opinion of her own behaviour on to Cassandra. Poignantly remembering Chloe Post on her wedding day beautiful in cream silk, and the bridal posy flying high over the heads of the guests, apricot ribbons streaming, all Cassandra said was, 'Believe me, Julia, you aren't the only one.'

After a tactful interval, Emily borrowed the car and drove to Armitage Lodge. There was still a lot of snow about, though the roads were clear, and a pale winter sun shining out of an equally pale sky threw long blue shadows across the drifts. The curtains of the house were drawn, giving it a blind, embattled look. She parked and got out. As she did so, something moving under one of the trees caught her eye. Whatever it was appeared to be making for the house, or, rather, trying to make for the house, not walking but dragging itself along the ground. Shading her eyes against the dazzle of light reflected by the snow, Emily went across to investigate, and found Jardine.

Morgan picked up his emaciated dog in his arms, and with Emily following, carried him into the house. He laid Jardine down on the rug in front of the fire.

'I'd better ring the vet,' said Emily. 'Do you have the number?'

'It's in the book by the telephone,' answered Morgan, not taking his eyes off his dog, who appeared unable even to raise his head. Once muscular and glossy, Jardine was now virtually unrecognizable.

'He says he has to go to the Murgatroyd farm first, there's a problem with the bull, and then he's coming straight on here,' transmitted Emily.

'That's all right, just ask him to get here as soon as he can. Say it's an emergency.'

Replacing the receiver, Emily said, 'I'll get him a drink of water.' She went into the kitchen, which was primitive beyond belief, and found a jug. Jardine was very thirsty. With Morgan supporting his head, Emily poured water in through the side of the muzzle. Jardine's tail stirred a fraction in thanks.

'Poor old fellow. Where do you think he's been, apart from coming home?'

'God knows! And God knows how he survived that fall. Though it explains why we couldn't find him. The main thing is that he *has* come home.'

Morgan sounded close to tears.

Emily stole a glance at him. Haggard and unshaven, he looked untidily Byronic, with tousled hair and dark circles under his eyes. Emily was dazzled and admitted to herself that in spite of his disarray, or maybe because of it, she found him very attractive.

'Morgan, I'm so sorry. Caro asked me to come. To be here for you, was the way she put it.'

Giving her a haunted look, he said. 'She's quite right. I do need someone who isn't part of this household. Aunt Clara, having been in permanent hysterics with both the others looking after her, finally collapsed completely and has gone into hospital. Of course, she saw it happen, so it's hardly surprising. There has to be an inquest, naturally.'

'What will you do afterwards?'

'I have to go to London. Not just to sort out the tangle Grandmama's affairs are in, but also to see Chloe's solicitor, who wants a meeting as soon as it can be arranged.'

The doorbell rang.

'That will be the vet. Would you mind letting him in, Emily? I'll get Cassandra. If Jardine survives, she's going to have to cope with the canine nursing while I'm in London.'

Emily rang The Gallery and spoke to Victoria Harting. She explained the situation, ending with the words, 'I hate having to ask, but it is a crisis, and if you could do without me for one more week…'

Victoria, who liked Emily, was both accommodating and brisk.

'I'll get a temp. Don't worry about it, Emily, I know all about crises,' she said, thinking about the ongoing Jack Carey variety with something of a sigh. 'We'll expect you back in harness Monday week.'

In the wake of the second funeral, Morgan travelled back to London. Emily had gone on ahead and Morgan missed her. Missed her more than he would have expected, probably because Emily had been part of the golden age before things had all gone terribly wrong. Leafing through a photograph album after her departure, he looked at pictures of the three of them fishing on the banks of the Tyne, Caro a narrow, angular child before womanhood set in and softened the lines, he himself also narrow and angular, and Emily, a pudgy, unconfident little girl with riotous curls and plump knees, scowling at the camera, stringed jamjar in hand. Apart from build, there really wasn't a discernible physical resemblance between Caro and himself. Not for the first time since Meredith's revelations, Morgan wondered if she had in fact got it right. Although whether she had or hadn't no longer mattered in one sense, for Chloe's cataclysmic death and his belief that his own actions had indirectly caused it had effectively cauterized his passion for Caro and caused him finally to turn away from the old obsession.

He went on turning the pages. Dates and locations were written in white ink beneath each picture. Emily had changed, he recognized. Emily was now lissom and very pretty indeed, and her hair, rather than always getting in the way as it had when she was eight, or whatever she had been when the picture had been taken, now enhanced her face. Funny that he should suddenly notice it. Maybe he had been too obsessed with Caro all these years to really *see* Emily for what she had become. He wondered what had happened to that awful man she had had in tow. What was his name? Larch, wasn't it?

The Prince's Gate flat, shortly to be put on the market, smelt stuffy. Since Chloe's solicitors, Wagstaffe, Wagstaffe and Wagstaffe, were extremely up-market, Morgan changed into a suit before going to his appointment with them in St James's. On arrival, he found himself being shown with reverence into some sort of inner sanctum. 'Mr Tertius Wagstaffe will be with you directly,' intoned an acolyte, handing Morgan a copy of *The Times* to be getting on with.

Tertius Wagstaffe, when he arrived, was revealed as small and improbably bow-tied and looked old enough to be in danger of crumbling into dust at any moment.

'Ah, Mr Steer. Forgive my tardiness. Another, rather verbose, client held me up. Before we go any further, please accept my condolences on the untimely death of your wife. Sad! Very sad! Now, down to business.

Had Mrs Steer made you privy to the contents of her will?'

'No. But to be honest, I wasn't aware that she had made one.'

'She did so on my advice. As you know, Mrs Steer was a very wealthy woman, but as you also no doubt know, she was not a very businesslike person. She therefore relied heavily on us for that sort of thing. My further advice to her was that in the event of her death, her money should be left in trust for the child you were both expecting, with the income for you to live off for the duration of your life. And that in the event of both predeceasing you, Mr Steer, the whole lot should go to you. Plenty of Post money. No point in ploughing it back into the family. Spread it about, I say. So that's it. You get it all. To do with as you will.'

'All! How much is all?'

Mr Wagstaffe named a heroic sum.

Christ! One minute I'm practically in the poorhouse, thought Morgan, and the next I'm seriously rich.

Aloud he observed, 'What about my father-in-law? I feel sure that if he can, he will try to overturn the will.'

'Do you? Then I should let Mr Post get on with trying, spend as much money as he likes trying,' said Mr Wagstaffe with some satisfaction. 'He won't succeed. Will's watertight. I should know, I drew it up. I have, I may say, already had Mr Post on the telephone. I had to explain that my client's confidentiality is absolute. He became quite agitated, but finally was persuaded of the correctness of what I had to say. Yes. Now, turning to another matter, the only other question you have to address, but not necessarily today, of course, is whether you wish to retain us as your solicitors or would prefer to use your own.'

Reflecting that Mr Wagstaffe appeared to have the measure of John Post to a very useful degree, Morgan said, 'Oh, I shall retain you, Mr Wagstaffe, no question about it.'

He stood up.

They shook hands.

As Morgan was leaving, Mr Wagstaffe said, 'Forgive me for asking, but am I right in thinking that Mr Post did not attend the funeral?'

'He did not. He has proposed his very own memorial service instead. With no reference to me, I may say.'

'And the mother?'

'As I understand it, she's going to organize the memorial service.'

'Really! Well, well! A very complicated family, I fear. You will be hearing from us in the next few days, Mr Steer. Allow me to show you to the door.'

Back in the Prince's Gate flat, Morgan paced up and down in front of the large oil painting of Leonora Steer. It was hard to believe that he was suddenly in possession of more money than he knew what to do with. No need to sell the house now, or the flat he was standing in, come to that. The juxtaposition of tragedy and good news was both confusing and unnerving. It was difficult to know whether to weep or celebrate. Weep first, celebrate later perhaps.

Spread it about, I say.

The words of Tertius Wagstaffe came back to Morgan. I'll settle enough on Mother and the aunts to make them independent, he decided. It's the least I can do. But tonight I need company. I need to talk to somebody. Where once the image of Caro would have risen before his eyes, it was now Emily, the little sister, who came to mind. He looked up the number of The Gallery and dialled it. An efficient, upper-crust voice answered.

'Is Emily Barstow there, please?' asked Morgan.

'Who shall I say is calling?'

'Morgan Steer.'

'Morgan?' said Emily, when she finally came to the telephone. 'Are you all right?'

Ignoring the question, he said, 'I need to see you. Are you free for dinner tonight?'

From one of America's best-loved authors...a story about what life, joy and Christmas are all about!

DEBBIE MACOMBER

Shirley, Goodness and Mercy

Greg Bennett knows he's made mistakes, hurt people, failed in all the ways that matter. Now he has no one to spend Christmas with, no one who cares.

Greg finds himself in a church—and whispers a simple heartfelt prayer. A prayer that wends its way to the Archangel Gabriel, who assigns his favorite angels— Shirley, Goodness and Mercy—to Greg Bennett's case. Because Gabriel knows full well that Greg's going to need the assistance of all three!

Shirley, Goodness and Mercy shall follow him...because it's Christmas.

On sale October 22, 1999, wherever hardcovers are sold!

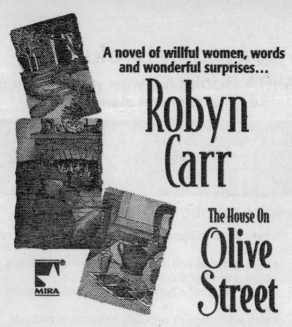

A novel of willful women, words
and wonderful surprises...

Robyn Carr

The House On
Olive Street

MIRA®

Elly, Sable, Barbara Ann and Beth. They have been drawn
together by the sudden death of their friend Gabby—and the
favor she has asked of them. For these four women, whose
own lives have become unhappy works of fiction, a summer
spent sorting through Gabby's personal papers offers the
perfect challenge—and the perfect escape.

In the house on Olive Street, away from their menagerie of
troubles, these women will discover something marvelous:
themselves, each other and pieces of a dream that only they
can make happen. For in telling the hidden story of a
remarkable woman, their own lives are about to change....

**"A warm, wonderful book about women's friendships,
love and family. I adored it!"
—Susan Elizabeth Phillips**

On sale mid-November 1999 wherever paperbacks are sold.